Integrity

Clayton Lindemuth

COPYRIGHT

Copyright © 2022 by Hardgrave Enterprises LLC and Clayton Lindemuth.

All rights reserved.

No portion of this book may be reproduced in any form without written permission from the publisher, except as permitted by U.S. copyright law.

Publisher's Note: This is a work of fiction. Names, characters, places, and incidents are a product of the author's imagination. Locales and public names are sometimes used for atmospheric purposes. Any resemblance to actual people, living or dead, or to businesses, companies, events, institutions, or locales is completely coincidental.

INTEGRITY/Clayton Lindemuth

Contents

Acknowledgements:		VIII
Special Thank Y'all		X
Dedication		XII
1.	ONE Jocular fiber...	1
2.	TWO Tap the brakes a little harder...	9
3.	THREE Talk to her...	13
4.	FOUR Just the right thing...	17
5.	FIVE How to drive...	23
6.	SIX Truce...	29
7.	SEVEN Lucky cows...	37
8.	EIGHT General Sherman	41
9.	NINE "That's all of us."	45
10.	TEN Their own desires. Needs...	49

11.	ELEVEN	55
	Run until he couldn't...	
12.	TWELVE	63
	Whatever rage did...	
13.	THIRTEEN	67
	Penance...	
14.	FOURTEEN	73
	Monster inside...	
15.	FIFTEEN	75
	It'll be a favor...	
16.	SIXTEEN	81
	What delicious pain...	
17.	SEVENTEEN	89
	Trespassers...	
18.	EIGHTEEN	93
	Acknowledgement...	
19.	NINETEEN	99
	The gun in his hand...	
20.	TWENTY	103
	The clay jar...	
21.	TWENTY ONE	105
	You're a country boy, ain't ya?	
22.	TWENTY TWO	111
	Moxie...	
23.	TWENTY THREE	117
	I guess you brought Him.	
24.	TWENTY FOUR	123

"You missed."

25.	TWENTY FIVE	127
	"Now I'm bullshit."	
26.	TWENTY SIX	131
	Wrroo woo rrr whoogggd.	
27.	TWENTY SEVEN	139
	"I woulda."	
28.	TWENTY EIGHT	143
	A bind with the truck stuck...	
29.	TWENTY NINE	147
	"Mind what I taught you."	
30.	THIRTY	151
	"It'll come to you."	
31.	THIRTY ONE	155
	"Most people's shit for thinking..."	
32.	THIRTY TWO	161
	Intent.	
33.	THIRTY THREE	165
	"You saw his teeth."	
34.	THIRTY FOUR	171
	"In case, is all."	
35.	THIRTY FIVE	175
	"Next time you won't see me."	
36.	THIRTY SIX	181
	The hardest lessons...	
37.	THIRTY SEVEN	189
	A flash of orange...	

38.	THIRTY EIGHT "Run!"	191
39.	THIRTY NINE Sewers...	195
40.	FORTY "Linc did it."	199
41.	FORTY ONE Grace...	205
42.	FORTY TWO Whispers...	209
43.	FORTY THREE The rubber...	213
44.	FORTY FOUR Spare her a terrible decision.	217
45.	FORTY FIVE Spitballs...	221
46.	FORTY SIX Significant stores of jocular fiber.	225
47.	FORTY SEVEN "Pretty sure two could."	229
48.	FORTY EIGHT Mercy, not sacrifice.	233
49.	FORTY NINE Yes Yes Yes!	243
50.	FIFTY "I can beat them!"	249
51.	FIFTY ONE	257

What remained was spider webbed.

52. FIFTY TWO   259
Don't quit lookin'...

53. FIFTY THREE   265
The only thing that feels peaceful

54. CODA: BAER, TAT, and JOE   273
Who sees everything, at once?

55. CODA: FRANK   277
This town knows you.

56. CODA: LINC   283
It's called jocular fiber...

What's Next?   285

From Clayton   289

Acknowledgements:

First, I'd like to thank Chrys, who helped with editing. I appreciate you greatly.

I'd like to thank the many awesome readers who make up the Red Meat Lit Street Team, my Facebook group. (Download my favorite novel Strong at the Broken Places FREE when you join).
https://www.facebook.com/groups/855812391254215/

For INTEGRITY I asked the group for suggestions regarding Frank Buzzard's tractor repairs, and within a couple hours had more real-life experiences and wisdom than I could use in five novels. I also asked what language they heard growing up to describe a backside flogging, and I asked the women how they would spell what they said giving childbirth. Other questions too.

I'd like to thank the following for their suggestions. Any errors in the book are mine alone.

Ken West: for suggesting the tractor's needed repair was the points, and for the insight the old timers would gap them with a book of matches.

Renee Shishka: for suggesting rust-rotted wheel rims, and water pump that had been repaired so many times it couldn't be done again.

Dutch Denson: For much of the language for and scenario for the tractor's distributor problem and solution. Many of the words in the book are taken directly from Dutch's explanation of problems he experienced and solved back in the day.

Dutch Denson: for the line about using a coat hanger to leave question marks on Linc's skin.

Landon Johnson: for help with the homeowner's insurance scenario.

Beverly Smith: for Tat's childbirth language: AAASRGHHJIO8YFFHPPUTT!! *(I love having the number 8 in there!)*

Connie Leamon-Hall: for Tat's childbirth language: Uhng! Uhng! Eeeeaaahhhhh! Uhng!

Colette Bivens: for the detail of Tat's burst blood vessels in her eyes after giving birth.

Deana Jones Coyner: for the Tat's repeated and rhythmic "Uunnhh..."

Dave Brown: Insight into F-150's in snow.

Ken Button: Weight in the bed of the truck.

Paul Kunkel: Skinny tires behavior in snow.

Roger Hutchins: "Lead sled" for Eldorado.

Special Thank Y'all

INTEGRITY benefitted from the editing help of Chrys, and with the incredibly talented and detail-focused readers of the *Virtue Series Beta Readers Team*.

A special thank y'all to Chrys Wilkins and the Virtue Series Beta Readers Team: Your time is important and the fact that you're willing to use it to help me make the book better is a warm and generous thing, on your part. I appreciate you.

Virtue Series Beta Readers Team
Carl Hughey
Cindy Wasson
Neil Cummings
Deana Coyner
Donna Fisher
Easy Dub McKraus
Frank Costa
Kathie Marold
Kim Saint
Kim Collins
Lawrence Stonebreaker
Marty Campbell
Ralph Bush
Toni Miller Vance
Tracy Gandin

INTEGRITY

Dedication

This novel is dedicated to young men, but us older farts too.

ONE
Jocular Fiber...

February in Oak, Pennsylvania, made sane people shiver. No two ways about it.

Locals told the kids as a matter of town pride, if you start in Oak and drive straight north, there isn't a single hill all the way to Santa Claus. Arctic wind comes straight and fast, downslope over ice two thirds of the way.

Kids understood that back in the day — which meant, somewhere deep in the yawning chasm of history before they were born — at least a good twenty years back — every single aspect of winter was even worse. The snow came sooner and piled up deeper. The air was more frozen; they didn't plow the roads because they didn't need to, on account people got super-strong walking uphill coming and going, everywhere they went.

Even though the winters weren't as horrible as they used to be, the people of Oak, Pennsylvania, prided themselves on besting them. Old folks taught the young that embracing the cold improved the experience, so they didn't think of it as a hardship so much as an annual test that proved their mettle. Oak kids knew they were tougher than kids from other towns, where mollycoddling hills slowed their weather.

Some older kids played along with their elders, declaring they'd be satisfied if there were no hills going south either, so their summers caused equal torment. The old folks nodded and smiled. Any kid bright enough to say something like that was going places. Such a clear display of good cheer, wit and grit — or jocular fiber — would see to it.

But that, Frank Buzzard thought, wasn't his son at all.

Linc didn't have the imagination to make light of colossal snow drifts and temperatures that sometimes lingered around ten below zero for a week or two before heading back to the low teens. He was tough enough for a kid, but he didn't have the jocular fiber that helped men endure the most challenging hardships.

When Frank left the house to head into town on Friday, right after the school bus dropped off Linc, the thermometer on the porch read five degrees, not bad for a late afternoon.

He sat in the truck with the engine off, shivering, watching his son walk the driveway toward the house. Could the boy move any slower and still make progress?

To Frank, a man's pace gauged his fitness as a human being. Anything less than one hundred percent effort pointed to a character deficiency of some sort.

When Linc was twenty feet away Frank rolled down his window and said, "Let's go."

"Uhhhh — where?"

"Tractor Supply."

Linc stopped walking.

"C'mon."

"Can I put my bag inside?"

Frank waved his hand.

It was nonsense. Linc's bookbag could fit on the seat between them.

"Go. Hurry it up."

Now angled toward the house and his face unseen, Linc allowed himself a few muttered syllables of profanity. As his breath froze and drifted from his mouth he wondered if his father might interpret the fog.

But what about the evening's milking?

Fitting in a trip to town and getting to the cows on time seemed mutually exclusive. But if his father said to do something, he'd learned a long time ago not to spend more than half a second figuring out how to obey, so he improved his speed, kicked his boots on the steps, opened the front door and dropped his book bag on the living room side, where his father would find it impossible to trip over.

Sue Cooper had been floating prettily in Linc's mind all day since lunch when she smiled at him, but now she vanished. She fought hard, smiled big, turned a little to demonstrate how well she filled her blouse, but —

"Holy — "

Jaw agape, feet frozen in place, Linc stared at an array of guns on the sofa.

Rifles, pistols, shotguns.

His eyes bulged. Where had they come from?

There must be twenty rifles lined up side by side like how they used to make forts by sticking poles in the ground. The entire back of the sofa was hidden by stocks and barrels.

He counted another eight pistols.

Linc's father had said he was going on an errand all day after the morning milking, driving into the city — but there was no way on earth Frank Buzzard had the money to buy that many guns.

"C'mon!" Frank called.

The F-150 engine turned over and finally grabbed.

Linc spun, grabbed the doorknob behind him and pulled; shoved the screen door and let it slam too. He jogged to the F-150 and jumped inside. Linc let his wide eyes ask all forty of his questions about the guns — but Frank never met his gaze. Instead, he put the transmission in gear and crept forward. For a man always pushing others to go faster, he drove like a blind man.

A gentle glitter of snow had been falling for days, never enough in the air to threaten accumulation. Then in the last day, after a week of nonstop ice crystals dropping through the sky, but never accumulating because the temperature hovered above freezing all day, the temperature dropped twenty degrees. A giant storm front rolled across the sky and in the last full day, more than eighteen inches of snow had accumulated. With so much land given to fields, some of the drifts encroaching the road were eight feet high.

After turning left where his driveway met the county road, Frank still drove slow knowing the plows didn't fight the drifts but instead tended to see how far they could extend the road on the opposite side. If he wasn't careful, he'd find his right wheels dropped into a perfectly smooth, snow filled ditch. He kept a crowbar and a sledgehammer in the truck and could likely winch himself out of almost anything, but with the ground frozen, there was no way he could get stuck and make the evening milking on time.

He drove slowly.

If he could only teach his boy to think about bad consequences before they happened...

Even though Linc was impossible to talk to, Frank had brought him along to the Tractor Supply hoping he'd see something that would spark his interest or give him some sort of ambition for his life; by osmosis, maybe, since nothing else seemed possible.

And also, because he'd noticed dollar bills going missing from the clay jar he used as a poor man's safe in the lower kitchen cabinet.

Frank was still trying to think of how to bring the whole thing to a head without blowing his temper. Truth was, all it took was one insolent sideways glare from Linc, and father wanted to beat son back into the original dust he came from.

For the last year or two Linc had two main speeds, sulking and moping. If he had a third gear it was back sass; kid didn't have a fourth. He did as he was told but didn't seem to have any zeal at all, except Frank had noticed that if a girl close to Linc's age was nearby, his kid was a human gyroscope, always oriented to keep her a quick glance away. He'd walk half sideways to hold her butt in the corner of his eye.

Frank indulged a stray thought: if he suddenly blindfolded Linc and told him to point to the nearest fifteen-year-old girl, he'd better be standing clear of both his son's arms.

Heaven forbid he raise a boy whose lust was several hundred magnitudes stronger than his work ethic. That was exactly what the world didn't need. Maybe he'd better deepen his understanding of his son's biological progress.

"You ever talk to that girl you told the story about? In school. The one with the yellow pants?"

"What girl?"

"You know. You said she wore yellow pants and had flowers in her boots, for Halloween."

"That wasn't a story. She just had flowers in her boots."

"Is she pretty?"

"I dunno."

"What's her name?"

"Susan."

"What's the rest of her name?"

"Cooper."

"Ahh."

"What?"

"I knew some Coopers growing up. What's her mother's name?"

"How would I know?"

"Questions."

"What?"

"When you're talking to her. Ask her questions."

Linc looked out the window.

Frank looked at Linc.

"Well... you can't go wrong with a Cooper girl. What kind of flowers did she have?"

"Daisies."

"See, that would have been a story if she'd had Lazy Susans, wouldn't you say?"

"Not really."

"But if she did."

"She didn't."

Silence. Road. Snow.

"So?"

"So what?"

"You talk to her?"

"No."

"You gonna?"

"Gonna what?"

"Oh, come on, Linc. Talk to her."

"So I can ask her mother's name?"

Silence. Road. Snow.

"Or what kind of flowers she had in her boots. Didn't we talk about, you know? The birds and all."

"Dad."

"Well, that's why. Girls want you to talk to them."

"No, they don't."

Linc crossed his arms at his chest and looked out the opposite window. There was probably an eye-roll in there too, which made it fortunate that Frank was paying close attention to the road.

"I don't know nothin'," Frank said. "Made you outta dirt and spit."

Those eye-rolls made his blood boil. Jocular fiber or not. When Frank was a teen, if he would have disdained his father the way Linc did him, he'd have earned a fist in the face.

Still, Frank huffed like he found the lone kernel of humor in it and finished the conversation with his mouth cocked in a slight grin. The boy was a budding thief, but he didn't have the genes to be all bad. His mother was an angel and Frank had defended every square inch of her integrity every day of his life. Integrity was all he had, and the only thing he'd take with him.

There had to be hope for Linc somewhere.

TWO
TAP THE BRAKES A LITTLE HARDER...

Frank had read in a magazine at the barber shop a week back how training dogs was all about capturing their interest in something they were already excited about, some kind of play, or game, and associating that with a new behavior. Smell this sock, and if you find the boy with the foot that made it so wretched, you get to play with your ball or get a belly rub; something like that.

A wild thought — just to see where it goes: with Linc so interested in girls, maybe Frank could get him to stop stealing by taking him to a broth —

Nope.

Dead end thinkin', right there.

But if he could get Linc as excited about homework and farm work as he was about that Cooper girl, it'd be an act of fatherly genius.

Senior's Tractor Supply was outside town on the left, past a long-closed motel and burger joint that used to be — back in the day — where Frank took the girl that one day became his wife, and many unplanned years later, Linc's mother, and immediately after that, a hole in Frank's heart so big the wind blew right through him.

All too soon, Linc would be looking for a destination like the old motel and burger joint, with similar convenience.

Would his son ever get his head on straight?

How had he raised a thief? Stealing family money.

"You better get your game together, you want to land a Cooper girl," Frank said. Then thinking about the general ambiguity of what he just said, added, "You better crack the books. Cooper girls ain't just pretty, they're smart, too."

Linc kept his head pointed out the window.

Frank shot an easy fist to Linc's shoulder, like when they used to roughhouse for fun, but his fist stopped short and he found himself grinning like an idiot, wondering why his son couldn't be a regular guy who understood good old fashioned demeaning humor was only intended to make him both strong and humble.

There was something wrong with the boy. Winters were depressing but it wasn't that.

He was a thief.

And like usual, as soon as he thought more than a split second about Linc's crooked ways, Frank's ribs drew tight on the hole in his heart. Anger was the only thing that made it small enough to forget. The boy stole from his own father. What kind of disrespect was that? As if Linc didn't see Frank work until he couldn't work any more, every single rotten cheerful day, to put clothes on his back, food in his belly and a bed under a roof.

Linc didn't see that?

Or didn't care?

Frank clenched the steering wheel while his face chewed itself like gristle.

The insurance man's office was open.

Frank clung to the thought while his stomach churned.

He'd have to remember to pay his homeowner's insurance. Since paying off the house, the insurance bill didn't escrow with each mortgage payment like it used to, and he had to set aside the money in his checkbook all year so there'd be enough when the annual bill came due in a few days.

Up ahead, the sign for Senior's Tractor Supply turned on while Frank watched. He looked toward the sky and a dark wall of clouds had blotted the sun.

Clouds like that meant snow. A lot more of it.

He'd started winter behind on firewood and on average the temperature had been colder than usual. He could kick himself for not getting the task done in the summer. That was a lesson right there. Just because he felled the trees and let them age in place didn't mean the job was anywhere close to finished. He still had to saw logs and haul them across five hundred yards of field — and to do that he'd have to fix a rotted rim on the wood trailer — and if he was going to do the one it'd be a waste if he didn't knock out the other at the same time.

And there was work all over the barn. Boards needing replaced. Corn to shuck. After getting fired at the clay plant two years ago — the only place with manufacturing jobs in the county — Frank had thought maybe he was close enough to turning on Social Security that he could eke out a life on his own terms, ramping up the farm's productivity enough to add a couple dollars of income, and not just food. With the mortgage paid, he wouldn't have needed very much good fortune to make a go of it.

But good fortune disappeared into work, and the pile of work ahead never seemed to diminish. The product of his labor was consumed in maintaining tools, machines or ten thousand smaller expenses that cropped up better than his corn. Profit, nowhere to be found.

Meanwhile, his son turned into a thief.

And Frank knew as soon as he asked Linc about the money missing from the clay jar, his son would turn into a liar too.

Senior's Tractor Supply was a hundred yards ahead. Frank shifted in his seat and got a full look at the vehicle driving behind him without its headlights on.

Frank put on his turn signal, braked, and waiting for an oncoming car to pass, glanced three times in his rearview and twice in his side view.

"Easy, guy. Tap the brakes a little harder. A little harder..."

Frank released his foot from the brake pedal. Let the truck ease forward. He looked in the mirror.

The car was in a skid.

"Lincoln! Put your back in the seat! Now!"

THREE
TALK TO HER...

Linc froze at his father's shout. In his mind's eye he was at the county fair where he'd gotten a glimpse of Sue Cooper last summer, in a dress showing off her achingly beautiful bony knees. Except this time, she and he were tucked where all the power cables ran behind a food truck that sold hot sausage sandwiches.

The irony was not lost.

The gathering evening made it a perfect place for Sue to lean toward him with her lips puckered, slick and juicy with cherry lip gloss — her eyes softly closing —

Linc's heart almost bounced free of his rib cage. He expected something like the taste of a Luden's cough drop. He bent toward her.

In the truck seat he was leaning forward too, and when the car behind them slammed into the F-150's bumper, the kinetic jolt knocked Linc back into the seat at the same time Sue's lips painted gloss on his.

The girl could kiss.

The truck burped forward a couple inches and rolled another foot.

Frank grabbed Linc and peered into his face with such intensity Linc recoiled.

"What?"

Frank let loose a long slow breath. He placed both hands on his thighs and stared forward while emergency seconds ticked off the clock, each one seeming a mile long and two deep, so after three seconds of silence, to Linc, the whole catastrophe seemed like it was days ago and a county away.

"What happened?" Linc said.

"Car hit us. I expect he got the worst of it. Better see."

The oncoming car in the opposite lane had passed a moment after the collision. Frank cut the wheel, pressed the gas, bounced over the rut and entered the empty Senior's Tractor Supply parking lot.

The Toyota that hit him followed into the lot and parked behind Frank's F-150.

Still in the driver's seat, watching the sideview, Frank pressed the brake and watched his taillights reflect red off the Camry's front bumper and the nearby snow.

"You all right, son? Your neck okay? Turn your head a bit."

"I'm okay."

"Do as I said. Turn your head back and forth."

Linc complied.

"Nothin' feel funny?"

"I said I'm okay."

Frank opened his door and stepped into a fresh six inches of snow that had accumulated since the lot had last been plowed. You'd think with all the tractors around...

He limped to the back of the truck, glanced at his bumper then to the man in a black and yellow coat stepping out of the Camry. Never saw him before... some idiot from the city.

"You all right?" said the man. "Your leg all right?"

"Huh?"

"Your limp."

"Nah, that's nothin'." Frank said. "The war. Shrapnel."

"Oh. Good. I mean — any damage to the bumper?"

"Yours a little. Got some scratches and your grill's messed up. Looks like my hitch was just short of going through your radiator. You all right? No whiplash or anything?"

"I'm still in one piece. Hey listen — I'm sorry. This whole thing was my fault... any damages or whatever... I think there was some ice under the snow or something."

The man unzipped his Pittsburgh Steelers coat and fished for his wallet.

Frank paused him with an open hand. "You're admitting fault?"

"Uh – yeah, I guess that's what I mean."

"Then don't worry about it. My bumper has so many dents, more don't matter. And you can likely fix your grill for less than your deductible. You turn it in, and they'll just kill you on your rates the next forty years. How they operate."

"Uh... you don't want my information in case something comes up?"

"My son and me are fine. Just give us a surprise, is all."

"Okay. Uh. Thank you?"

"Stay safe."

Frank caught Linc's look, then turned his gaze toward the building entrance. He put his hands in his gaping pockets and found snow had already accumulated inside.

The Camry door closed behind him, but Frank didn't look. He opened the door and held it. Linc was ten paces behind.

"C'mon!"

Linc scooted his boots.

Frank released the door and headed for the counter where a platinum blond he recognized from the week before was still standing, wearing the same turquoise sweater, accented by old woman glasses with six feet of beads off each side of her head. She wasn't anywhere near antique enough to pull off the look. In different light, actually... maybe...

She had decent lines but came from somewhere else. If she'd have grown up in Oak, he'd have known her. As it was, he could only place her to last summer. Any more hesitation while he studied her form, she'd take it to mean something. Probably already did. Should he apologize?

Frank cleared his throat while Linc smirked. "You gonna talk to her?"

FOUR
Just the right thing...

Frank smiled, hard.

"My name's Buzzard. I think it was you that left a message. I ordered a distributor last week for a '52 8N."

"Frank, right? That came in a few days ago."

She tapped the keyboard.

"I just got the message today."

"No worries. I called three days ago and again this afternoon. Let me go grab it."

"Wait. Three days ago... did you leave a message that time too?"

"Sure did, sweetie."

She stepped from the register and disappeared into a ceiling-high framework of steel beams and boxes. Parts everywhere — probably enough he could build a new tractor from scratch.

Frank glanced to his side. She hadn't called him sweetie last time. Last time it was mister. He blinked. Blinked again. The fluorescent lights flickered but no one else seemed to mind. He had a tooth abscess starting. Maybe. Frank hadn't noticed the lady called him sweetie until she walked away. Linc was eyeballing the candy bars.

Frank rubbed his eyes.

Some people couldn't see fast enough to notice a jittery fluorescent. But they knew how to sell a candy bar. Everybody selling everything — and not because a man hunting a distributor for a 1952 Ford tractor required chocolate and peanuts to go with it. They put nuisance products up by the register as a form of deceit, knowing they were more likely to snag interest at the last minute. The afterthought sale.

Whole world was full of people like that. John Senior. Tricks and subtle deceptions that over time always accrued to the business. Like the casino always winning in the long run — not that Frank would ever fool away a dollar at a game of chance. He wouldn't risk losing a dollar at a game of skill either — even if he thought he had the skill to win. Best thing to do with a dollar was save it or buy something that would last a hundred and ten years.

Frank Buzzard: the poorest financial genius in Oak. That's what refusing to play fast and loose with your morals got you.

Platinum returned while opening a box that fit easily in both her hands, timed so the top flap revealed the distributor as she arrived at the counter. She held the box open — her fingers were long, and her nails painted soft blue — hey! they matched her beads — then offered the box to Frank.

He glanced at her name badge and grinned.

"Susan, huh?"

She smiled big and with the added wrinkles her glasses looked more at home.

"Something funny?"

"My son — his girl's name is Sue — we were talking on the way in. You ever put Lazy Susans in your boots for Halloween? That'd be — "

Linc rolled his eyes. "Really? We're doing this?"

"That'd be funny," she said. "But I'm not a lazy Susan. I work my tail off in here."

Frank fought a compulsion to scope her body again and say something both predictably clever and regrettable.

"I didn't mean... we were just talking on the way in."

She shrugged. "Hey, it's funny enough for February. You look familiar. Weren't you in here last summer?"

"Yeah. The radiator finally let out. It's a constant restoration job. Believe me, I don't like comin' here."

"Well, we like seeing you."

Frank pulled his wallet from his pocket and nodded beyond the register to a closed bay door.

"I noticed last week you didn't have the maintenance garage open. That some new winter thing?"

"Lou died."

"Nah. Shucks. Man, that's rough. How's — what's his wife's name?"

Frank pulled out his bank card. Kept it in hand.

"Gloria."

"She holdin' up all right? How far back'd Lou pass?"

"He died, what, six-eight months ago? June, July, something. Not too long after I started here. And his wife passed — I dunno. Only heard about it, you know? I think she passed a couple years before him."

Frank looked at the floor. "Guess I haven't been paying attention. That's too bad for both of them. They was family to John Senior, right?"

"He called him Uncle Lou — but I don't know if Lou was anybody's uncle. He was a Fortunato, not a Senior. But he was one of those guys, you know? Here so long he was everybody's uncle."

"Wasn't nothin' made of metal he couldn't make work again. I'm sorry I didn't hear. Real sorry."

Frank offered his debit card and Susan took it. He noticed how long her fingernails were, and then realized he'd already noticed once before. Such a range of functions, for long fingernails. Drag them light and create sweet delight. Drag them heavy, say, down a man's back —

"Uh, that's weird," Susan said.

"What?"

"The computer says it went through, but the prompt never came up. It never asked you to sign. Or for your PIN."

Frank looked blank.

"It's never done that."

Frank maintained his half-smile. The skin on his back tingled like he needed to press up against a barn timber and give it a good scratch.

"Well, the receipt's ready to print," Susan said.

She hit a key. A tiny printer spat paper. She ripped it off and placed it on the counter. Pointed to the bottom line and pushed a pen from her side of the countertop to his.

Frank watched her face instead.

"I guess it went through," Susan said.

"But you don't know?"

She shrugged her eyebrows. Her eyes bulged behind her lenses. Susan pushed the receipt closer to Frank.

"I guess the distributor's yours."

"But we don't know if the charge went through?"

"I don't know how it did, but the computer says it did."

Frank leaned closer. That fluorescent light — he blinked, and it felt like he had grit under his eyelids. Must have been from coming in out of the cold.

Wait.

What?

"Uh, Susan? I asked when I ordered, and the part was ninety something. Niney-three, I think. This says one thirty-six niney-four."

"Let me see something."

She tapped the keyboard.

Frank shook his head. Clamped his teeth. This was just the thing to expect at a store run by John Senior.

Susan turned the monitor.

"There's two models. The warehouse was out of the cheaper one so we ordered the other. You don't have to take it. We'll just keep it in stock. Plenty of 8N's out there."

Frank saw his checkbook register in his mind's eye. Wished he'd brought it along, but it was easier to use the debit card and reconcile his book with the receipt. Forty bucks. With the homeowner's insurance due...

"Well, I don't have a choice. Tractor's got to run. If I ordered the other, how long would it take?"

"No telling if we can get it at all. Computer says out of stock."

Frank clenched his teeth. Tried to ward off the feeling that having no money was about the same as having no worth.

"I need the distributor, so I guess... Yeah. Ring it up."

"I already did. Here's your receipt."

"Oh. But we still don't know if — hey, can I get my card?"

She slid his plastic across the glass countertop and Frank thought maybe he'd break his insurance bill into semi annual or quarterly payments, like he'd considered driving in.

"Can I borrow your phone a second?"

"Here you go, sugar."

He flipped the card and changed the angle until the glare vanished and he could read the numbers, then cradled the phone to his shoulder and tapped the keypad.

With his head tilted he noticed Linc, again eyeballing the candy bars.

"Uh, hello; yeah, Miss — this Cindy? Oh, Joy. Thought I recognized your voice. Yeah, this is Frank Buzzard. I'm at the Tractor Supply and we have a glitch or something with the computer. Can you see if I've had any transactions in the last couple of minutes?"

He read half of his card number, changed his angle under the long white bulbs and read the rest.

"Okay, good. Thank you Joy. No, that's all. You have a nice day. Okay. Yep. Uh-huh. Uh-huh. No, I'm not interested. Bye."

Susan watched.

Frank shook his head. "Didn't go through."

"Oh, you're such a dear. I don't know why I didn't think of calling the bank."

"It's no trouble. You have another machine to use? I only brought the one card."

"I'm going to cancel out the whole thing and start over."

Susan pressed her glasses farther up her nose and struck the computer keyboard with her index finger only, as if her main ambition was to get a resounding crack! out of each stroke.

"Okay. That's cleared out. Let's try it again."

Frank gave her his card. She rubbed it on her sweater under her right collarbone. Frank watched. Linc's head snapped around. Susan ran the card through the reader.

"This is debit, right?"

"Yep."

Susan gingerly pressed a key. Her face tightened. Her smile puckered. Her eyebrows ascended dizzying heights. Then her mouth split into a wide grin.

"Okay. Good! Look. It wants your PIN. It's working this time."

Frank pressed 6574, the last four of Linc's Social Security number.

They waited. Frank looked at Susan and found her watching his eyes and fought an irrational fear that his card would be declined even though the funds were in the account.

ACCEPTED

Frank exhaled. Looked around. Linc had wandered farther down the counter and seemed interested in nuisance-sale LED flashlights. Or — more likely — the magazine rack had a cover showing cleavage that looked good at fifteen feet.

"I can't thank you enough for calling your bank," Susan said. "Otherwise, I think that distributor would have come out of my paycheck."

"Knowing John Senior."

Her mouth partly opened. No words.

"Thank you," Frank said.

She gave him his receipt. "Thank you. Seriously, thank you."

"Just the right thing to do," Frank said. "Gee whiz."

Near the door, Frank half-turned. Susan had pulled her glasses off her face. She waved and Frank nodded.

"C'mon Linc. Let's go."

FIVE
How to Drive...

Following Frank to the F-150, Linc watched the way his father walked with his right leg bowed out. Through the years he'd seen his father in every conceivable configuration: walking like now in loose pants, bent at the knee, folded up tight while he squatted next to a tractor hitch. He'd even seen his father's crippled leg with the foot twisted halfway around, clockwise, stuck in a trench while Frank fell away, such that his knee should have blown into a hundred pieces. Later Linc learned the shovel-wide trench they were digging had a pocket, and Frank's foot rotated into a space opened up from the last big rock pried out with the heavy steel digging bar. Then he learned his father never laced his boots tight since the war. His foot had only rotated a quarter way around, not a full half circle.

But what stuck with Linc — because it was wrong — was that his father kept a lot of play in his boots.

Frank Buzzard didn't permit slop anywhere in his life. He spent every waking moment looking for opportunities to be rigid. To be consistent, he ought to have worn his boots so tight his feet turned black and fell off.

Still, Linc had seen his father's right leg in every configuration possible except in a pair of shorts, and from the various contours, the way his pant leg pressed at various times, Linc had noticed a sizable part of his father's right thigh was missing. The only thing Frank ever said about it was, "artillery shrapnel," as if a couple nouns described what happened.

Linc's father was a slop-booted hypocrite.

And just now, worried about every penny in his check book, given the opportunity to save a hundred and thirty-six dollars, he chose to make a big show of his principles for the heavy racked woman at the farm store.

Did old people even get horny?

And another thing: if the family finances were so bad Linc couldn't have school clothes, why didn't Frank clutch his neck when he got out of the truck and sue the guy who hit him? Did he want to survive or didn't he? He complained about money but didn't take advantage of a golden opportunity to make a bundle. Josh Ward at school — his father was side swiped, and the insurance company paid out ten grand.

The money situation couldn't be as bad as Frank let on. Anywhere you look, desperate people never missed an opportunity to capitalize on someone else's mistakes. That was the first rule of survival. If someone's dumb enough to give you a distributor you desperately need without paying for it, you take the distributor.

That meant Frank *chose* to not buy Linc school clothes. And that meant Frank deliberately made Linc stew in shame every minute of every day at school.

Linc knew if he climbed inside the cab that moment, it would be a sore challenge to keep his mouth shut.

Struck by fortuitous curiosity, he kept walking to the back of the F-150 and observed the bumper. He'd hung back earlier, listening, while his father spoke with the man in the Pittsburgh Steelers coat. Frank had said there was no damage but to Linc the impact seemed too powerful to have not dented the truck.

He needed to see for himself.

"C'mon, son."

Frank slammed his door. Roused the engine. Got the wipers blasting fresh snow off the windshield, then turned them off. He stepped back outside and beat the first wiper against the glass, breaking ice from the blade, then did the same to the other.

Linc stepped farther away from the truck and beheld the bumper from a wider angle. Snow landed on his neck and he turned his collar higher.

He studied the truck's back end and smiled as a mental image formed: he dropped the tailgate and sat under the hot summer sun with Sue Cooper, a load of hay bales and a blanket behind them. Sweat wet on his brow. Her skin was shiny with it. Maybe they had a couple wine coolers. He'd heard at school the girls liked them. Maybe if he pressed Sue's boot with his, that magnificently curved calf of hers would — or better still, if he dared tuck his leg behind hers and bring it forward, she could wrap her foot around his ankle, and they'd be tangled.

One limb down. Three to go.

Mercy.

Linc swallowed. Her nipples showed through her top. She squirmed in her jean shorts and took a sudden breath the way a person does before getting psyched or taking a plunge.

Linc felt woozy.

"What're you doing back there? C'mon! We got to milk."

Frank reentered the truck and slammed the door.

Linc discovered the rear of the F-150. How long had he been standing there with his mouth gapped? He'd better make sure to see something worth the delay.

Most of the purple-hued parking lot lights were on and if his father hadn't noticed the new dents in the bumper, he wasn't looking. The whole thing hung at the wrong angle, as if the hitch wrenched the bumper downward in the middle so it took the shape of a shallow V.

Linc joined his father inside the truck.

"What?"

"Nothing."

"What were you looking at?"

"The bumper."

"Why?"

"I dunno."

"Of course you do."

"To see how hard the Steeler fan hit us."

"What'd you see?"

"Bumper's bent to hell."

"Language. Watch your mouth."

Frank put on his seat belt. Waited.

Waited.

"Strap in."

"Forgot."

Linc clicked his seat belt.

Frank drove, now even more hatefully slow than before.

Looking out the window, Linc practiced crossing his eyes until he got dizzy.

His friend Tony had an older cousin named Steve who had a smoking hot sister and a primer gray Chevelle that didn't run. Steve worked at the clay plant in the summers — his father was an executive and got him the job ahead of college-age boys — and he saved his money until he could go to Sears Brothers' junk yard and buy a new used engine and all the other parts he needed. Steve talked it up the whole time it took him to figure out how to put the Chevelle on the road, working nights in his father's garage at home. His father liked to tinker with cars too. By the time Steve was sixteen, since he didn't work on a farm year-round and had loads and loads of free time, he and mostly his father had the new engine in and the Chevelle road ready. Steve bragged for a month that the junkyard engine came from a Vette and everybody teased, what, like a Chevette? A big fuel injected two-liter? My dad's chainsaw has a bigger engine. But after his birthday when Steve got his license, he drove the beast to school and lifted the hood for everyone to see. He and his father had installed a 6.2 liter, 525-horse engine from a wrecked Corvette that only had two thousand miles on it. When classes let out, Steve took a bunch of kids for some donuts in the grass next to the bleachers at the football field, a good mile from school, down past Sawmill Creek and across the railroad tracks. Then he drove all six of the kids who were crammed into the car home, doing his best to stay on dirt roads so he could fishtail every inch of every mile. He took one turn so hard Linc — crammed tight in the back seat and leaning forward so everybody's shoulders would fit — couldn't help but land in Steve's sister's humongous right boob. It was like landing in a pillow. He wanted to open his mouth or nestle his head but instead bonked it against the window as Steve corrected the fishtail. Steve's sister called him a cretin and knuckle-punched his leg so hard she gave him a charlie horse.

  THAT was how to drive.

  Frank inched along the snowy road.

Six
Truce...

Linc inhaled deep and let out a breathy huff.

"Something on your mind?"

Another huff, drawn out longer.

"What's going on in that head of yours?"

"I could have had the milking done already. I have homework."

"It's Friday. You have all weekend for homework."

Driving through town, Frank slowed and rotated his head while passing the insurance man's office.

"You see anyone inside?"

"Lights are on."

Frank shot his arm out of his coat twice and then removed his other hand from the steering wheel and pushed back his sleeve. He looked at his watch. Frowned. Noticed the fuel gauge getting low. Kept driving.

"Why you so ornery this afternoon?"

"I'm not."

"Lord, give me a straight answer from this boy, one time. I'll be your bondservant."

Linc blinked three times with his teeth clamped but they failed to stop his words.

"Oh, you want a straight answer? You gave away a hundred and thirty-six dollars and I'm wearing last years' floods[1]! You're nothing but a hypocrite."

Frank recoiled.

His boy was correct about one thing even if he was dead, dead wrong about the meaning of hypocrite. By any fair estimate, Frank was a mediocre provider. But wait a damn minute —

"You say I should steal from John Senior, and you got the gall to question my honor?" Frank drove the side of his fist to the truck door. "I could spit!"

Unbid, he recalled the prior night as he lay on his back in bed, finally situated so the covers weren't pulling his toes one way or the other. He'd been reliving the day's troubles and in the twilight of consciousness before sleep he considered the full of his life in a single broad stroke and thought, I'm weary of it.

The memory brought a hopeless hue to a moment that otherwise seemed a natural opportunity to mention Linc's theft from the money jar. But Frank considered the yawning black void of his anger and how close he was to falling into it, crossing a line he'd sworn to never cross again. He kept his eyes forward, scanning the road, the drifts, the thin black line the plow had cut that revealed the edge of the pavement.

He thought of his wife Jenny, just her face, not doing anything. It'd been so many years, Frank mostly saw her as a mind-photo where her expression changed to reveal if she was proud of him in the moment, or less than proud.

Seemed like a long time since he'd felt better after seeing her.

"We'll have more money, eventually. Just got to get caught up with all the repairs and maintenance. You see everything that's gone wrong. It takes money to make it right. Takes money to make money. That's the first rule of business."

"Your pants fit."

Frank shook his head.

"I'm wearing last years' floods. You could have just taken the stupid distributor and kept the money. She was giving it to you."

"That's not how it works."

"That's how it would have worked."

Frank thought of the dollars missing from the clay jar.

INTEGRITY

"Pull up your socks, if you don't want people to know you have ankles."

"Whatever."

Frank's right fist hardened around the steering wheel and his arm tingled. But he remembered Turquoise Susan looking at him at Senior's Tractor Supply, and him feeling like having no money was the same as having no worth, and his ambition stalled.

That stink think about the money wasn't exactly true. He had assets and they had far more value in terms of what they could provide, if exercised, than in terms of what someone else would pay for them.

Take the Ford 8N: it looked like junk, but it would probably run another four hundred years, so long as someone gave it tender love and care and maintained it with new parts every now and then. A magazine at the barber shop said human beings replace their whole body over and over, cell by cell, many times over the course of a regular lifespan. Tractors were no different. They needed parts, and just like the case with people, the more TLC, the less repair. But the point being, the tractor was just as work capable as the day Hank Ford drove it off the line. It wasn't Frank's fault the government wanted inflation, so the prices of old things went down, and the prices of new things went up. The big wigs in their gray suits, with their monogrammed and cuff-linked shirts thought no one understood how the government and the banks conspired to destroy the working man's money. And with the sorry condition of high school education in the country, it was true: almost nobody did understand; especially not the young people — like Linc — being fed into the machine.

Fat lot they could do about it if they did, other than keep their rage bottled up like so much fuel for the next day's labor. How could a working man have time to keep bankers and politicians in check, anyhow?

No way on earth Frank would be a willing slave to the consumer mentality, buying new cars every couple years; running up debt, abandoning tools just because they got a couple dents and the paint chipped off.

Frank owned his house, barn and land, free and clear.

They sure liked to wet their beaks with taxes. Every which way they could figure a claim on a man, they'd stake it. And the banks would be all too happy to take a lien on his property if Frank ever was foolish enough to ask them for money. Point being, there were forces all around, some more successful than others, that wanted to make Frank work like a dog for them instead of work like a dog for himself.

Another metaphor came to mind, and another. He was almost ashamed to think in such lowbrow terms, but if the shoe fit... He'd spent his entire life until two years ago like a hooked fish fighting the line, finally losing his temper at the clay plant and breaking free. All of a sudden, he didn't have the weight of rod, reel, man, and boat dragging him into something that looked, walked and quacked like indentured servitude.

When he thought about trying to find a new job in a town that only had a clay plant, five fast food restaurants, two gas stations and little else save the churches, he considered employing himself.

The farm had supported two generations of Buzzards before Frank's father failed at it. Frank had bought the place after getting married, thinking between him and Jenny, they'd be able to decrease the food bill, grow some help and build something worthy of the heart and soul they'd invest in it.

But that didn't happen. Frank got on at the clay plant because Jenny's uncle had worked there twenty years and he put in a good word. Jenny didn't get pregnant until the end, and fifty-hour weeks at the clay plant didn't leave a lot of time or need for tilling fields. It was a hobby farm, under Frank's tenure.

— However, after speaking up at the plant about practices that looked borderline criminal, and not having the sense to close his mouth and stop poking around outside his area of operation, his job at the clay plant was no longer a lead weight at his feet, holding him down.

Why not run the farm full time?

Linc was old enough to do real work. Together they could build something for the boy to inherit, meaning, Frank might spare Linc from ever entering the trap of working for another man.

Betting on himself felt like gambling, but self employment felt like self ownership, and the benefits would accrue not merely to the remainder of Frank's life, but to Linc's as well. And likewise, the opportunity cost of not owning himself would be charged to him and Linc as well. That made the risk appear small compared to the mountain of reward.

He could do it.

The farm's assets were like different parts of a machine. Getting the enterprise up and running again was like fixing an engine. An engine needed gas, spark, and air. A farm required smarts, labor, and half decent weather. Combine the three and it ought to kick when he turned it over.

Two years in, Frank wondered which element he lacked.

It wasn't labor.

The weather had been accommodating.

Was he too stupid to admit he was stupid?

How would he even know?

Frank turned his face from Linc and blinked until the road was clear again, then rubbed his eyes as if they were bothered by dust.

Each generation grew up thinking they were free because their schools told them they were. George Washington never uttered a lie. Shining city on a hill. Manifest destiny and American exceptionalism and all that other horse manure. All Frank's life he'd been watching how the rules kept changing. Each generation was more encumbered by the tax men and educated so poorly they become enthusiastic slaves of the debt men too.

End result: any man or woman, not just Frank, could have his or her body maimed in service of a government whim, come home and get robbed with every paycheck for forty-plus years, and split what was left with the usurers. The best of his labor was skimmed off the top and bottom too, and the gain of his labor, the dividends, compounded in the account of the man who had enough capital in the beginning to entice other men to trade their hours for dollars.

In short, Frank understood the benefit of his labor was not the simple task he completed, but the sliver of the profit his work made possible. A company was more than the sum of its labor — and to those who would scoff that he had no capital at risk and didn't deserve a share of the gain, he would agree. He didn't risk capital.

He took capital risk.

He based his household economics on a company that could do foul things and stain his name, that could discard him as easily as retain him.

Who stood to suffer the larger loss?

Why did the profit go to those with the least to lose? Especially now that the government used taxes to bail out the moneyed class every time their own incompetence caught up with them.

Frank had spent most of his life with his head buried so deep in work he never looked up to take in the full picture. Then one day, his productivity all but shot, he saw how prior generations plotted to harness the sons of the next.

Just like the generation before that, and before that, back to the beginning.

He worked hard, lived clean, small and diligent, and still had nothing to show for it. He wanted to slam Linc into the nearest wall and scream, "DON'T FALL FOR IT! DON'T BE A SUCKER LIKE ME!"

But the boy wouldn't understand.

The young lived on hubris like it was a bottomless bowl of spaghetti, always gambling they had plenty of time to figure things out. Plenty of time to get serious... later.

Cresting the last hill before his place, Frank began tapping the brakes. His frozen land stretched before him.

If he could get the farm running just a little more profitably — if he could keep his health, get a couple good years' weather, plus a little luck, his son could inherit a better life. Possibly attain a level of freedom that had evaded Frank, and at the end have something to show for his pain and sweat. He might spare Linc years of drudgery, exchanging his most energetic and creative work for wages instead of equity in his own dream.

Coming to his driveway, Frank braked. Linc was still enamored with the view out the side window.

With thumb and pointer finger, Frank again swept his eyes free of wetness.

"We'll need to get after the milking, right away."

Linc half-faced him; a mutual sobriety seemed to bind them.

"I'll get on it," Linc said. "Then homework."

"Okay."

---

1. Floods is a regional term for pants which are too short. As in, the pants were worn in a flood, and subsequently shrank.

SEVEN
Lucky cows...

Linc kicked his leg out of the truck door after he opened it and then he stepped to the ground. Each year he'd grown stronger and stronger and each year his father grew weaker. It wouldn't take very long until their paths would cross.

Linc would be the smarter one; he'd wait until the outcome would be perfect.

It was strange to imagine himself in a future state of total rebellion against his father. A true fight to the death if Frank didn't learn to treat him with basic respect and honor the time Linc spent busting his back without pay on a farm that would only be worth something if it was sold to a competent... anything. A competent human being.

Linc wasn't blind. He'd grown up watching how his father thought things through like a cave man studying quantum physics. Linc was a million times faster to understand whatever he looked at. Puzzles. Math. Measurements.

He just wasn't filled out enough. Standing six foot flat and weighing a buck forty, Linc truly was a bean pole.

A rice-and-beans bean pole, with venison or some other game just about every day.

Linc tromped through the day's fresh snow, which had long since buried his footprints from 5AM that morning.

When he moved against his father — whatever avenue he took — he'd only be fighting for the right to take care of himself because he knew he'd do a better job of it than his old man was doing.

Wasn't self defense a basic right?

Wasn't that fair?

Behind Linc, still at the truck, Frank closed his door and said, "I'll be there in a minute."

"Fine."

Linc waved without looking back.

How could his father not grasp how humiliating it was to wear floods to school? There were programs for degenerate liar wastoids that couldn't keep their acts together well enough to hold a job. The school sent letters each year to make sure a kid wasn't in need. But Frank would rather pretend he was a fit man and competent to raise his son, just to avoid accepting help. He lied about his income, basically. Not the amount: the school didn't ask that. But it did ask in a way if Frank's income was sufficient, and that's where Frank deserved a giant neon HYPOCRITE sign over his head. And the result was even less money in the household because Frank had to buy food for his son to pack to school each day. Such a great businessman! Instead of Linc getting both free lunches and new pants each year, bought with reclaimed lunch money, Linc ate a peanut butter and jelly sandwich each day at 11:30. Not that he wanted the embarrassment of free lunches. But pit the humiliation of a couple kids hearing a rumor of what they already knew — Linc's father was poor, hence Linc was too — versus everyone who saw him being unable to refrain from smirking, or all-out laughing in his face because his pants were crazy short, Linc would take the free lunches.

Every cent was important to his father. Just not the pennies that would spare Linc his daily humiliation.

A few days before, Pete Dickey called him Ankleman in the hallway outside of Biology.

Ankleman.

Linc went berserk but Pete never went anywhere without his jock pals and they each got a hold of Linc somewhere and pulled him off Pete. They left him on the floor on his back, but rage returned Linc to his feet. He lowered his head and charged the retreating line. Unable to tear through, Linc didn't stop thrashing until a junior year heavyweight wrestler punched him above his ear so hard he collapsed against the wall lockers.

Not that Pete didn't have a point calling him Ankleman.

Linc's floods were not the kind you'd miss if your eyes swept the room. Linc's floods were halfway up his calves. He'd grown eighteen inches in three years. He was a beanpole. An Ichabod. His waist had only expanded from 27 to 28 inches, but he'd lengthened from four foot six to six feet, half coming from his scrawny, bony, humiliating ankles, which his pants left out in the open for everyone to mock.

And his crotch was so tight! His pants were designed for boys standing four six!

Linc's groin ached.

Sue Cooper!

Aagh. She was wonderful.

Linc had to milk.

Aagh. Lucky cows.

At least he'd thought to snag a couple Snickers Bars from the Tractor Supply. If he only took a single good-sized bite each day he could prolong the Snickers Experience for a week.

Outside the lower entrance, Linc stomped snow until he could open the door.

He stepped inside. Smelled cows and their waste.

But in his mind, he heard Sue Cooper moan as he drizzled *I love you* in melted Snickers on her naked torso, and it was like the cows and barn weren't there at all.

EIGHT
General Sherman

Frank parked the F-150 in front of the barn. As Linc angled toward the lower entrance, the most direct route to the cows, Frank said, "I'll be there in a minute."

Linc didn't look back but mumbled something and added an arm motion Frank could choose to interpret as either "I'll take care of the milking" or "I reject planet earth."

Hard to tell — and probably why Linc did it.

His son was capable of milking all ten cows without Frank's help. But if Linc was working then Frank ought to be working too.

But first he wanted to verify the distributor he'd bought at Senior's Tractor Supply matched the one he'd be replacing. The Tractor Supply had screwed up another part Frank had ordered a few years ago, blaming the mistake on the part number being wrong in the computer, an error that made Frank's repair job take ten days instead of five. Ever since, he made a practice of comparing the new part to the old right away, even if he didn't have time to do the repair until later.

Usually, he brought the old part with him when he picked up the new. But the night before — Thursday — he'd found a letter in the mail from his old war buddy Jake Walsh, and Jake's handwritten scrawl provoked Frank to drive three hours to Pittsburgh first thing Friday morning after milking. After a couple hours for tearful hugs, sitting at Jake's deathbed while his painkillers and meds kept knocking him out, a small amount of time telling stories, and an even smaller portion given to Jake explaining his gift of the arsenal now resting on Frank's sofa, then the three-hour drive home — Frank failed to muster the minutes required to remove the old distributor before driving to the Tractor Supply.

Frank hadn't even performed a true inventory of the weapons he'd received and couldn't speculate on their condition other than that they seemed well cared for.

And he still had to ask Linc why he'd never heard about the message Turquoise Susan left after her first call on Wednesday.

Walking to the barn Frank removed the distributor from the box and turned it over in his hands. He slipped. Found his footing.

The barn door required extra muscle to slide open but as Frank glanced upward a snowflake landed in his eye and he didn't spend another moment wondering what was jamming the track. Instead, he mused about how nice it would be if his other tasks would similarly melt when the sun returned.

Door opened, enough of the day's decaying light entered the barn to reach the 8N and a few rays glinted off a pair of stainless-steel dog food and water bowls hung on the wall like hub cabs found on the roadside.

At the tractor Frank held the new distributor next to the old one, still mounted on the side of the 8N's engine.

Perfect match.

Frank grinned, warmed by a tiny blue nub of optimism ignited within him. Life was nothing but work and trouble, and to have a project look like it was going to be work and no trouble — that was the kind of thing a man might enjoy, so long as he didn't feel entitled to easy living in the future.

Work and no trouble... as if that happened more than once in a blue moon. Frank thought a moment. Every day seemed a gauntlet of mechanical breakdowns, shortages, weather, his budding-thief of a son testing his jocular fiber.

For something Frank had been joking about his whole life — jocular fiber — he didn't seem to have much. Life was damn hard, and it wasn't funny most of the time.

If he didn't have the jocular fiber, what sinew held him together?

Frank leaned on the tractor's rear tire and drained his lungs. Let his shoulders sag and his back curve. Allowed his head to droop, stretching tendons down his neck and spine.

A day spent behind the wheel looking at bright white snow had made his eyes tired and sitting all day in the F-150 seemed to allow his body to realize it was tired too.

Good thing there was plenty of work to think about.

The 8N would be running in prime form in no time. He'd replace the distributor, then tackle the welding job on the wood wagon's rusted rims, and by then with luck the sky would be snowless blue, and he'd clear a path to some of the hardwood trees he'd felled, up at the wooded top of Kroh Hill. In the worst case, if he couldn't follow the tractor road at the edge of his fields, he could take the long way around: five and a half miles of dirt road to get to the same place he could reach in a half mile following the perimeter of his fields, or five hundred yards, cutting across.

Regardless, firewood would be cut within days, or the house would go cold.

Enjoying his moment of quiet in the rapidly dimming daylight, Frank climbed onto the tractor. The original 8N had a sculpted, flat seat. Frank had swapped it with one from a junked Cub Cadet lawnmower, with a comfortable backrest. Leaning backward, Frank slid downward so his spine pressed the top of the backrest, popping each joint capable. Once he was sitting like he did in high school, slunk low with his legs way out, as if to provide his crotch the best view of the room, his gaze again crossed the dog food and water bowls hanging like ornaments on the barn wall.

Three years had passed since General Sherman died. Frank thought of Linc's moody, mopey demeanor and wondered if the dog's death coincided.

Three years since Sherman died... and two years since Frank had been fired from the clay plant.

Which meant, two years since he'd forever stained his soul by beating his son until he couldn't move.

NINE
"That's all of us."

Frank hadn't gotten a new dog after General Sherman because dogs were overrated as guards, unnecessary for hunting, and only cost money. That's what he told Linc, the only time he asked.

Truth was, none of his dogs ever liked Frank.

Sherman had growled every time he walked past, like the dog could see something was wrong in his head. Heck of a thing to want to commiserate and the dog doesn't tolerate you, and all you ever did was feed him and keep a warm rug in front of the fireplace for him to lay on.

One day when General Sherman was old and had been having difficulty getting around for a while, Frank saw he couldn't power himself off the rug.

Frank drug the rug outside, eased Sherman off as best he could without upsetting the dog's insides, and for the first time in years sat close without the animal growling.

Frank eased a .22 pistol out of the small of his back where he'd tucked it, and rested it on the ground, and without a word slipped his fingers to the back of the dog's head.

He rubbed Sherman behind the ears and marveled that the dog allowed him.

Frank had planned on slipping the pistol up, only using his fingers as a quick deception, but General Sherman's weak, high-pitched grumble-mumbles stayed Frank's execution of his role. He worked his fingers in small circles until they tired, and his back hurt where he suspected he had a rib that somehow loosed itself off his spine when he was tugging a hay rake that was stuck when he as a kid. The wound had never healed, so much as disappeared from notice time to time.

Eventually General Sherman stopped growling.

"Goodbye," Frank said.

He eased the pistol next to the dog's head and noticed the dog's chest wasn't filling or falling, and he waited a long time, knowing Linc was at school, and no one was watching. Though his heart felt like it was going to explode with love and misery, and no one, not even God was paying attention, his eyes remained dry and his mouth flat.

Even still, he wondered if someday Jesus would say to him, *Here is one in whom there is no deceit.*

In his emptiness it was too much to hope.

I saw you under the fig tree.

Frank buried Sherman in a field where his decaying body would do some good, but deep enough the plow wouldn't catch it. After washing the rug in mild bleach, he let it hang a week on the line and then returned it to the living room. He placed Sherman's food and water bowls in the barn, on nails on the wall, and let the dog food sit in the basement until a year passed and he dumped it in the field at the edge of the lawn, where he threw table scraps and everything else that might compost back into soil.

Frank observed the dull sheen of the stainless-steel dog dishes go gray as dusk and dark clouds overwhelmed the Buzzard farm.

Much as Frank pondered, he couldn't attach the dog's mistrust of him to any deed he'd done. He never abused the dog. Never cussed him, hit him, anything. Yet, it wasn't some anomaly with General Sherman. He tolerated others, fine.

Frank sat erect in the tractor seat, swung his legs down and dismounted.

Time to catch up with Linc and the milking — but Frank stopped walking.

The day's routines were jumbled.

He'd only thought to set a hog out to thaw that morning. It was sizable and would likely still be frozen inside.

Leaving the barn's main level door open Frank limped to the house. He couldn't help staring at the rifles leaning against the back cushions of the couch. He'd transported some of them in cases, most in blankets that Jake had suggested he bring along for the purpose. Some of the rifles appeared to be gems. Stocks like polished glass. Others — the real workhorses — were beaters. Marred bluing and flat varnish, worn to bare wood at the grips. So perfect they'd earned use, year after year, like that lever action Winchester Model 94, the .30-30 at the end of the first cushion.

One of the rifles was a flintlock carried by one of Walsh's ancestors during the Revolutionary War. Frank had heard the story in Vietnam and had wanted to ask again, but Jake slept most of the time Frank was there, and after loading all the rifles in the truck, Frank didn't have time to stay.

"All I think about is the old days," Jake said. "But I don't like to talk about them."

Frank leaned in. "That's all of us."

There was a lot of money in so many firearms. Even if each was only worth a couple hundred dollars, combined, six thousand sat on his couch.

Which would Linc steal first?

The Ruger 1911?

The world was crumbling.

Frank had raised a thief.

He'd either have to find a good place to hide the guns — from his own son — or have a conversation with the boy that was so unmistakably clear, he'd never dare steal from his old man again.

Frank hurt to think about a conversation that clear. Growing up, he'd received several.

Frank stepped to the sofa and reached for a magazine fed, sawed-off twelve gauge semi automatic, and after a prolonged moment remembering why he'd entered the house at all — to start some rice boiling — he pushed aside a few of the pistols on the bottom cushions and placed the shotgun in the center.

That would be the one to keep handy — the only long gun that was loaded.

Frank added three cups of rice to six cups of water, set the electric range's burner to LOW, and joined Linc at the milkers.

TEN
THEIR OWN DESIRES. NEEDS...

Frank Buzzard owned two sets of milking machines, but Linc had to warm up the cows before he could pump milk.

(One early conversation:

Linc: Is it pumping, or sucking?

Frank: What?

Linc: They suck it out, right? Mechanically — it isn't a pump.

Frank: Son — is that all you think about? You gotta learn to think about other stuff. Uh — never mind. It's a pump, not a vacuum. No, I don't know. So! What'd you learn in school today?)

Linc had been doing the process so long — usually making a joke of it — he never questioned the efficacy of the procedure. Thinking now as a rebel, he wondered if his father wasn't punking him. How many times had Frank laughed inside that his son was stupid enough to be tricked?

He should skip warming up the cows.

But what if they wouldn't milk?

What if, like Frank had told him years before, cows really do need a little psychological ramp up to get the milk hormones juiced?

Frank had said cows were female, and a wise man always paid extra mind when dealing with the fair sex of any species. They were wired differently. Bottom line, if you come waltzing in and shove a milker on her teats, you won't get near the output as by talking to her in a soft voice for a couple minutes first.

"I know three girls that cheat all the time. Mostly on tests but their boyfriends too."

"What? What's that have to do with milking a cow?"

"You called them fair."

Frank snorted.

"Fair doesn't mean, like, they play fair. It means they're beautiful, inside and out. Heart and soul. A woman's got virtue on her mind all the time. On account they have to live with tougher consequences to bad decisions, I guess. Shouldn't be that way but it is."

"That doesn't make sense."

"Well, uh, how do I say this? You're twelve now?"

"Thirteen."

"Good. That's better than twelve. If a woman makes a bad decision with a man, it isn't like a man making a bad decision with a woman. I mean what comes during the bad decision, or after. Plenty of men are cruel. Plenty run off. A woman can't escape her mistakes as easy. She's wired to love, and forgive, and nurture. Half the time — now I'm talking to you like an adult, right? So be a grown up in your thinking, here — half the time, her mistake winds up making a baby inside her. So, she has to pay attention to little things, and that makes her more clued in. A woman has to ponder goodness and virtue because her situation on planet earth punishes her if she doesn't. Moreso than men. And the more a person thinks about virtue, the harder it is to be bad."

"But she doesn't play fair?"

"We're talking the philosophical realm, here. Fair means... wonderful. Delicate and sensitive. But like your mother — tough as nails. You read about that Chinese girl, gives birth in a hut then goes out to work the fields? I read that in school. If Grejda's still teaching English lit, you'll read it too."

Linc was silent.

Frank was too. Then:

"Lotta folks think God messed up humans on his first try and got them right on the second."

"I don't get it."

"Wait until you love a girl so much, just thinking about her makes you a better person. You'll know what fair means."

Sue Cooper!

At this exact space in the barn, two and a half years prior Frank demonstrated the cow-warming concept. He placed his cupped hand on the jowl of a milker named Ophelia and stroked her cheek with his thumb.

"The female loves a gentle touch," he said. "Women, cows, whatever. It changes their hormones."

Linc watched.

"Get thee to a nunnery," Frank cooed. "That's right baby. Mmm. A nunnery." Still charming Ophelia, Frank cocked his head. "You learned about that Pavlov guy in Russia, right? And his dogs?"

"I dunno. I guess."

Frank stroked Ophelia's neck and stopped at her shoulder.

"Pavlov. He rang a bell before he fed his dogs, and it wasn't long 'til the dogs'd start drooling for the bell instead of the Purina. You get it?"

"Get what?"

"We want the cows to get in the right frame of mind for milking. In the mood. That means we go through a nice, easy routine so they know what's coming. To get the milk flowing."

"You sweet talk cows."

"You need to take an Ag class at school. I know you want the academic track, but we're talking basic farming knowhow here. Thousands of years. Remember you have to get the tone right."

Back then it was Linc's first time, but now upon reflection, he knew Frank wasn't playing him because going back as far as Linc could remember, his father always warmed up the cows with the same speech before he did the milking.

"Okay," Linc had said.

"I've tested all manner of words and here's the ones that work best."

In an awkward but cow-seducing voice, Frank began.

He later wrote down all the words for Linc to read from, and it wasn't long until Linc warmed the cows from memory too.

He stood now in the aisle with five girls on either side of him, stared deep into the black eyes of the first, and as if courting Sue Cooper on bended knee, began:

"It is not the critic who counts; not the man who points out how the strong man stumbles, or where the doer of deeds could have done them better."

At the second cow — Maureen — he pressed his thumb to her muzzle and stroked. He adjusted the bite out of his voice and eased from cow to cow to cow to cow until he finished:

"The credit belongs to the man who is actually in the arena, Colleen, whose face is marred by dust and sweat and blood, who strives valiantly, who errs, who comes short again and again, Layla, over and over. Because there is no effort without error and shortcoming; but who does actually strive to do the deeds; who knows great enthusiasms, the great devotions; who spends himself in a worthy cause — that's right 'Tilda baby, a worthy cause; who at the best knows in the end the triumph of high achievement, and who at the worst, Anna darling, if he fails, at least fails while daring greatly, so that his place shall never be with those cold and timid souls who neither know victory nor defeat. All right ladies. Teddy Roosevelt said that. We're in the arena; let's milk."

Linc placed suction tubes on the teats of the first cow on each side of the aisle.

Two started. Eight to go.

It'd be an entirely different chore if they had boobs instead of udders.

Linc congratulated himself on the thought then listened to the gentle mechanical sounds and after a moment, convinced everything was right, stepped from between the cattle stalls.

He swiped the light switch on the corner eight-by-eight and dropped a foot into a long shed-like room that had been added to the barn in his grandfather's day — the cornery — and took his place at the corn sheller. The device looked like a crank-operated sausage grinder and was mounted on the drain end of an old white cast iron bathtub.

Cranking the knob Linc thought it'd be useful to know how many ears he could shell during one milking session, before needing to hook up the next cow. Sure, each cow was different. But knowing the average would provide a handy rule of thumb that would make him more efficient with his time.

That was the kind of thinking his father seemed incapable of.

Linc had counted several times before but never concluded with an answer.

Each time he started, he never lasted more than three cobs before Sue Cooper delighted him by showing up — in his mind — in varying stages of undress.

This day she was fully clothed but in a thin cotton dress. The sun was scorching, and the light glowed in her yellow hair. Sweat glistened on her skin and made the cloth snug every place it most delighted Linc.

No lines around the triangle, but a little brillo poof that stood a mite proud of her hips.

She approached him naked under her clothes... slid her dress to the side and exposed her right shoulder but the fascinating part was how her breasts moved beneath the damp cotton as if they had their own awareness, their own desires.

Needs.

I've been waiting for you, Linc. Saving myself...

ELEVEN
Run until he couldn't...

Linc inhaled but his chest was tight and his heartbeat clunky underneath. How many corn ears had he run through the grinder? Four? A hundred?

Were the cows dead yet?

One of the milking machines beeped.

Linc chucked another denuded cob into a 55-gallon drum next to the sliding door. He returned to the cows and removed the udder suckers from the first on the right side, spun around on his three-legged stool and placed them on the next. He did the same on the other side of the aisle, then went back to the cornery.

Why his father usually joined Linc for the chore, he never understood. There weren't enough milking machines to serve all the cows at once and running only two milkers concurrently left so much space between tasks, Linc had plenty of time for the corn... and with no end to the corn needing shelled, the situation seemed balanced, even perpetually efficient, so long as one man did the job.

Frank's presence was one more way his father proved he didn't have enough sense to run a business. In the time he'd waste with Linc, he could have swapped out the distributor on the 8N tractor.

But something in his old man's brain didn't work. While his father paid lip service to running a tight operation, the so-called bottom line never seemed to guide Frank in how he spent his time and money. (Micky Sager's dad owned Oak Lumber Company, and one time when Linc and his pals were visiting

Micky and watching the Steelers get their asses pounded, he overheard Lou Sager mention that in business, the bottom line was paramount. The terms were so intriguing, Linc looked them up.)

His father didn't think that way. To Frank, the bottom line was what he was left with after running all his decisions through a bunch of highbrow principles that no one else encumbered themselves with. To Frank, the point of business was less about earning a living and more about making sure everybody knew how wonderful he was. Hence his idiocy with the distributor. The bottom line move would have been to take the free part and save the money. That's what people who cared about the bottom line did — and it had nothing to do with virtue. The business world was raw and cold. If some random company overcharged a buck thirty-six, they'd never tell. They'd hope you didn't notice and lie as long as they could if you did.

That was what Frank always said.

But even as Frank led a sermon on how rotten people were in their business dealings — successful people — turn the tables and he just had to be different. It was like he knew how to play the game and refused. Linc's father believed people thought about him, apparently, so he wanted to make sure they found him super honest.

Truth was, no one thought about him.

Same with the school lunches. Proud Frank couldn't let Mrs. Donovan at school know he couldn't cut it as a provider, so Frank cut his nose to spite his face. He wasted money buying what he could obtain for nothing, somewhere else, so a beaked hag that no one ever thought about either wouldn't know he was broke and could use the financial help.

Everything Frank did — wait! Whoa! Check that!

Everything Frank did — except beat Linc with his belt — he needed to run through whatever arbitrary, ancient, moronic virtue code he thought he upheld.

But beat his son so bad it was criminal... screw that! No code!

Hypocrite.

Either way the outcome punished Linc and allowed Frank to keep himself catatonic to his faults but with all the glazed glory of his virtues climbing down into the hole with him as he dug his own failure.

Paying for a distributor they were giving him for free. Wasting his time watching Linc do a chore he'd handled mostly alone for two years. Forcing Linc to ride along to the Farm Supply, when he could have spent the hour doing homework. Or making supper.

The kicker: Frank didn't pay Linc a wage or allowance. Mister Morals was down with slavery.

Child labor.

Linc thought of the pair of Snickers bars in his outer coat pocket. They had to be near-frozen by now. He ran his tongue over his teeth. The vision of Sue Cooper had left his mouth pasty.

Still in the cornery, Linc listened.

The milk machines sucked.

Linc retrieved a Snickers, gently pulled the top open without ripping the plastic down the side and slipped out part of the bar.

He bit, worked his teeth like chisels, then jammed the bar into the side of his mouth so his molars could get in on the chocolate busting.

The candy bar was a rock.

Linc glanced at the door.

With his palms on either side Linc pressed the bar to the edge of an ancient two by four that still had hard, square corners. He added weight, lunged, and the nougat core snapped.

He tossed half of the broken bar into his mouth and after a few seconds of lathering the chocolate with his tongue and spit, flavor exploded into his awareness and Sue Cooper was back, now with her mouth open like she wanted some too.

She changed his whole world.

Trying to penetrate the stolen candy bar with his teeth, Linc recalled that the last time Frank started in on him, his eyes seemed to stare at a different world. Linc read the beast in his father's face and knew deep down that the beast wouldn't need many opportunities to cause Linc brain damage or death.

Frank always, eventually, swung for Linc's head.

Sue Cooper.

A single thought of her — even a clean thought, seeing her cute little tongue squeeze out between her luscious cherry gloss lips — made Linc jump from his track to hers.

Sue rescued him, over and over.

Impossible to guess if it could happen, but he hoped she would be with him when he was the Buzzard everyone meant when they said, "the Buzzard place." Except with Linc at the helm and Sue at his side it'd soon be the Buzzard Family Farm, and then one day when he was ready for the next world, some ancient future date impossible to comprehend — Linc being old — when he passed away it would be the Buzzard Estates.

And the hope that was too much to hope was that Sue Cooper would marry him before any of it started because the more Linc thought about it, the more certain he was that his life wouldn't truly begin until Frank's ended. Or until Linc got away and did his own thing, with Sue, if he could convince the girl of his dreams, who probably didn't think of him twice a year, to abandon her world for his.

Linc rolled the candy wrapper back on itself to protect the remaining bar from pocket lint and continued to gnaw the other Snickers.

Back to the cows, he changed the milkers from the second to the third on each side.

Now in the cornery the Snickers began to yield to Linc's teeth. The outside chocolate was a wonderful goop of flavor while the caramel and nougat were like pond mud sucking to keep hold of his foot.

Linc grabbed an ear of corn and fed it into the grinder. He rotated the handle one time and before the cob seated, before any kernels fell from the spout, he froze.

A snow-scrunching sound arrived from outside the barn.

Linc tried to swallow but the gooey clump stuck to his teeth.

The lower-level barn door groaned open. That'd be his father uselessly joining him, and as soon as Frank didn't see Linc out with the cows, he'd look in the cornery.

Linc stopped trying to free the glob from his teeth and hurried his hand back to the grinder to keep it rotating and the internal teeth yanking corn kernels.

Appearances.

He worked the bar back and forth with his tongue. It wouldn't move. Quick — his father was just outside the door — Linc reached into his mouth and pried nougat from his teeth.

Frank's boots clomped on the grungy barn foundation stones like he was trying to knock snow from them. A moment later Frank filled the entry to the cornery, and Linc stood at the far end of the tub, facing him. To Linc's right or left there was nothing plausibly worth looking at, so he continued to look at his father while his cheeks were puffed out and his mouth was gag-full of Snickers.

Frank offered Linc a weak smile indicating his mind remained elsewhere and Linc tried his best to work his jaw without appearing to work his jaw, but the caramel was like glue on his teeth even while a glob of nougat was at the back of his throat about to drop down the chute.

Linc forced his mouth to be still, but the muscles did their automatic thing. He began to swallow but the lump of candy jammed sideways, and with a single heave Linc coughed the mess of chocolate, nougat, caramel and peanuts — and a foot-long trail of brown spit — into the shelled corn in the bathtub.

Frank looked as if a turd came out of Linc's mouth, and for a split second Linc humored the idea of explaining it away as just that — too much peanut butter in the day's PB&J, his intestines were so plugged they worked backwards — but while Frank was stupid in a million ways, he wouldn't long mistake a partly chewed Snickers bar ejected from his son's mouth as a bowel movement.

"Son?"

Linc ran his tongue all over the inside of his mouth pushing whatever melted candy he could down his throat and when he'd cleansed his palate well enough to talk, Linc said, "Yeah?"

"What is that, on the corn?"

"Nothing."

"We're not gonna dance this time, boy. I asked a question."

Linc closed his eyes and felt even skinnier and un-tougher in the dark. He opened his eyes.

Frank remained in the entrance and Linc watched his stance change from concerned — when Linc first spat the lump of candy — to closed-off, with waves of furrowed forehead sliding after his brows into his eyes.

Next, his lower eyelids would twitch. Frank would clamp shut his eyes and when he reopened them, the beast would be looking through them.

Linc's knees went weak and his hands trembled. He panic-flashed ahead to an image of himself curled on the floor with his arms protecting his head because the beating was getting so bad, and it was the safest posture to endure his father's rage until it was exhausted.

No. Not this time...

Still standing behind the tub, Linc glanced to his right and his peripheral vision reminded him that the cornery extended another five feet to his rear. He'd use the space. That was his plan. When Frank began striking him, Linc would stay for a bit of it, so Frank could later call it mission accomplished instead of chasing him.

Then Linc would summon the madness he felt when Pete Dickey called him Ankleman, the fearless thrashing berserk rage that made five jocks retreat to the lockers then walk half-backward as Linc stalked them another twenty paces after getting clocked in the head so hard he forgot his name, until realizing Sue Cooper was looking at him through frightened eyes.

He'd spin through the space he'd just retreated and rip Frank's hair and kick his balls until Linc could dash out of the cornery, and from there he would run until he couldn't anymore.

Then Linc remembered all the new guns on the living room sofa.

TWELVE
WHATEVER RAGE DID...

Frank studied the shiny blackish lump that Linc ejected from his mouth, and which now rested in a dune of corn kernels.

"Son?"

Linc's mouth moved but he didn't say anything. He cleared his throat.

"Yeah?"

"You okay? What is that on the corn?"

"Nothing."

Electricity tingled in Frank's fingertips. Linc could have provided a real answer. He knew what had been in his mouth. Instead, he chose disrespect, testing boundaries, all of it like so much bleating of a child. Real challenges faced them, but Linc was so wound up in his own importance he'd rather fight the workday's progress at every turn.

Still eyeballing the brown lump, Frank said, "That's not nothing."

Linc glowered.

Was Linc setting him up to get outsiders involved? Some child's advocate social worker? Knowing Frank couldn't string three coherent syllables together whenever someone claiming authority started trying to push him around.

Frank labored every day to ensure his son had three meals and a warm bed, but the kid hated him... He stole family money from the clay jar. And now he dangled the irresistible provocation of a baldfaced lie in front of Frank, saying there was nothing on the corn while four feet from his mouth, the slimy object denied Linc's words as he spoke them.

Frank's choler rose and his throat tightened.

"I asked a question."

Linc was mute.

Frank stepped to the iron tub, grabbed the object and bringing it to his nose observed a fractured peanut nested in nougat.

"Where'd you get a candy bar?"

Linc held Frank's glare while his hand worked inside his coat pocket. He pitched the remainder of the candy bar to the corn. Then with a snarl, he chucked the second bar to the corn too.

"Tractor Supply."

"Uh huh. And you paid with the money you stole from the clay jar? That it?"

"I didn't pay at all... Dad."

Frank stepped closer. Linc stood shoulder to shoulder with him, but the boy was a skeleton with an attitude.

"You stole from the Tractor Supply — the one company we can't survive without. The only place within two hours' drive that has the parts and supplies we need to keep afloat, pay the bills, put food on the table."

"Notice you didn't say clothes on our backs."

Frank's lip twitched. "Your name is all you got. My name — "

Linc braced.

Frank swung with his right fist but while his arm shot forward and his shoulder followed and his body twisted, Frank saw his dead wife Jenny's terror in Linc's eyes.

Frank understood reason had departed him.

He had no mind. He was vulnerable. His zoo had opened the gates and his animals were running loose. He would do whatever rage did. Whatever teeth and claws did. He would destroy...

And later he would weep until his eyes bled.

His fair wife Jenny had passed within hours of delivery. She'd given Frank a son in exchange for her life. Somehow in the boy's adolescent confusion, he chose poorly, and Frank was about to destroy him.

Crippled by sudden insight, Frank dropped his fist mid-flight and instead of punching his son through the wall, Frank's forearm rode Linc's shoulder. Linc dodged. Momentum carried man and son into an awkward embrace. Frank grabbed Linc's coat with his left hand and cupped the back of his head with his right. Linc drew up both arms to push back, but Frank held until they both steadied.

Each stared at the other's eyeballs, bloody veins in the whites. Nostrils flaring wide. Brows yet quivering.

Tears filled both men's eyes.

Frank smelled chocolate. He released Linc. Stepped away. Folded his right arm then secured it with his left.

"My God! Lord! I love you, son. We can't have this anymore! Whatever this is, we can't do this anymore!"

Frank climbed the foot high step out of the cornery and left.

THIRTEEN
PENANCE...

Frank Buzzard stomped across the snow toward the house. Arms thrusting, elbows too. Pointing and muttering.

Linc had tried to bait him with the candy bar, knowing his rage would follow.

Good thing Frank ditched the barn. If he'd have stayed Linc would have gotten the fight he desired against a Frank he didn't — the Frank who sputtered words that didn't go together because what was inside him could only be communicated with fists.

The moon was up. Dusk arrived and deepened while man and boy occupied their minds with other things, but when dark came it struggled against a thick white blanket of snow that, had Frank noticed, he might have taken for a holy rebellion against night. Instead, he tramped across frozen footprints mindful only of his own light dimming.

According to his conscience Frank had taken discipline too far — truly too far — one time — two years ago. He was working at the clay plant until right before it happened. Doing right in the midst of a hundred doing wrong felt like fending off a physical fight every day, only scrapes, bruises and anger for his gain. The constant friction raised his temperature and the day Big Red Hlavacek fired him, Frank left work early so mired in frustration he remained in it when he arrived home — early — and caught Linc tending a fire made of dried pinecones in the woods. Needles and twigs all around, willy nilly, like to catch the county on fire.

Playing with fire again.

Frank stomped among the hemlock and eastern pine in the narrow stand of evergreens on either side of the creek that ran adjacent his lawn and driveway, all the way to the old sawmill they named Sawyer Creek for. He got hotter and hotter watching over the fire while Linc raced to the house and struggled back with a five-gallon bucket of water between his legs. Not a full five, though. Linc splashed half against his knees, reducing his burden when the burden was supposed to be part of his punishment.

Always trying to get over.

Always thinking he was... what? Frank couldn't find the word. Entitled? Superior? Smarter?

Sovereign.

Frank clamped his teeth while Linc doused the fire.

Irresponsible brat could have burned the farm. What then? Lose a twenty-year job and the family farm all in one afternoon. What was the kid thinking?

Frank spoke through his teeth.

"Get everything soaked, then feel around with a stick and make sure none of the coals are live, yet."

While Linc worked on his knees Frank unfastened his belt. When the steam abated Linc stood and wiped soot from his hands to his pants.

After a moment the water absorbed into the ground and Frank pushed the coals with his steel toe boot until he was satisfied no embers survived, then he beat his son back to the ground and continued until his back hurt from lashing Linc while stooped over.

Afterward, tears fell from Frank's eyes and Linc's blood soaked through his sleeves while Frank carried him back to the house.

Grieving the loss of his goodness, Frank decided he wasn't right for the world and the time had come to make his exit.

INTEGRITY

All that day — all his life — the injustice regular people endured at the hands of the selfish class provoked Frank's ire. Some people used any power held over other human beings, legitimate or corrupt, to enrich themselves and impoverish their neighbors. Then defended their cheating by saying if people weren't so gullible there'd be less trickery.

They didn't actually say that. They'd have to be honest to say that.

In truth, Harold "Big Red" Hlavacek, a monster-sized Czech who was good at following and giving orders, actually said, "You got a problem with authority, Buzzard."

"I have a problem with thieves in authority, Red. This is stealing!"

"It isn't stealing from you."

"Doesn't matter."

"You're the only one saying it."

"We stamp two hundred on the crate and there's only one hundred and ninety eight inside. A lie's a lie whether anyone says it — and you better believe that just because everyone here's too kowtowed to call it what it is, that doesn't mean our customers can't see they're being robbed."

Big Red's eyes betrayed how little occurred behind them. "Robbed? Come on. What'd you see? A couple light crates?"

"Every single one. I've been counting."

"Who hired you to count?"

"Red, listen to me. It's every crate."

"One-percent slippage."

"One percent fraud."

"Look. I don't care what the count is. We're allowed a fail rate."

"It's a scam. We're cheating."

"No we're not."

"Then put ONE NINETY EIGHT on the box."

"Get out of here! Look. I got work to do."

"A lie is a theft," Frank said. "Can't you see that? How can we — all of us — I mean everyone — how can we function when half of what we say to each other bears no semblance to reality? How long will people do business with us when they can't trust what we say? Everyone a liar; everyone a thief. How's that supposed to work? Someone has to call this out."

"What do you expect me to do? I got a wife and kids."

"I expect you to do what I'm doing. Go to your boss and call this out, and stand there calling it even though he says he has a wife and kids! You call out the lie! Until he goes to his boss to call out the lie. I'm not off the hook until you take me off it — and then I'm your backstop. I follow up and if you didn't take responsibility, then I still have it and I have to advance the truth again. Accountability. That's how the little man changes things. Because it matters, Red! And you don't get off the hook until your boss does the right thing, and he becomes accountable to the truth. Then you backstop him. That's how the righteous advance. That's how we take this world back from the lies. Don't stand for things that shouldn't be stood for. That's what the hell you do, Red! BE THE FUCK ACCOUNTABLE!"

Big Red's eyes remained unexcited and small. Frank had known from the get-go that Red was pulled from the ranks to manage them because he possessed exactly the skill to do so, and no more.

"Well Frank, I am making a call. Don't wait until the end of your shift. Go now. Punch your timecard, and don't come back."

"That's it?"

"That's it. You'll get something in the mail from HR."

"You know, Red, when you stand with liars, they take your name."

Red kept his eyes pointed at a form on his desk. "Like I said. Don't come back."

"You let them take your name for something small, and later on you learn they used it for something big. A company that'll steal one percent will steal ten percent. Or a hundred, if it can figure the way. You're all the same, though. Truth doesn't matter in the little things, so it can't for the big, either. People like you, truth doesn't exist at all. What a mess you people have made."

Frank backed out of Red's office, went home and worked his son with a leather belt until well after Linc stopped blocking the blows with his arm. Then Frank carried him from the woods to the house.

After dressing Linc's wounds, blubbering apology after apology until Linc asked to be left alone, Frank sat in the basement under a sixty-watt bulb with a .38 revolver in his hand. He placed a single cartridge in the wheel and confessed his misery to his Savior, asked what sense it made, him trying to model virtue when he carried so much rotten ass evil inside.

If the Lord hadn't given him the idea of working the farm for a living, so he would have a future to give to his son in penance, Frank wouldn't have seen the next morning.

FOURTEEN
Monster Inside...

Frank kicked his boots until compressed snow fell from the treads then opened the screen door. He stood in silence and grappled with a stray awareness he'd sensed many times — but never at a moment so pregnant with an answer.

Why did his soul feel more at ease under the sky and constricted under a roof? Why did he feel more suited to the wild than among the civilized? Why did the secret thought at the back of his mind so often come forward? How was it possible that a living man could wish he wasn't? Or see that it would have been better for all involved, even the one who wouldn't have been born without him, if he had never existed at all?

Why could he forgive others — chronically, almost as a weakness — and not forgive himself?

Why did the part he played for darkness so profoundly outweigh the part he played for light?

He was doing his best. In every moment, his ultimate best.

Rage felt like a disease, a compulsion, not a choice. And the monster inside him that pulled the lever never showed his face — so Frank never had the chance to murder it.

He may as well punch a shadow.

Instead, he bumbled around like a God-forsaken marionette with strings stretched to the depths of hell, ruled from afar by a being whose sole purpose was to cause hate and chaos in men.

Frank lowered his head a moment and closed his eyes as the hole in his chest appeared again.

That place where his soul was supposed to be.

"Jesus Christ, look at me. You ever see a piece of shit like me?"

All those guns were inside on the sofa. The only thing between them, a door that wasn't even latched.

FIFTEEN
It'll be a favor...

Frank opened the door. Closed the screen. Stepped inside. Closed the door. Transferred snot from his upper lip to his sleeve and hesitated a long moment before glancing through the half-light toward the sofa.

He had work to do.

No time for self indulgent, woe-is-me stink think. It was time to summon his last reserve of jocular fiber.

Cheerful grit.

Hope — despite absolute certainty everything in life was by cosmic design intended to crush his identity and leave him weeping in misery.

Onward, pawn!

Entertain us!

The house seemed cool. His skin didn't tingle or itch with the heat after being in the cold so long. Hands still ungloved, he wiped the wetness from his eyes and tromped to the kitchen. He checked the boiling rice and turned off the burner. It wasn't done.

So what?

At the wood stove he raked forward the embers and loaded the last of the firewood he'd brought inside that morning. He returned to the porch, filled his arms with logs and carried them inside. Then went back outside and followed a path made from his earlier boot prints, lifted a ridiculously giant 20x20 nylon tarp sheltering a tiny stack of logs, and filled his arms twice, bringing to the porch the last of the wood cut for the season.

The rest of his needed firewood was still on the top of Kroh Hill, trees felled and dried but not yet sawed into eighteen inch segments.

Frank studied the logs stacked on his porch next to the house. Three days. Then the house would go cold.

He turned and looked to Kroh Hill and the sky beyond.

In the past when he dwelled too long on his sins, stepping outside and sensing the expanse of the created universe reminded him he wasn't intended to have a significant part. A gnat compared to planet earth was infinitely larger than a man to God's universe.

Being down on himself was in truth a wholesome moment of clarity, unblinded by the arrogance of claimed significance.

"The show must go on," Frank said. He kicked each boot once against the bottom of the log pile, removing snow. "Anything for a laugh."

Back inside, Frank's boots gritted the kitchen linoleum and gruffed the living room rug. His coat sleeves rubbed his coat torso. A single *tick!* arrived — fired from expanding water pipes. Turning his head Frank caught the gentle *whoosh* of air feeding the front vents of the wood burning stove, which he'd placed before the fireplace on a pedestal of bricks.

Silence was richer in the cold.

Although two years had passed between the moments Frank relived during his walk from barn to house, he found himself in the same metaphysical space.

Would his death solve any problems? Linc's problems?

Would the life insurance and the farm provide for Linc's future better than Frank and whatever was left of the farm after he quit trying to make a go of it? He'd wanted the farm to be a sanctuary from the world's madness. Was Linc better suited at fifteen to bring that about than Frank was at sixty? Would Linc even want a sanctuary from the world?

Did Linc even understand what an honorless mess of a society he would inherit?

INTEGRITY

Unlikely. His biology was just beginning to demand he fight for his place in it. Seeing flames on the battlefield, he'd pick up a flame thrower.

Maybe Linc would find the lie more comfortable than the truth. He'd make a home of the world that only fed Frank's frustration.

Frank closed his eyes but sounds prevented him from drifting. He opened them again and turned. Light projecting from the wood burner's air vents glinted off the rifle barrels on the sofa.

"Lord God. Jesus. I can't do this. I can't fix myself. Take this evil out of me."

He flipped the light switch and broke the spell.

At the kitchen drawer he removed the check book and placed it in his pocket. A quick inventory of his billfold yielded a five-dollar bill. He had a card, cash, and checks.

It was only two Snickers.

Frank glanced at the gun collection on the sofa.

Carry a pistol?

Sometimes he thought it'd be smart to carry, given the armies of idiots advancing across the country. Soon they'd be in Oak. They were already passing through, rear-ending folks. People on the news, shooting up the country all the time.

But in his present state, arming himself seemed like kind of move he'd later regret from a prison cell. Or kneeling before his Maker.

Nonetheless Frank found himself in front of the sofa, ensuring the wheel of a snub .38 Special contained brass. He slipped the revolver back into its holster, then shoved both into his coat pocket.

Frank closed the kitchen door and tramped to the F-150, fired the engine and with the truck in reverse carrying him to the barn, he stopped.

Leaving the door open and the truck running in neutral with the parking brake pulled, he walked to the lower level and entered the milking room.

Linc was standing in the middle of the aisle between cow rear ends, faced away, as if he'd frozen mid-step when he heard Frank enter.

Frank waited.

Linc didn't move.

"This isn't easy, Linc. Listen. You're practically a grown man. That — back there with the candy bar — I won't say any more about that or the money you've been taking. Whether you choose to be a good man or a rotten one is up to you. I really wish you'd at least pay me the courtesy of looking at me while I'm talking to you... ... ... I guess being stingy with respect isn't always a bad thing... ... ... so... ... ... well, there's that."

Frank turned. Stopped and turned back. Linc hadn't moved.

"I was saying in life, you'll choose to be a good man, or you'll choose to be a bad one... I'm being as humble as I'm capable right now. To give you the truth. You don't choose all at once, though. Lotta folks wind up somewhere they didn't expect. Couple bad decisions here, a couple there. They get on a path. You hear what I'm saying, son?"

Linc's back was mute.

"Doing wrong starts a man on a path and that's why I don't budge an inch, ever, on my principles. If I allow myself to cheat an inch one place, there's no reason I won't cheat a mile someplace else. So, I make damn sure I'm not open to the inch. The only principle I fail to live up to is how good a job I do taking care of you. I get so angry — not at you so much as me, and the world — I get so damn mad I don't know what to do with it. And I hate me more than you do. That's why I'm putting this out man to man. I try to push you the right direction, but you push back, mostly because you don't want pushed. That's how I know you're good inside. You stand up. But you don't know as much as you think, and you still need pushed every now and again. For your own good."

Frank waited.

"You know son, even a fool can say something worth hearing. Still nothing? Can't make peace with your old man?"

Linc lowered his head.

"Well, son, I'm done with it. You can stay under my roof if you want. I welcome you. But I can't have a man working on the Buzzard Farm if he doesn't fight to uphold the same principles I do. I'm talking about the stealing you did, before. If you're here when I get back, that means you're not going to do rotten things. We're going to work together and build something. This place is going to be yours someday if you want it, so there's no reason you shouldn't start having a say in how we do things. But that means you have to be all in. You have to know the finances, the repairs coming, all the costs of business."

Linc turned, his thumbs looped in his pockets.

Frank paused. The F-150 mumbled behind him. The milking machines pumped in chorus.

"I'm going to go pay for the Snickers bars and wipe the slate clean. I'm going to trust you to come clean to yourself. Do it while I'm gone. Come clean — to yourself, you understand? Do the hard thinking. Hold yourself to account. Acknowledge you know the difference between right and wrong and pledge you're going to live an honorable life. And not be a damn thief."

Linc removed his hands from his pants pockets.

"Great deal, until you decide to beat the fuck out of me again."

"I know. Like I said, I hate me more than you do."

"Easy words."

"I know."

Frank pulled the holster and pistol from his pocket.

Linc sucked in air. Stepped backward.

Frank squatted and placed the holster and pistol on the cement.

"You keep that on you. It's a short .38 — best for close work. Put the holster on your belt. I ever touch you again... do what you need to do. It'll be a favor."

SIXTEEN
WHAT DELICIOUS PAIN...

Frank turned from his driveway toward Oak. He pressed the gas farther down now that he'd successfully navigated the route only a half hour before.

Wipers off, snowflakes bounced from his windshield. The glass wasn't warm enough to melt a snow crystal — though now they were more like pellets.

In town Frank drove twenty miles per hour, five below the limit. His eyes tracked the insurance man's office. Most of the rest of the 9 to 5 businesses were closed with their lights off, but the insurance man stayed open. Frank had his checkbook register, checks, debit card, everything but his last statement.

Senior's Tractor Supply would be open until at least seven.

His rearview mirrors showed an empty street. Frank tapped his brake and once his forward motion all but stopped, he angled to a parking space opposite the insurance office.

He stood beside the locked truck a moment before crossing the road. Experience had taught him to never enter an insurance man's office without knowing exactly what he intended to accomplish. Walter Truby's agency had as clean a reputation as any business in town, but in the end, men were men.

Especially businessmen.

Frank pushed the glass door. It was frozen. He leaned and saw Walter at his desk, back to the door. As Walter turned in his seat Frank pulled the door and it opened. He stepped inside.

"Hey Frank."

"Hey Walter. Still open? I saw the light on."

"Last meeting went long. Been trying to get out of here for an hour."

"I'll come back. You go home to the family."

"How's the roads?"

"Worse than you think, probably."

"I grew up here."

"Didn't you move to Oak in the fourth grade?"

"Okay. I grew up in Maine, then here. I understand bad roads. Let me finish signing three more pages so I don't... Hey? Everything all right? Your eyes..."

"Wind's blowing pretty good out there. Eyeballs sting."

"Sure. Okay. Be right with you. Have a seat and check out that new Guns & Ammo. There's a good article in there on the Howa 6.5 Creedmoor."

Frank looked around. Walter Truby's office wasn't like other brokerages Frank had worked with — certainly nothing like the agency he worked for, many years before. Walter didn't have a staff. He kept his business small so he could do every task himself.

"You want one hundred percent accountability," Walter had said in his opening pitch, "do business with a man who can't pass the buck."

Frank was sold. And though no man could entirely vouch for another — not knowing his soul — Walter Truby seemed to play it straight with his customers. Heck, Frank stepped from the sidewalk straight into the office of the man whose name was on the window.

It felt like respect being offered.

Frank looked over the wall. Lotta diplomas. Certificates. Trophies with dust and photos of Walter when he was thinner and had more hair.

Long ago Frank had asked Walter why he didn't hire help and he shook his head then glanced at Frank with a message in his eyes he'd never put on his lips.

That said something.

INTEGRITY

Walter rocked in his chair and scribbled.

This whole thing with the distributor costing more — who was Frank kidding? He was behind. His account was lower than it was supposed to be. His income came from selling milk and cows when they were too old to calve but not too old to be a bunch of hamburgers for a fast-food giant. He leased out a twenty-acre lot that was too far away for him to work; land his father inherited late in his life, by surprise, from his mother's side; and handed to the next generation not too long after. Frank hadn't gotten the process down well enough to match his feed production to his cattle population, partly stemming from not fully understanding the implications of a cow's age when he paid top dollar for his first ten milkers. Three of which he received bottom dollar for several weeks later, sold to a company that turned old cows into steak burritos.

Sometimes he sold cattle. Sometimes, not.

Erratic as his income was, Frank knew it was lower than it should have been. Any fool could project two lines forward and anticipate their crossing. At some point every penny he ever saved would be spent, and he'd either start flipping burgers for a living in the greatest irony ever, or sell the land, leaving himself nothing and his son less. Misspending thirty some dollars meant not making good on the promise he'd made to God, that he wouldn't take his life, that his punishment instead was to build the farm into something worthy of passing to his son, thereby freeing him from serving other men as their tax or debt slave.

Lessons came hard for men who depended upon themselves and no other. One foot in front of the next. It got easier...

Ah!

The ghost of jocular fiber: someday there'd be nothing left to do but giggle at the world's madness, and the ridiculousness of him thinking he could navigate life without succumbing.

Frank corralled his stunned eyeballs and stared at a blank spot on the wall:

It was getting easier because he didn't care as much. Didn't have the ambition to think well of himself. The best future he could hope for was a downhill path all the way to his grave... and on a certain level, he was okay with that.

That wind from outside must have done something to his eyes. He pinched each in turn between thumb and index finger, pressing the wetness to his finger and then corner of his eye, then off his face.

What about the guns?

Jake Walsh hadn't made him promise not to sell his guns, only to look after them and uphold the purpose that animated Jake when he bought them to begin with: defending the republic against its government.

Jake had reminded Frank that morning: you want to live in a free country, you keep guns, and if you have the means, you keep a lot of them. No one thinks like us anymore. Everybody's watching Wife Swap. Not much courage out there. People do their thinking after they've already been stampeded over the cliff. But for those smart enough to swerve, they'll realize it was never the guns they had to fear. They'll look for the only tool that can make them equal. And since it behooves the patriot to have well-armed patriots beside him, it'll be good to have plenty of weapons to go around when there are plenty of people with no purpose left but to squeeze a trigger.

You dig, my brother? Tell me it ain't righteous.

Frank nodded. He'd had those thoughts a million times... just never had the means to build and stock his own arms room.

God forbid it ever come to that, except in truth, while Frank couldn't dream of the country falling during his lifetime, it probably would during Linc's. That was the awful shame of it. People just didn't think like they used to — and they were proud of it. Intoxicated by their own lack of education and the heady sense that the present was enlightened and the past a relic.

To sell Jake's guns Frank would have to sabotage Linc's future freedom, which resolved the matter: no way, period.

INTEGRITY

And truth was, Frank was aching to fire a couple rounds through that .570. The rifle could likely drop a deer — or a jackbooted thug — from a mile.

Walter Truby's chair groaned. Frank swiveled his head.

"All right. So, you wanted to take care of the homeowner's bill tonight?"

"I'm considering dropping it."

"Reducing the coverage amounts, you mean?"

"Altogether. Dropping it altogether."

"Going uninsured?"

"Self insured."

"Frank. We've worked together a long time, so you know I'm not being smart with you. Self insured is a... well... it's words without meaning. Insurance transfers risk. You can't transfer the risk to yourself and think you've accomplished anything."

"I don't have the money."

"Well... No money? At all? Or not enough for an annual payment?"

"That."

"So, let's change it to monthly."

"Pay more for less, on account I have less money? Is that smart?"

"It keeps you from losing everything you've ever worked for when an accident happens."

"All my life I've only seen one house fire. Sixty years."

Walter kept his smile far from his lips and the thought far from his vocal chords, then spoke it anyway. "Long ago, I was trained to say, *that means you're due*."

"Yeah. Good thing you didn't say that."

"I understand you're going through a rough time, but we have plenty of options. I can shop new companies for you, different coverage amounts, different riders. We can get the bill down. If I remember, you have the extended replacement cost type of policy."

Frank remembered the term.

"Is that good?"

"Sure. Very good. But expensive."

"What are you saying?"

"A homeowner insurance policy can be set up to pay the cash value the house was worth when the loss was suffered — its market value. That costs the least. Often times, the market value isn't close to enough to rebuild the house the way it was. So, another option is to buy a policy that covers the replacement cost of the house."

"So, you get it back just like it was. I remember, now."

"No, actually. Replacement cost gets you back into a similar house. If you had granite counter tops and the price is high on granite, but a similar quality — Formica maybe — costs less, the insurance company pays for the Formica."

"Not a problem, at the Buzzard residence."

"Well, here's the thing. You don't have replacement cost, you have the next level higher: extended replacement cost. Meaning, if you had marble, you're getting marble. It's the most expensive coverage, and it's what you have."

Frank was still while Jenny gathered into a memory.

They were younger, sitting with Walter when his office was new. He'd sent them a piece of mail saying he might be able to beat their current rates. Jenny was pregnant with Linc and said she'd feel more comfortable, free from worry and capable of living her best, if she could rest assured everything would be taken care of if the house ever blew away in a tornado. And since they'd just gone through Frank's benefits package at the clay plant, and increased Frank's life insurance because of the baby coming, they might as well get set up right with the new homeowner's insurance too.

"So how big's the price difference?"

"Big. If we bumped it down to the middle of the road, the Formica —"

"Walter, you know I don't have granite. I don't need Formica. I'd be content with plywood."

"You really shouldn't go with the lowest cost option, market value. What could you sell your house for, today, if you needed a buyer fast?"

"Not much."

"That's what the policy would pay. How do you build a new house for not much?"

Frank wished he had a toothpick. If he had a toothpick, he could pry on that one molar. He hadn't thought of it all day. Just pressed his tongue absentmindedly against the swollen gums next to his crown. Maybe his frustration with Linc caused the inflammation to spark up. Maybe it was a rogue strand of venison. He'd forgotten to brush last night, like most nights since Jenny died fifteen years ago.

He'd been distracted and not thinking about his tooth, but talking to Walter, trying to think when it was so hard, trying to think while a man sat behind his good reputation and tried to use fear on him... Frank really wanted to shove a toothpick in the abscess and release the pressure. What delicious pain, a stab in the middle of a mind-numbing throb. He'd need a place to spit blood for a few minutes.

Of course, the dentist had said the infection would occur inevitably, and be very painful — more fear mongering to make a sale — and Frank said he'd deal with it when the time came.

Cutting off the nose to spite the face. Frank unpacked the wisdom. Not many things were powerful enough to get a person to destroy their identity. Spite was. Hatred — well placed and deserved hatred — was. If the dentist had given Frank a rundown, this happens then that happens... Cause, effect... You decide. Frank would have decided. But explain something relying on hyperbole instead of facts? On fear instead of logic? Go to hell. I'll let my teeth rot for the joy of not doing business with someone who disrespects my mind. You are not the only one who gets to harm my health for your pleasure.

Was Walter talking down to him? Manipulating him?

Every salesman wanted money and loved painting a picture of future destitution.

"You know what, Walter? Drop the policy. Drop the whole thing."

"What?"

"You heard me. I'm assuming the risk. Enjoy the rest of your day."

Frank kept his eyes disciplined while leaving the office; couldn't risk looking at Walter too long and having him translate the directness of Frank's stare into the rage boiling beneath. Frank opened the door with a quick yank. He slipped crossing the road. Caught himself on a hand and an elbow, which sent a bolt of pain right through him.

The truck engine was still warm. Frank cranked the heater, backed onto the road and with all four wheels spinning, drove away as Walter Truby came to the door and waved his arms.

SEVENTEEN
Trespassers...

After Frank exited the milking room, Linc stood with his boots close to the .38 barrel and toed the pistol, so it pointed at the opposite end of the barn instead of Colleen's hooves.

Two years before, when Linc lay beside a steaming mush of coals in the woods and Frank lashed him with a folded belt until he lost consciousness, he could have used a snub .38. He didn't know what to do with it now, so he left it on the floor.

Linc completed milking the last two cows and standing at the door as if to return to the house, he instead reversed, crossed to the other end of the lower deck and climbed the steps to the middle bay with the tractor. He considered shooting the new one hundred and thirty-six dollar and ninety-four cent distributor with the .38, but that would mean returning to the lower level to get it.

Instead Linc climbed the ladder to the upper hay loft.

He crawled across the bales to a two-foot square door that opened outward. He twisted the six-inch wood latch, pushed, and looked at Kroh Hill. The house, coop, fuel pump — the full raggedy Buzzard catastrophe was on the other side of the barn. The house was all Frank, run down, disrepair, shutters hanging sideways and paint that looked like the white hide under a cow's ass.

But from Linc's position on the opposite side of the barn, the window opened to empty space. Fields and woods. Snow.

The beauty of it was too big to be tainted by a small man's cruelty.

Three deer emerged from the forest near the top of the hill. The sun had been down awhile and the moon was up, keeping the snow-covered land lit like dusk. A bold yellow swath of headlamps disappeared where the road briefly angled toward the Buzzard place then turned away. The hill was the highest in three counties, so a PennDOT genius put a lookout up there, right where the headlights disappeared. Or a county road genius. Whatever genius built the stupid roads. Linc had been there a dozen times, the first time to see what merited a lookout.

There was no merit. The hill overlooked the Buzzard situation on one side and a bunch of swamp land on the other.

A fourth deer bounded from the woods and charged past the other three, then they galloped across the field through the snow, which was thinner on the side of the hill, where wind kept blowing it into the bottoms.

Linc watched until the deer disappeared under a roll in the field.

Frank told Linc to come clean with himself but the only thought that looped in Linc's mind was that no man had the authority to command another to think, or when to think, or the proper conclusion of his thoughts. The only authority Frank had originated with his violence — and that wasn't authority so much as power. Power had no justification. It was a tool anyone seeking destruction could wield. Absent a higher purpose, a right, it was like the tooth or claw of an animal.

Frank Buzzard.

Each year after planting, when normal people rested in the evenings, Frank — and that meant Linc too — cut firewood along the field's edge and left the smaller limbs for cover for rabbits and ringneck.

Linc watched another deer emerge from the shadows to the moonlit snowy field.

Frank hunted from this perch, though he never called it hunting. It was meat on the table, not sport. The official term

INTEGRITY

would have been harvesting, but in Frank's parlance it was, 'I'm gonna shoot a deer tonight. Be ready to go get it."

So Linc would have to find a can of starter fluid and drive the F-150 inside the barn to jump start a jalopy lawn mower that never mowed but putted along well enough to drag a wagon with a head shot deer in it. One more item Frank had found at a dump (the tractor) and decided to resurrect, like the black and white television in the living room.

Frank hung the deer by splitting the tendons going into the back ankles and hooking them over nails hammered into the ends of an eighteen-inch length of two-by-four. He let the deer rest over night and butchered the next day, unless it was summer, when everything had to be done at once.

The deer never stopped coming to the field.

That's what animals did. They kept coming back for more. None of them ever posted a sign with a pictogram of Farmer Bob with a gun. Being able to think, as humans could think, was an advantage not lost on Linc. His mind could help him avoid walking into the same terrain again and again.

He could escape.

Or throw the king off his perch.

Linc crawled a few feet, yanked up a bale and rolled it next to the window where he could use it as a backrest.

Getting situated, he stretched his legs and leaned against the repositioned bale. His coat was jumbled at his back and his butt was cold. He leaned far to his right and lifted his hips, dragged the coat beneath, and caught a flicker of orange light from the bottom of the field, next to the woods, where no light ought to be.

Trespassers.

The glow flickered.

There was no way down there without driving past the house and barn. There were no tracks on the field road that led there, so unless he went down there before the snow, the trespasser had to have snuck in through the woods adjacent the Buzzard land — woods owned by a hateful codger named Kelley James who, when Linc was nine, threatened he was a direct descendant of Jesse, so stay the hell outta my woods! Linc looked up Jesse James and was duly impressed. Linc had a pair of wooden pistols that shot fat rubber bands and joined Jesse for a few train robberies down by the creek. But a man with a woman's name (Linc knew a girl named Kelly in school) seemed strange, possibly adequate cause for being so mean, so Linc looked up Kelly at school on the internet and discovered it was a man's name and meant *War!* to the Irish. No wonder Kelley James was a (the new term trickling down to the nine-year-olds was) dick.

Reclining in the loft, the entire illuminating experience flashed through Linc's brain as a singular awareness.

That five-acre parcel was posted with yellow signs nailed to trees every ten or fifteen feet. Linc could see about thirty of them from the barn, where James and Buzzard land abutted.

Linc leaned to his right, folded his elbow and cradled his head in his hand. The fire was small. Two hundred yards, most likely. And from the angle and tree line, the trespasser was on Buzzard land.

EIGHTEEN
Acknowledgement...

"Hello, uh, Sue."

She smiled then tilted her head. "Everything all right with the distributor?"

"Oh yeah, it's not that. It's just I need a favor."

On the drive from the insurance man's office to the Tractor Supply, Frank had stabbed the abscess like planned, and with the toothpick fully inside his mouth managed to stab his cheek too. His gums had bled and that felt wonderful after the nervy pain. But the holes in his cheek kept attracting his tongue, as if he'd eventually rub them smooth. As Sue watched and waited for him to ask his favor, Frank's cheek bulged outward three times while he considered how to bring up Linc's theft of the candy bars.

Sue raised her brows. Looked to her left, then gracefully, enchantingly, to her right.

"I think we're alone," she said. "You want to slip inside the mop closet?"

"What?"

Sue tongued her cheek.

Frank choked on air.

She snorted.

"I thought you'd be back." Sue stopped talking while a round of giggles bounced her.

"That was... uh, not what I intended. I just popped a blister and... To tell the truth I could shovel a hole and die in it. I can't believe I did that. No, I have this situation... a humbling situation."

Sue wiped her eyes. "You're here about the Snickers?"

Frank caught her shiny gaze. "You saw him steal the candy bars?"

"I did."

"But you didn't say anything."

"I didn't."

"I wish you'd have clued me in. I'd've put an end to that on the spot."

Sue swept the merriment from her face and delivered her soft voice through a warm smile.

"Let's go back. When I saw your son pocket the candy bars, it was at the same time that I realized you saved me from having to cough up a hundred and thirty dollars for giving you a distributor without taking any money for it. Nobody does what you did."

"Well, I... You know. Anybody woulda — "

"No, Frank. Not *anybody woulda*. You did."

"It doesn't make me happy to admit it."

"So that's why I didn't say anything. That and one other reason."

"Thank you, Susan. I'm going to square that up right now."

Frank sank his hand after his wallet.

"You said that and one more reason," he said.

"A long time ago I heard an American Indian proverb. Or Japanese. One of those wise cultures, you know? Anyhow the proverb said for every hundred things your kid does wrong, correct only one."

Nodding, paying strict attention, Frank nonetheless wondered if the mop closet was nearby. Which wall was it on? He hadn't done anything that crazy since the seventies. Nothing like a good old fashioned knee-trembler.

She couldn't have been serious.

It didn't matter. Frank could never do something like that. It was too soon after Jenny.

"Did you hear me?"

"Uh-huh. I'm thinking. It doesn't make sense. Correct which one thing? Why not the rest?"

"I think the proverb means kids are smart. They figure things out."

"That why most kids today are feral."

"I think the point was the world teaches the lesson, so you don't have to. You get to set a good example, like you do. And be the kid's champion, not the person always saying no." She shrugged. "It's none of my business. When I get nervous, I talk too much. That thing you did with your cheek threw me off my game. You raise your kid your way. If you're any indication, he'll be fine, too."

There was that smile again. She said he was fine. And Lordamighty, her shape was persistently, gloriously female, each time he looked. If she had the pillows she had the folds.

Frank held Sue's look —

Two. Three. Four.

"It's okay, Mister Frank Buzzard. Just a compliment from an old lady."

"Old lady my eye. What're you? Thirty-five. Ish?"

"Liar. Don't stop."

Frank lost himself in a smile. Got confused. Forgot, then remembered his purpose.

"I came to pay for the candy bars."

"How many?"

"Two. That's what I'm aware of. Did he swipe more than that?"

"I don't think so. Can you grab me one, so I can scan the code?"

Frank passed her a Snickers from the rack below the counter. Fished inside his wallet and passed her three singles. He couldn't look at her without imagining her face close to his, so near her breath warmed his cheek and her perfume intoxicated him.

Frank swallowed and diverted his attention to cardboard taped to the swinging door that led to the maintenance shop behind the main building.

HELP WANTED

"That's new."

"Just put it up. I was going to call you later, so you'd know. But I figured I'd give you time to get in from your evening chores."

"Um, Miss Susan, it's been a lot of years. No offense. Are we flirting?"

"At first I thought so, but now I'm pretty sure it's only me."

"Flirting you mean?"

"Frank — Dear — it's complicated when you try to talk about it, but easy as pie if you go with what feels right. You know what I mean? Yes, I'm flirting. If that makes you feel nice and comfy, you can flirt back. I won't bite. But if not, that's okay too. The worst thing that could come out of it is I cook you a nice dinner sometime."

"And the best?"

"It's unbecoming to force a woman to brag."

Frank closed his eyes. So cold today. Windy. So many tears. He allowed his lids to remain closed too long and when he opened them a new moment was upon them. Sue was passing him a handful of coins. He extended his hand and she dropped them. He'd wanted to feel her hand in his, a short moment. Nothing too forward. Just a sign.

But an ill-timed customer entered and tripped a door buzzer that shat all over the moment.

Frank turned his head half sideways to the sound, saw some guy bundled up in his coat with a pointed hood. A Green Bay fan.

"Dinner," Frank said. He nodded small and saw her eyes glow small and her smile lift small as the new customer's squishy boot steps arrived in line behind Frank.

Frank widened his grin and Sue did too, capping it with a fire burst eye twinkle.

"We'll have to set that up. As to the sign, did that go up since I was here last? An hour ago?"

Sue nodded. "Mister Senior's complained so many times about not being able to find good help I thought I'd remove an obstacle, you know, and let people know he's looking."

Her gaze drifted beyond Frank to the man behind him. Her eyes signaled recognition but nothing special. Frank capitalized on the moment and again appraised her full form, neck to thighs — where the counter cut off his line of sight. The job couldn't be right for him. He'd stand at the swinging doors behind Sue all day, hoping she'd turn sideways.

When Frank returned his look to Sue's eyes, they were already locked on his.

She was smiling. Eyes like Christmas tree lights. Was that cinnamon in the air? Lord, imagine making a home with a woman like Sue. Imagine putting your feet up, and your heavy wool socks fit loose and comfortable. Body so tired it could quit but doesn't. A cup of coffee before you doze off, looking out the fogged window to the whiteout. Two weeks' firewood on the porch and what is that? A chicken roasting in the oven? She comes over, kneels, and says, "I know what you want. What you need." Then she rubs your feet.

Says you work so hard she loves you for it.

Respects you for all you do. All you are.

How you treat her.

And she's right: the acknowledgment is all you need. You'd give your life to know if you were actually good. Hearing her say it would justify what you've given up, trying to be.

"Frank?"

"Uh, yeah. What kind of help? Doing what? Out of curiosity."

"Same as Lou Fortunato did. Anything and everything. I'll tell John you asked about the sign."

"I don't think that's a good idea. John and me – we haven't gotten along since we were kids."

"Well maybe you'd both benefit from sorting things out. He only says good things about you."

Frank backed from the counter and bumbled into the man behind him. He turned, fast —

"Hey Frank. Good to see you."

"John Senior — "

Seconds passed. Frank took in John as if he was an apparition while Sue switched her smile from Frank to John and back, each time, the corners of her mouth dropping a little.

"Sorry I startled you," John said.

Frank watched the remainder of Sue's shiny happy smile collapse as she studied his eyes. She whispered, "I'm sorry."

Frank backstepped.

"We could use a man with your skills," John said. "Pays good."

Frank limped to the exit and before stepping back into the cold, blowing dark, turned for a last look at Sue — but as soon as he saw her, he shuffled into the snow.

NINETEEN
THE GUN IN HIS HAND...

George Smith had video games.

Back before Linc's ankles shot out of his pants and he was a regular kid at school, George invited ten kids to his eleventh birthday party. He had the privilege of being the eleventh, the most prestigious number. And so on. The next year he invited eleven to his twelfth, and the next twelve to his thirteenth, but Linc wasn't one of them.

By then he was Ankleman!

But they didn't say it to his face anymore. Now they called him Berserker, and bowed.

George's parents had crazy money, at least back when Linc was eleven. Frank said no, he couldn't go, but Linc did what chores he could in advance and hurried through the rest on the Saturday of the party. He begged until Frank said he could go if he walked. It was only three miles as the crow flew. He would also need to carry a slingless .22 — he was a skilled plinker — and bring a rabbit or three home for the freezer. Tree rats were okay too, since Linc would have to clean them.

Linc carried the .22 and stayed his trigger finger when a red squirrel sat on a stump and barked at him. Not enough meat for the trouble — and the little thing had a lot of spunk. He seemed more adamant about living his life than Linc was about taking it. Another mile in, following another farmer's tractor road around a field, Linc stumbled on a grouse that stood looking at him. The Game Commission had just stocked the bird. Linc didn't know. He drew his .22 but the bird was so pretty and so perfectly unmindful of Linc that he lowered his rifle and determined to see how close he could approach walking slow, with no subterfuge, straight forward. At ten feet the grouse thundered to flight and Linc walked the rest of the way with his face split open in a grin.

If there were animals on his path, he didn't see them.

A quarter mile from the Smith house, Linc stashed the rifle inside a rotten stump at the corner of a field.

One Christmas when Linc was even younger Frank had gotten a bonus check and spent a good deal of it on presents for Linc. Frank never bothered with a Christmas tree. That was for people with time to cut one and time to look at one in the living room. Frank said he had neither. Christmas morning, Linc emerged from his bedroom and was stunned to find five gift-wrapped boxes in the corner of the living room, piled under a photo on the wall that his father stared at, every time he passed. Those gifts are from your mother and me, Frank said, before wiping his eyes and leaving Linc to open them alone.

George Smith's birthday presents looked like Christmas for a dozen people in the best of times. When the paper was scattered and the boys had whoa!'d themselves to dizzy delight, George's father set up the new Play Station (by unplugging the old and tossing it aside) and the boys stomped while chanting:

"Call of Du-Ty."

"Call of Du-Ty."

"Call of Du-Ty."

"Call of Du-Ty."

The Smith family television didn't come from a dump. It was huge, with a sound bar underneath and a block of bass Boom beside the cabinet. The battle was in the living room. Soldiers almost fell out of the screen. While the other boys yelled and cheered, Linc kept his butt cheeks tight because the concussion of the first grenade almost made him lose control of his sphincter. Almost. No shame.

INTEGRITY

Twenty minutes in, he won his chance to hold a controller and never gave it up.

On the walk home he shot three rabbits through their heads, and a red squirrel through its guts, for the kill.

• • • ● • ● • • •

Linc removed his right glove, tucked it in his left pocket and wrapped his fingers around the grip of the .38 Frank had left on the barn floor. After a moment gathering familiarity, he pocketed the pistol, gloved his hand and set off.

The Buzzard driveway continued past the house and barn in the form of a tractor road that circled the lower field and after two thirds of a mile, to the top of Kroh hill. When the fields were planted and Frank shot deer on the top of the hill, Linc drove the lawn jalopy on the tractor road to retrieve them.

But the tractor road appeared to lead straight to the trespassers, as if they'd camped right there in the open.

Frank would have said it took a lot of cheek.

If Linc approached the trespasser on the tractor road he'd be seen. If he came up through the woods, Kelley James might put a bullet in his back — though he didn't really believe that anymore.

Instead, Linc walked from the barn on an angle that would have taken him to the top left side of Kroh Hill — the side with the lookout on top — and when the field rolled the first time, he cut left in the bottom to avoid creating a silhouette. He counted his steps and when he imagined he'd traversed far enough, he stopped.

Moving slowly, Linc stooped and shuffled through six-inch snow until he saw the man's fire. The snow didn't rise above the top of his boots, but he'd kicked a lot onto his socks because his pant legs were short. Linc bent forward until he could barely walk without dropping to all fours, then plodded forward. Next time he spotted the fire he knelt and propelled himself on hands and knees.

Linc stopped and tapped his pocket. The .38 hadn't fallen out but his pockets were filled with snow. He emptied them then closed and snapped their flaps.

He'd been outside so long he was used to the cold. But close to the snow, his face reported a new dimension of chill as if the cold came in waves.

Linc pushed and created a pocket where he could rest on his forearms and watch the activity below without snow right next to his face.

The trespasser's light came from two sources: a campfire and a lantern. The lantern rested on the hood of a car — some old-fashioned job, built when cars resembled aircraft carriers.

A lanky man with no hat and disheveled hair crouched at the fire and no sooner had Linc found a comfortable position in the snow, without any next to his face, falling into his boots or resting against his socks, he observed a rapid sequence of events.

A dog existed — it moved.

The man observed the dog, too.

The man's head snapped square on Linc's position.

The man waved Linc forward.

Linc squirmed but was buoyed by the snow. His hand flashed to his pocket. He jerked free of his glove and with the pocket beneath his weight, struggled to remove the pistol. With it free in his hand, he wondered what to do with it.

Linc noticed, however, the gun in his hand changed everything.

Instead of wondering how to escape he mused about how to advance his interests.

TWENTY
THE CLAY JAR...

Frank allowed the engine to run an extra minute after arriving home. The lights inside the house remained off.

He sat in the cab.

The fuel gauge showed the F-150 close to empty. The extra trip burned some gas, sure, but he'd forgotten to fill the tank in town because his mind was exercised.

He preferred to use the underground fuel tank near the barn for farm-specific work, meaning, tractor work. He recorded details to the penny and while the F-150's work and the tractor's work both benefited the farm, he'd set up his mental ledgers the way he'd set them up, and to his thinking, even though he knew it was not the way a fancy accountant would do it, he had a better handle on his resources versus the work they had to accomplish if he only used the fuel from the tank for his tractor.

But the rule wasn't so hard and fast that it made sense to drive back to town to fill the gas tank. It was just enough of a rule to feel bad about himself when he failed it.

Frank pulled the truck around the loop so the nose was headed back out the driveway and parked a dozen feet away from the fuel pump.

The tank was old, but the hand-operated pump worked, albeit with a faulty gauge. Fill a five-gallon can and the meter could read anything between four to five and a half gallons, depending on whichever ghosts haunted the machine that day. To keep a fair estimate of his fuel supply, Frank dispensed fuel into five-gallon cans and recorded the usage on a chart tacked to the barn wall.

Frank tromped to the barn, wrote on the chart, grabbed two red, plastic five-gallon containers. He filled them at the pump and realized while pumping that he hadn't eaten since breakfast and his stomach was a pit. He remembered the rice he'd put on the stove and wondered if he'd ruined it by leaving it in hot, unboiling water.

There was probably a rule for that.

The first fuel can full, Frank swapped it for the second and pumped.

A life without rules, boundaries... how could a person live without constant mindfulness of how badly he was screwing up?

Frank knew every one of his rules and lived by them. That was the definition of honor. You do what you're supposed to do. And what you're supposed to do is follow the rules. Don't blaspheme, don't cheat, don't lie, don't covet, don't steal, don't murder, don't look too long at a woman who's only going to stick a knife in your back.

They were probably still laughing, back at the Tractor Supply.

"Did you see the cripple ogle you?"

"I wore this sweater just to make him drool."

"He doesn't even deserve tits."

That's why Frank's rule about women was that Jenny, albeit dead, was his only safe choice.

The second fuel container was full. Frank twisted on the cap for each and left them in the snow at the base of the pump. If the rice was ruined, he'd have to start over or create a new recipe out of rice mush.

Where was Linc?

All this time he'd been home, he'd forgotten about the ultimatum he'd given Linc.

Was the money in the clay jar still there?

Frank crossed to the house and opened the door.

TWENTY ONE
You're a Country Boy, Ain't Ya?

The glowing lantern rested on the hood of a gold car better suited to an old Paul Newman movie than a snow-drifted field road. The trunk was toward the fire and the passenger side toward the field. The man who'd waved now ignored Linc and seemed bent on some emergency. The dog was gone, possibly hidden in shadows created by clumps of grass and stumps between the tractor road and the posted forest. He'd lifted his hind leg to the snow, stepped behind the car and hadn't returned.

Linc sniffed. The breeze had carried his scent away from the vehicle when he started across the field, but he hadn't earlier considered the person who'd built the fire might have a dog with him. The things could smell anything, it seemed. Unless the wind was strong, eddies could easily circle back and inform on him.

Frank had taught Linc the basic principles: when a hill cools after sunset, the valley is relatively warmer, and wind flows in that direction — useful to know while hunting because animals had better noses than people. With the sun already down, the breeze ought to be changing direction soon. When it did, the dog would reliably pick up Linc's scent.

It wouldn't matter. The trespasser had already spotted him.

Linc watched with the .38 holstered inside his pocket. He could remove his glove faster than a man or dog could cross fifty yards.

Frank had taught Linc a hundred times about situational awareness, that it was better to hunt by ambush than by stalking because high awareness of a well-chosen, static situation was a million times superior to a low awareness of a changing situation, such as when a predator stalked prey — or a boy with a gun he'd never fired approached a strange man with a car and dog, out where they knew they shouldn't be.

In the former situation, the ambush, the hunter easily noticed changes. In the latter, every step created a thousand changes in perception. Any one of them could provide cover for an enemy making his move.

Frank drilled Linc until he understood the concept. It wasn't only important for hunting. It was important for life because even a sunny afternoon in the park could become hostile; bad actors were always capable of intruding.

"Sit still and pay attention. Best lesson in life."

Knowing the terrain and knowing the enemy meant survival, while ignorance of either was a sure path to death.

Closer to whimsy but still a valid intellectual point, Frank also taught Linc to never toss grass into the air.

"That's movie nonsense. Garbage for city people. Just one time I'd like to see one of those grass tossing — you know they always say some crap like, he could track an ant across a mile of bare rock — then he tosses grass in the air 'cause he doesn't know which way the wind's blowing. Just once I'd like to see one of them genius TV trackers get a bullet in the head right after he flashes his arm all over the place. People see that a mile off. On TV, you know?"

If a breeze was strong enough to blow grass and man didn't feel it on his face or hair, he ought to get his ass beat on principle. A lot of folks needed their asses beat on principle.

Thus Sprach Frank Buzzard.

Sometimes he wasn't a total — whatever he was. Self deluded, egotistical, hypocritical.... What?

Phucktard?

Abusive phucktard?

Sometimes he seemed to be doing his best, and somewhere inside he had to care about Linc, or he wouldn't be such a moron about so many things.

Sometimes... some rare times... Linc pitied him. The man didn't seem to know what planet he lived on. Or during which millennium.

He seemed to believe that back in earlier times everybody shared his code. How anyone who claimed to enjoy reading history could find evidence —

Linc stopped himself. He was ranting in his mind the way Frank ranted with his mouth.

The brain boggled. There wasn't a single word for his father. He was a Frank.

Instead of tossing grass, Frank had taught him to be still and pay attention to the terrain. Did the leaves flicker? Did the grass bend as waves crested across the field? Were the clouds moving fast or slow? Which direction? Did you feel anything on your face? If the air seemed still, did it still seem that way if you wet your finger and hold it aloft? Not high like some idiot saying, "over here," but close and low as possible.

Be still, be quiet, be nothing, and whatever game moves nearby, you hold the advantage. The other way around, he does.

Linc was still even after the trespasser spotted him. The grizzled man tended his fire and kept adding snow to a kettle hanging from a tripod. From time to time he stepped away and looked inside the car. His guttural syllables arrived across the snow in no particular order, perhaps carried by the engine's exhaust, sounds meaningless but urgent.

He sounded like a crazy man.

Linc lifted his head and crawled forward — aware he wore a deep blue coat and crawled on moonlit snow.

The passenger door opened and the car's dome light awakened the scene. The man sprang from his crouch and before he'd moved a foot a girl's painful cry arrived and Linc crawled another yard closer. Her voice sounded young. Linc could tell.

Had the man kidnapped her?

As snow floated from the sky the man lifted the lantern, opened the trunk and removed something that looked strikingly like a gym towel rolled around a pair of white shorts and rubber banded in place, like Linc carried on Tuesdays and Thursdays to school for gym class.

At the fire the man whipped open the towel and lowered the bottom end into the pot of melted snow and returned to the car. Again, Linc smelled the car's exhaust. The direction of the breeze was changing.

The car's passenger door remained open but at an angle that blocked the interior from view.

The girl moaned.

Was he killing her?

Or was it... the unspeakable... a violation of her pristine sex?

Linc's heart thudded like it had flipped sideways and from somewhere in the blackness at the back of his mind emerged an image of a girl like Sue Cooper, but her forehead stretched, eyes bolt open.

And from that same blackness sprang the rage that launched Linc forward.

The man returned to the car mindless of Linc witnessing the harm he was about to conclude on the woman. Crouched, Linc rushed further across the field until he obtained the correct angle to see inside. The man was folded into the entry and the girl cried again, and again. Linc stood erect. His feet hammering snow, he flung his hand free of its glove and plunged it to his pocket. He withdrew the .38 from holster and aimed to his right where any ricochet would send the bullet skipping across the snowy field.

Linc fired.

"Stop!"

He fired again.

"Leave her alone!"

The dog barked — still unseen. The man withdrew from the car and waved Linc forward.

Behind him, the girl lay on the seat with her head the other way, her bare legs folded, her sex concealed only by black underwear.

Linc pointed the .38 at the man.

"Put the gun away, son!"

Son?

What?

"Put it down! My woman's in here. I need your help!"

Left of the man and lit by flames, the dog stepped into the trampled snow behind the car with its head low and teeth bristling. His growl came slow and heavy, clear enough to separate each throaty rattle. Linc swung the pistol toward the dog.

"Leave her alone!"

"Shucks — You're a country boy, ain't ya?"

The man again turned his back to Linc and bent inside the car.

Linc was close. Was it a trap? Some deception to confuse him? The man's body again hid his actions inside the car. Linc resumed his sideways path until he was toward the rear of the car, and he could see between the man and the seat, her legs, the blankets she lay on, the towel he'd just fetched.

The trespasser dropped to his knees and from his waist up, disappeared into the car.

"AAASRGHHJIO8YFFHPPUTT!!"

The growling dog now stood beside the rear bumper.

Linc lowered the .38.

"Uunnhh, uunnhh, uunnhh, uunnhh, uunnhh..."

The girl was giving birth.

TWENTY TWO
Moxie...

Linc's brain was blank. The air was cold. His knees were weak. His gun hand was numb. Empty field all around, he felt cornered.

"Uunnhh."

After a long moment Linc withdrew the holster, slid the pistol inside and returned both to his pocket. He patted the other, but his right glove was gone. Spotting it twenty yards behind him, he jogged, then walked, then felt self-conscious, then jogged. He slapped the snow from his glove and with his hand again covered headed directly for the gold car.

"You need help, mister? Hey!"

"Uunnhh —- Uunnhh —- Uunnhh"

The man's voice was directed at the woman and indecipherable.

Linc stepped closer. The dog advanced. Linc stopped.

The man's voice was urgent but not strident, intense like his gym teacher urging another rep with the barbells.

As Linc neared the car the dog positioned himself between, no longer growling. The man leaned back and revealed the girl's bare calf, her leg hanging off the seat.

"C'mere. Give me a hand. Go around. Get in the other side and grab the keys."

"The dog —"

"That's Joe. He won't give you no trouble."

"Good dog. Hey Joe." Linc put his arm out.

"Need you to hurry it along. Thought I had everything ready and shit, nope."

The man returned his attention to his woman and Linc stepped around him and the dog and the car to the door on the other side. He opened it and heat blasted.

"You want me to shut the engine off?"

The girl's back was to him, arched against the console. She had raven-black hair and wore a heavy sweater. As she moved her head back and forth, he saw the bottom part of her face was very tanned.

She grunted, loosed a long airy groan and said, "Baer I'm going to shoot you."

"Yuhp. Take the key from the ignition. The trunk release in the glove box don't work. And don't mind her. She's tough as cowhide an' happy as a lark."

Linc killed the engine and took the key. The seat was covered with a shower curtain — brass rings gave it away. Linc expected blood and there was some, from what he could see of where the girl was sitting, but mostly it was just a shiny opalescent mess.

At the trunk he inserted the key, but it wouldn't twist.

"You mind if I steal some of your hot water? Lock's frozen."

"I just had it open."

"Want me to tell it?"

"Smartass, ain't ya?"

"I'm kinda freaking out."

"Use some hot water. Do it fast but don't spill the vice grips. I need a blanket out the trunk."

"Use one of these," the girl said.

"Lemme do my thing," said the man. "You just push that critter out. C'mon Tat. You're almost there."

Linc grabbed the wire handle of the pot with his gloved hand and tilting it, heard metal clank inside. He trickled steaming water on the trunk lock, attempting to open it every few seconds.

"Mister we got a house — "

The trunk opened. Linc stared inside at a white five-gallon bucket filled with gold coins. Beside the bucket was an array of camping equipment: back packs, sleeping bags, paper bags of groceries...

"Grab that blanket there on the right. Blue one."

Linc struggled to find the blanket without removing his gaze from the gold. The man was a bank robber or something. A shiver shot up Linc's back. He rested the pot of hot water in the snow and brought the blanket to the man, noticing as he did the girl's underwear weren't black — they were red, and in the footwell.

"One more push Tat. One more. Give 'er hell!"

"Uhng! Uhng! Eeeeaaahhhhh! Uhng!"

Linc reeled. Gold — a million dollars' worth of gold and a real woman's vagina in ten seconds.

A baby with black hair and a slimy body lay on the shower curtain.

The man used another white towel to wipe clean its nose and mouth, then covered it from the cold.

The man half turned. "You got that yet?"

Linc handed him the blanket and the man said, "Okay Tat, I'm gonna close your legs here and get you covered, but I got to work underneath a minute. When you feel the rest comin' you go ahead and push it out too. Nice and easy. The hard part's done."

He joined her right leg with her left at the seat back, opened the blanket Linc provided and covered her.

"Hey son. Start the engine again. Need heat in here. And where's that bucket with the water?"

Linc lifted the bucket from the snow and held it. The man pulled back his coat sleeve, dipped his hand straight in and withdrew two six-inch needle nosed vice grips.

"Good. Go ahead and start the engine. Then get the bucket on the fire again, case we need more hot water. Understand?"

"Yes sir."

"Alrighty. Let's get about it."

"I think it's coming," the girl said.

"Yuhp. I got it. You're doin' fine. Just fine. Moxie's breathin' fine."

"Moxie?"

"We got a son."

The girl's voice carried no words. Then: "That's a girl's name."

Linc keyed the ignition and twisted. The engine rumbled.

He placed the pot on the fire and looking back saw the car door closed, the interior dark but for the lantern on the hood, and the man carrying a stringy slop of afterbirth a few yards into the field.

"We have a house up the way, Mister. It's too cold out here for a baby."

The man said nothing as he washed his hands in snow then snapped them free of it. After six long steps he arrived at the fire and dipped his hands in the pot and washed again.

"We live right up there. You can see the barn. And how come you came down here? Right past the house? There's a hospital —"

The man crouched beside the fire and for the first time Linc noticed a holster strapped to his leg. A very large holster with a very large pistol grip at the top.

Linc recalled the gold and wondered if he'd made a mistake putting the .38 back in its leather, then his pocket.

"That gold back there's mine. Earned it makin' shine, and been totin' it all over these United States. I ain't a thief, since that's what you're thinkin'."

"No sir."

"Uh-huh."

"It's just — you don't make much sense."

"I'll give you that."

"Who's she? Your wife?"

"She is."

The dog joined the man.

"This here's Joe."

"You said that. Why are you here with your wife having a baby in a blizzard. In my field?"

The man grinned.

"Fifteen? Sixteen?"

"Fifteen."

The man nodded. Beamed.

"That's my boy in there. Moxie."

"You're crazy."

The trespasser grinned wider and then laughed.

"Look around! Miracles everywhere."

"Uh. Yeah."

"We have a tent, but I wanted Tat to deliver in the car on account it has a heater. But it won't be long afore the exhaust give us trouble. You came right on time — a sure sign you're an instrument of the Almighty. Why don't you head back the house and bring your old man down here so I can holler at him a minute."

"What'd he do to you?"

"Hunh?"

"Holler at him?"

"Have a word, son. Have a word."

"You are nuts."

"I am nuts. Appointed by the Almighty, goin' where he says, doin' what he says. In this world I am nuts. A sane man's gotta be."

TWENTY THREE
I GUESS YOU BROUGHT HIM.

Frank stood looking at the F-150 while Linc tramped ahead. Deciding against, he followed his son.

The plastic holster belted on his hip didn't feel right and being under his coat, it would be useless in a snap situation. Rigid, with hard edges, its greatest charm was that it was fully concealed. He'd decided to arm himself — of course — but instead of presenting the menace of a slung rifle on his shoulder, or the aggression of carrying one at port arms to meet a stranger, Frank opted for a nine-millimeter he'd never fired, toted in a holster he'd never worn.

A perfect example of letting concern for another man's opinion get in the way of good thinking.

Some fool drove to the bottom field right before a blizzard, then delivered a baby. The trespass against good sense was worse than the trespass on his property. Frank braced himself to meet a fool.

Or worse.

Fact was, when Linc said the man was strapped with a holster that went halfway down his leg, Frank's first thought wasn't to lend assistance. Inside his heart, he steeled for a fight. But it was hard to stage a fake childbirth for a farm boy, and it would be a uniquely rotten man whose first impulse after becoming a father would be to instigate violence against people coming to help.

But in the end men were men. Frank went armed — and even told Linc to take a minute and run his belt through the .38 holster, so his hand didn't have to think too hard to find it.

Linc also carried an oil lantern on Frank's instruction.

Linc said, "The moon's out. The lantern'll just mess up your night vision."

"It'll keep you from surprising a man with a gun."

"I don't think he surprises easy."

After passing the barn the tractor road curved a hair left and remained flat for a hundred yards. Then bore a little left again as it dropped a slight grade to the bottom of the valley that defined Frank's side of Kroh Hill. The woods on the other side of the valley belonged to a man Frank went to school with, several grades behind: Kelley James — spent ten years in prison for selling weed and came out blaming everyone but himself. The field road circled right at the bottom and started climbing again until after three false summits, it arrived on top of Kroh Hill.

Passing the flat after the barn, his mental wheels turning, Frank thought of the F-150. He'd forgotten to put gas in it. He'd have to remember to do that.

The snow on the flat after the barn wasn't so deep that he couldn't pull a vehicle, maybe with chains on all four tires. But arriving at the slight left and the downward slope he found the drifts too high. He'd have more luck towing the car across the field — unless the drifts at the bottom prevented the car from getting to the field.

So much useless thinking. Half the time a man's mind would do better to rest inert and wait for a couple facts to arrive. All speculation did was get the heart rate up.

Still, with a woman in labor, what fool man is going to drive a mile back a driveway then a field road before a blizzard?

Sometimes human stupidity seemed incapable of setting a mark so high that another stupid person couldn't surpass.

Turquoise Sue. What a rack. If she hadn't tricked him like that at the end. Oh, the glee in that wretched woman's eye, seeing him squirm in front of John Senior. Frank had wanted to pop him in the nose the last forty years after high school, and John just renewed the contract for the next forty.

Farther down the slope Frank saw the orange of the stranger's lantern sitting on the trunk of a —

"A Cadillac," Frank said. "What is that? Seventy.... ?"

Frank stopped and let his heart catch up. Walking downhill in knee high snow with a bad leg wasn't as easy as it sounded.

Linc arrived at the vehicle and spoke to the man, who seemed affable enough. Linc joined him leaning on the hood and watched Frank arrive.

"Get off the man's car, unless he invited you. What'd I teach you about property?"

Linc stood.

The other man lowered his head and when he lifted it his grin was big. He thrust himself forward from the hood and in a step offered his hand to Frank.

Frank watched long enough the man's grin flattened.

He accepted the shake.

"I'm wrong bein' on your land," said the stranger. "Shoulda stopped in — but it was too late. Lights was off. The lady was in labor. We needed someplace quick and I was cagey 'bout her givin' birth on the main road. I woulda come back to the house in the daylight, but not with her ready to drop a baby any minute. Regardless, I apologize."

"There's a hospital in town."

"If I'd a seen it I'd a parked there."

"When'd you get in?"

"Midnight."

"That's a long labor."

"Sixteen hour."

"I didn't see your tracks in the morning."

"On account it wasn't snowin' last night."

Frank nodded slow and the trespasser didn't nod at all.

He said, "We done sniffin' assholes?"

Frank huffed. Half smiled. "Why the piece?"

"Says the pot to the kettle."

"Yeah." Frank laughed, unconvinced. "Yeah, you're right about that. I don't have to tell you this doesn't look good."

"Matter of perspective, I'd say. Ain't lookin' very good on my side neither. Got the lady in there with a newborn baby, a quarter tank of gas for heat, and a tent that'll be under snow in another day, if it keep comin' down."

Linc stepped between the two men.

"He said he followed God here."

"Couldn't have. God's not here."

Linc stared at Frank.

Baer raised his brows.

Frank said, "That a fact?"

"Yessir."

"Then I guess you brought Him. I was thinking I'd offer you the barn, but the house'd be better."

"We'll appreciate anything you do and leave you better'n whole, soon as I can get a tow truck down here. Or a shovel. Long as my woman and son's warm I'm good."

"Dog got a name?" Frank said.

"Joe."

"You got a name?"

"Baer."

Frank held his look. Offered his hand. "I'm Frank Buzzard. That's Lincoln."

They shook hands again.

"I'm Baer, and the lady's Tathiana. Tat."

"And the baby?"

"Moxie."

Frank smiled. Sometimes men were rough because they were corrupt, sometimes because other men were corrupt, and they wouldn't stand for it. He knew which was on his land.

Still...

"Eldorado," Frank said. "No need for a tow truck. I can get you out — what is that? Seventy-seven?"

"Eight."

"I can get you out no trouble with the tractor, but I have to put on a new distributor. Do that tomorrow first thing. Tonight, you and the lady'll take my room — you'll want the bathroom right beside. I'll be on the sofa."

"We appreciate you."

"Can your lady walk through the snow with the baby? Or do we pull her on a sled?"

"Let's pull her, you don't mind."

"I don't mind. We'll be back in a bit."

TWENTY FOUR
"You Missed."

Frank and Linc walked side by side toward the barn.

"You do any of that thinking I asked you to do?"

"I thought you said you wouldn't bring any of that up again."

"I'm just asking if you did it."

They tramped along.

"You don't have the right to tell me when to do my thinking."

Frank grabbed Linc's arm and stopped him. They squared.

Linc moved his hand toward his hip but the .38 was under his coat.

"I made an offer. If you stay here, it's with the rules I said. I won't have you in my house if you're going to steal from the farm or lie to me. I won't have it."

"You ever think about how lucky it was that you beat me in the summer, that time? If I had to miss a week of school, and then showed up with my back tore up like that..."

"I know," Frank said. "What would you have me do, now? Turn myself in? Go to jail? Looking at cement all day would be a relief. Everywhere I turn around there's a reminder of something or another I've done wrong."

"So run away."

"I don't claim to be good, but I won't be a coward and quit trying."

Frank felt himself drifting as if he'd had a double dose of cough syrup. His heart pounded from walking fast, uphill in the snow.

"You know Linc, your mother always told me I'd be a great father. We tried a long time to have a baby and it never happened. But after that time out in the woods, when I did what I did, I was glad she was spared seeing how wrong she was about me. You're young enough, you haven't done anything horrible yet. That's what I'm trying to keep you from. There's no going back, once you've done evil. That's why I'm pushing you. I don't want you to wind up where I am, hating myself and wishing there was a way to take back what I did, and make the past different. C'mon, Linc! Look at me! I'm talking to you."

Linc looked up from the snow.

"I'll never be a great father. I can't even be a good one, at this point. But having integrity means you never give up trying to be good, even when you have no right to it. Even when you know you're hopeless, you keep fighting to be your best and do what's right even though you forfeited your ability to feel good about it. So, if you want to turn me in you can go to town as soon as you get the truck out. Have them put me in jail if you want. Show them the scars and I'll confess I put them there."

Linc stepped a pace away from Frank.

"If you think that's the path that gives you the best shot in life, it's your decision to live with. But you ought to think about what that'll set in motion. You aren't old enough to be on your own, unless you like being homeless and hungry. I don't know anyone who'd adopt you. Maybe you do. But if you believe the state can bring me to account more than my conscience has, every single day I've been cursing myself these last two years — "

"Bullshit! You never stopped! You took a swing at me tonight!"

"I caught myself."

"You missed."

"I froze."

"You lie."

"You're right. I should've never took the swing. And I gave you a pistol because I'd rather be dead than ever do it again."

"You're unhinged. This is such a shit show! This whole fucking thing!"

"I'm doing my best. That's why I'm trying to show you the basic respect it takes — "

"This is respect? This is what it looks like? You can keep it."

Frank lowered his head. "I asked whether you did that thinking because it was part of the deal. I was going to bring you in on the finances. How can I bring you into the finances if I think you're going to steal? Anyway, I had to cancel the insurance on the house."

"What? Why?"

"Couldn't afford it."

"Don't you *have to* afford it? Isn't that one of those things?"

"Yes."

"But — Dad — Buzzards don't seem to have the best luck."

"When there isn't enough money, there isn't enough money."

"But what if — "

"Once we have a spare minute, I'll show you the finances. I only brought up the thinking I asked you to do earlier so I could find out if we're on the same team, now that we're going to have strangers in the house."

"Can we just get the truck and figure all this out later?"

TWENTY FIVE
"Now I'm Bullshit."

Frank tossed the keys to Linc and angled for the barn while Linc tramped toward the truck.

"Back it up to the gate," Frank said.

He removed a toboggan from the barn wall and put it in the bed of the F-150 with the hook looped upside down over the tailgate. Below the toboggan the bed carried its regular winter load of dirt-filled sandbags, six inches deep.

Linc opened the driver-side door and shifted his left leg, but Frank gestured for him to remain and circled to the passenger side. He grabbed the back of the seat and tried to swing his bad leg first but that left an impossible angle for the good.

He backed from the door and studied the situation.

Linc's face was blank but his attention, great.

Accustomed to entering vehicles on the driver side, Frank had been leading with his bad leg and standing on his good so long — since he was a kid, after the war — that entering a vehicle never reminded him of his injury. His weak leg was flexible enough to fold and strong enough to lift itself into the cab, but it wasn't strong enough to launch his rear end to the seat, as he was asking it to do while entering on the passenger side.

Head down, he thought about leading with his bad leg and standing on his good.

Leading with his bad and standing on his good.

"I'll get out," Linc said. "You drive."

"Nah. I want you to get the practice. You ever drive in a foot and a half of snow?"

"All you need to do is use your other leg first and hang onto the top of the truck."

Frank closed his eyes. He opened them.

"I understand that, Linc. Just thinking something through."

"Yeah?"

Frank swung his bad leg, grabbed the roof, slipped onto the seat and closed the door.

"What were you thinking?" Linc said.

"Sometimes you see things about yourself. That's all. Patterns in one place that illuminate some others."

"Ok. What's that mean?"

"You're in four wheel, right? Go ahead and put it in first. I want you to go slow and easy. You haven't been in snow this deep. Can you get through it?"

"You got out the driveway this morning."

"And we've had another six or eight inches since then. Plus, there's no telling how bad the drifts are. You walk through them?"

"Some."

"How high?"

"I took the field around the heavy stuff. After the bend they're five feet, easy."

"We're only going to the bend."

"Two feet, mostly I'd say. We can get through that."

Frank was silent.

"Can't we?"

Frank shrugged.

"Why slow and easy? If I punch it, won't we go farther?"

"Sure, 'til we don't. Speed helps if you're going a short ways — long as your momentum holds out. Ten feet. But if we go slow, you know what you're in for. If the truck can make it ten feet it can keep going, so long as the snow doesn't get deeper. You'll know more about your situation."

"But if not, we still only went ten feet. Same as if I punch it."

Frank thought about leading with his bad leg, like he always did, and standing on his good one. Maybe something different?

"Tell you what. Whichever way you want, go ahead. We'll learn something either way."

"No, don't do that."

"What?"

"I'm trying to understand but you're not giving me enough to make sense of it."

"Do what you want to do. Some folks have to learn by making their own mistakes."

Silence.

"This is such bullshit," Linc said. "You're bullshit."

"Now I'm bullshit."

"Yeah."

"Keep digging."

"Why? You want to kick my ass?"

"No. I'm standing down. Do it your way."

"I met you halfway. I tried to understand. I figured maybe you knew something about driving in the snow. I don't even have a freaking license. But you quit. I try to understand, and you quit. Meanwhile the girl and her baby are freezing down there. Are we done?"

Frank unlatched his door and under the dome light met Linc's glare.

"You go hard charging in life and you'll smash through a lot of stuff. You'll move the world. Then you'll watch the whole godforsaken mess collapse in on you, and you'll have a heck of a time figuring out how to get back out. You go nice and easy, keep your traction, and you may learn the situation's beyond your ability. You need to start thinking about the consequences you don't want. They happen a whole lot more often than the ones you do. Go slow and give yourself a chance to find out which way things'll go before the mistake costs you too much."

Frank closed the door and stepped backward with his eye on the bed of the truck, in case Linc decided to tramp the pedal and whip the back around.

The sound of the engine changed when Linc put the truck in first. He eased to the driveway, turned left, gunned the engine, and with all four wheels spinning, blasted into the snow.

TWENTY SIX
WRROO WOO RRR WHOOGGGD.

Standing in tire tracks at the back of the F-150, Frank looked toward the barn and observed the trail Linc cut through the snow. He'd driven less than a quarter mile on the tractor road, then turned right into the field to avoid the heavy drifts at the bend.

Except his intended path and actual path diverged.

As Frank had suspected he might, Linc forgot about the dirt bank at the left-hand bend that emptied into a downslope.

Instead of driving as far as made sense and walking the rest, he chased four-wheel drive glory. He hit the bank at a weak angle and bounced into the deep drifts he was trying to avoid. The F-150 had skinny tires with decent treads, but without chains and more weight in the back, he wound up with all four wheels spinning about where Frank had guessed he would, with the nose of the truck hammered into a drift as high as the hood and saddled on snow beneath.

Anyone with a mind and the willingness to use it could see the future. Not down to fine details, most of the time. But certainly, broad enough strokes to avoid most kinds of trouble.

That was what he wanted Linc to learn.

A bonus lesson: Linc was momentarily trapped inside the cab. He slammed his door into the snow, gaining an inch or so each time.

Frank bent, scooped and packed a heavy ball of snow.

When the door opened enough, Linc placed one foot on the seat and the other on the door sill, then humped on top of the roof and squirmed over. He swung his legs to the bed.

Frank tossed the snowball.

Linc caught it.

"Have fun?"

"What?"

"That's what you should have done."

"A snowball?"

"See how dense that is?"

"We're doing this now?"

"You screwed up now. And we're not doing anything. Just talking."

"Great. Ok. Snowball. Your turn."

"You stampeded yourself."

Linc pitched the snowball aside.

"Sometimes a situation won't give you any time to think. Go to war and you'll see. But that doesn't happen very often, and it doesn't happen hardly at all if you get yourself in the habit of thinking before doing."

"I thought."

"You wanted to help people who need your help. But there's a big difference between wanting and thinking."

"I told you back there."

"Son — Linc. Listen. Saying you want to do something or believe you need to do something isn't the same as thinking through how to do it. I want this; bang! Off we go. That's nowhere near the same thing as taking the wide view and seeing the situation a bunch of different ways before deciding how to move forward."

"She's freezing down there!"

"Bang! Off we go. That's what I mean. She's not freezing down there. She's in a car with a heater. She might be cold, but she isn't freezing."

"She has a baby."

"I'm sure she's aware."

"But — I thought going fast would blast through. When the snow plow leaves a mountain at the end of the driveway, you punch through it. That's all I was doing."

"Nevermind that I told you different the last time you said that, before you got the truck stuck. When the snow's over the axles, you have to push it. This is wet and heavy. If it was a powder, you'd have made it all the way to the bottom and back up the other side, if you wanted. But this stuff? See how heavy that is?"

"So why didn't you tell me?"

"Uh-huh."

"I didn't try to get through the drift. I wanted to take the field."

"Sure. And now you have some shoveling to do. It did look fun, though."

Frank pulled the toboggan from the bed. He backtracked until he could follow their prior footprints to the field and there, considered the grade. Probably not steep enough for a quick ride to the bottom. He pulled the toboggan by its rope and before long, Linc was behind him.

"Can't we use the tractor?"

"You're saddled. Tractor's got big wheels but the engine's only twenty-five horse. Or so. I've heard twenty-eight. It'll pull some, but not what you just did. No way."

"So how do we get it out?"

Frank stopped. Turned. "If you want to talk, get up here beside me."

Linc forged a second path beside Frank.

"So how?"

"How's the truck stuck?"

"Saddled."

"What's the most basic way to think about what you need?"

"We need the truck to move."

"Hold on. This stopped being *we* when you decided to do exactly what I told you not to do."

Linc quit walking.

Linc caught up.

"I need to get the truck to move."

"Why won't it move now? Mechanically. How's that happen?"

"The tires. What? Just say what!"

"Traction, Linc. You said the truck's saddled. Your tires are slipping because there isn't enough force pressing them to the ground, compared to the weight in front they have to push. How do you change that?"

"Pull it out."

"You don't have a way to pull it."

"The tractor."

"Tractor's not running, and time you get the truck in a position the tractor could help — tonight after supper — you'll be able to back it out."

"Tonight? I have homework!"

"That would have been a good thing to consider before you got the truck stuck."

"This is bullshit. You set me up!"

Frank checked his step and resumed while he remembered the last time he felt the beast climb forward from the back of his skull, and how he clutched his right arm with his left, so it wouldn't disobey.

He remembered when he asked the Lord God Almighty by whatever name he preferred to pull the evil out of him.

He thought about leading with his bad and standing on his good.

Staring out across the glowing snow to the silhouette of trees and the deep gray sky, Frank saw fragments of his father congeal into a snarling face, a burly forearm with a faded tattoo of a naked woman, and a wire coat hanger with the bottom stretched like a bow. He saw himself from a few feet away, staring at his own backside reflected in the bathroom mirror, welts like question marks all the way from his shoulders to his thighs.

Because Frank had said, *Dad, you set me up.*

Instead of anger, he observed his memory as a solution to a puzzle and felt the peace of emptiness.

Frank stopped. Linc stopped.

"You made a mess, son. Be a man and own it."

"What am I gonna do? I'm fifteen."

"You're better than that."

"But — what about the bucket?"

"On the tractor? What good's that? You mean to lift the back end?"

"No. To scoop out the snow."

"From where?"

"Behind the truck."

"You already proved you can get through most of it. Which snow do you need to remove, to get the truck unstuck?"

"I don't know."

"Sure you do. Call up your jocular fiber. Reason it out."

Frank waved and thirty yards away, the shadow sitting on the car hood waved back.

"Go ahead and think on it a little bit. Come up with a plan."

Frank stopped.

Linc stopped.

"Your heart was in the right place. Just not your brain. Hey — that's a fact, not a criticism. I do it all the time. That's what I was thinking about back there at the barn. You had some adventure. Now muster some grit."

They walked.

Frank said, "So what do you think about this fella down here with the cannon strapped to his leg?"

"I thought he was trouble at first, but he just delivered a baby in a blizzard in a Cadillac. Can't be all bad."

"No man's all bad. None are all good. We just need to see which end he's closer to. What'd he say his name was?"

"Baer."

"Folks with uncommon names are usually —"

"Howdy!" Baer called.

Frank stopped short of the campfire.

"Mind if we spend a minute at the hearth? You can get the missus situated how you want on the sled, then we all three pull her to the house."

"Enjoy. All yours."

The man called Baer shoved off the car trunk and reached his right hand over the fire. Frank shook it.

"I appreciate you," Baer said.

Frank met his stare and something uncanny within it prevented him from looking away.

"It's an uncommon man that'll forgive a trespass and help the trespasser in the same half hour. I'm in your debt."

Linc had approached to Frank's right and when Frank stopped at the fire Linc advanced another few steps toward the car, thinking to catch a glimpse of the woman inside. But the short haired block headed dog seemed always to stand where Linc wanted to stand. Linc dropped to one knee and offered his hand.

"How you doing, Joe?"

I'm tired from all the excitement. You?

"That's cool. I've never heard a dog do that. *Wrroo woo rrr whoogggd*. It's like he's talking."

Baer turned his head. "Very much like talking. Very much. Well, I'll get the lady loaded up while you fellas warm your hands."

The snow around the car was plenty trampled. Baer stepped around Linc while he stroked the dog's jowl and neck.

"What breed is he?"

"Pit bull."

Baer leaned to the glass of the rear window and peered inside. He nodded and opened the door. "Your chariot awaits, Tat."

Her boots appeared, then her trousered legs.

"You're moving good."

Baer's flat mouth became a grin. Eyebrows high, he reached forward and when he pulled his arms back out of the car, he held a swaddled bundle. Baer tramped four paces to Linc and eased to a knee.

"This is Moxie," he said. "I got a son."

The heat from the fire made Frank's face tingle. Wavering light shimmered through the trees on Kelley James' side, sparkled off the Cadillac's gold paint, and made the snow all around pure and bright.

There was something about the stranger...

TWENTY SEVEN
"I WOULDA."

Frank joined at the rope. Baer slid his hand to the left and made slack. Frank grabbed ahold and behind them, on the side closer the hill, Linc maintained a short distance between himself and the toboggan.

"You feeling okay? Hungry or anything?"

The girl couldn't have been much older than him — she looked the same age as juniors or seniors, but without the snarling contempt that usually lit their faces while looking at underclassmen. She was mysterious. Among people like her, with dark complexions and black hair, she was probably ordinary. But in moonlight, with her teeth as white as the snow and her skin looking soft as pudding, she was exotic.

"It did not hurt as much as I thought it would."

What a stirring accent... Platonically stirring. Yet... if he hadn't already pledged his eternal heart to Sue Cooper, maybe an exotic girl would be the way to go.

"Have you... uh. Have you guys been getting enough to eat?" Linc remembered the bucket of gold in the trunk. "I mean — we'll be fixing supper when we get to the house."

"Yes," she said. "We have plenty. But I am tired."

"Yeah. Okay. You just had a baby."

She flattened her lips and as her eyes glazed with disregard, Linc remembered the six-shooter on Baer's hip.

These people weren't regular people. They didn't push; they didn't aggress. But they sure carried themselves like they were capable.

With Linc's pace matched to the men in front, Tathiana remained in his peripheral vision. She'd dismissed him but he still walked beside her — like some kind of a dick who didn't get the hint. Linc looked forward hoping to see something worthy.

Nothing.

Then off to the left, up on top of Kroh Hill, he again saw headlights. Lots of traffic up there, for a crap-weather day. The road was barely maintained in winters and signs at the bottom where the road connected — on each side — said Travel at Own Risk. There were several tight turns — right where the grade was steepest — coming down the other side. Usually, folks took the long way around since it only added a couple miles, most of it on a snappy four lane that connected to the interstate.

Linc chugged through the snow and got in front of Frank. He reached for the rope.

"I'll spell you."

Frank gave him the rope. Linc pulled harder than Baer, then throttled back to match.

"Plate on your car said Colorado."

"Yuhp."

"What's that like?"

"I grew up in country like this, south a here," Baer said. "Always wanted to see the big skies and big mountains out West."

"Yeah?"

"You too?"

"Some. So how was it?"

"Beautiful, out there. Beautiful here. You talk to Tat? How's my boy doin'?"

"She didn't say."

Cresting the small slope, Baer turned his head the other way for several steps then turned his grin on Linc.

"That musta been fun. I never seen a truck buried like that. How'd you get out the cab?"

"Just beat the door against the snow a few times."

"Old man give you shit about it?"
"Some."
"I woulda."
"He said I have to get it unstuck tonight."
"Got any plans?"
"I wanted to use the tractor, but it isn't running. How would you get it out?"
"Shovel. Tire chains if you got 'em."
"That your plan for the Cadillac?"
Baer caught Linc's look.
"The lead sled's sittin' where it's s'posed to be."

TWENTY EIGHT
A BIND WITH THE TRUCK STUCK...

Linc hadn't been inside the house since they'd left for Senior's Tractor Supply. Nothing was different except a lidded saucepan sat on the stove top, likely full of rice. Frank had been in the habit for the last few months of mixing a can of kidney beans with rice and adding fat from soup cans he kept full of drippings from any meat he cooked. He tinkered with spices each time and the recipe was still waiting to be discovered.

The dog slipped into the house between human legs, quickly found the rug Frank had washed after General Sherman died and lay there watching the orange glow coming from the wood stove air vents.

"You want to check the stove?" Frank said.

Linc added a log and twisted open the vent below the door a quarter turn more. It didn't take much to make the living room too hot.

"Looky looky," Baer said, staring at the array of firearms on the sofa, butts on the cushions, barrels lined like sentries along the back, standing guard.

"Someone woke the lion."

Frank stood beside Baer. "Nothing like that. That a Model 29 on your hip?"

Baer nodded. He glanced at the sofa. "That's a pretty collection."

"Where you from?"

"Colorado," Linc said. "I already asked."

"North Caroline," said Baer. "Arizona for a bit. Then Colorado. An' all the space between."

"I always wanted to see the country," Frank said.

"She's worth seein'. You got a bathroom? I'd like to let the lady freshen up, soak in the tub if that's all right. And someplace she can rest?"

"Yeah, I apologize. I'll put you both in my room. It's handy to the bathroom. You can have the run of it."

"Appreciate you," Baer said.

Frank hesitated.

Were they married? They had carnal knowledge no doubt, but the girl was so young, and the man looked Frank's age, maybe younger, definitely more grizzled by his years. His face looked healed after a country beating. Eyes that didn't have a color so much as a signal. Like looking at punctuation marks. Was the girl a kidnap victim, so intimidated by her captor that she didn't dare speak up? Should he wait for a better understanding of the situation? Ask her point blank? His house — his rules.

"I don't mean to overstep, Mister, uh — "

"Baer. That's all I use these days."

"Miss — Tathiana? You and he — uh — you want to share a room?"

Baer snorted. "Ask her how we come to be together. Shit."

Tathiana smiled small with her eyes and her mouth. "We are together."

"That's a good thing, you askin'. A good thing," Baer said.

Frank held Tat's look a moment longer trying to discern if she'd hidden a message within it.

"Baer saved me from the kind of people you are thinking about. He saved many of us. Now he is mine — but we have to avoid certain people."

Frank dipped his head, faced Baer. "I'd like to hear about that sometime. Better than television, I bet."

"What," Linc said. "Like, criminals?"

"Devils. We'll save it for another time. Bathroom for the lady?"

Frank crossed the living room to Tat and extended his arm to the bathroom. So far, the baby hadn't made a sound and considering the artillery piece the scrappy man carried on his hip, Frank wondered if Linc had been confused. Was it a baby or a doll? Were they strangers having a baby-Jesus-in-a-barn moment, or thieves with a Raggedy Anne ruse?

It was strange to have guests from nowhere who are into guns arrive on the same day you have a new truckload of firearms in the house.

Situational awareness...

But as Tat passed Frank, he beheld the baby's face planted snug against the upper swell of her breast and there was no mistaking the skin of a newborn.

It was ugly.

And Tat's eyes were red from busted blood vessels. How long did Baer say she'd been in labor?

Tat closed the bathroom door and Frank said, "Baer, take a look here."

Frank led a few steps to an open bedroom door.

Baer stood beside him.

"I'll swap out the sheets. You best figure on being a day or two, 'til I can get your car out the snow. Unless you need longer, and we'll see what we can work out. For the Eldorado, only thing I have that can pull it is the tractor, and that won't leave the barn 'til I do some mechanic work. If she needs the hospital, or you know, I don't know. If she needs something, we're in a bind with the truck stuck."

Frank watched Baer's eyes and unlike a moment prior, now they were blank. No fear, no judgment; he just took in Frank's words until he said his piece.

"We do appreciate you," Baer said.

"I'll get the room ready," Frank said. "You mind sending Linc back?"

"I'm here," Linc said from behind Baer in the hallway.

"Take the hog that's thawing and cut it in half. Use a saw downstairs if you need and put it in the oven in some water. I'll get the sofa cleaned off next."

Baer tapped beside the bathroom door. "You good Tat? Need anything?"

Frank heard her voice but no words, then Baer's boots on the boards.

Frank kept a spartan bedroom with nothing but a closet, bureau, bed and end table; the one that matched sat beside the living room sofa. He kept a Bible in the drawer but hadn't read it in years. Clothes in the closet — not many. A couple pair of boots. A wall covered in photos of Jenny, opposite the bed, so he could bunch up his pillow and look at her — but he hadn't done that in years either.

Last couple of years, all she did was judge him.

Frank pulled a folded set of flannels from the shelf in his closet and swapped them with the ones on the bed. He changed the pillowcase too, then stood looking into the hallway a moment. The other pillow was in Linc's room. He and Jenny'd had two pillows in the house when Linc was born, and since there were only two people in the house afterward, he'd never gotten a new pillow. They were both thin enough they needed to be folded double to be any use.

Maybe he'd give Linc the pillow from the sofa, and he'd use a boot, like he did in the Army.

TWENTY NINE
"Mind what I taught you."

Linc carried the half-thawed, freezer-paper wrapped meat to the basement while Baer dragged a chair from under the kitchen table. They had four chairs and all of them were at the table. It didn't seem strange to Linc until the chair leg scraped the floor — Baer had grabbed the outcast chair, the one Frank two years before pulled from a dump because it looked similar to the one he shattered against the wall after losing his job at the clay plant. Frank had placed that one on the side with the smallest clearance to the wall, and neither of them ever sat in it.

No one ever sat there.

The Buzzards never hosted supper for other people. Linc had eaten with extended family a couple times, way back when Frank talked to them. And Frank made Linc attend a church thing at the pastor's house, back when Frank went to church. The pastor had too many people at the table and Linc sat trying to figure out how to scoop food to his mouth without elbowing either of the old ladies next to him. But they'd never once in fifteen years had another person at the Buzzard kitchen table, let alone two. Or three, counting the baby.

Guests for supper!

Between the new guns on the sofa, the .38 under his coat on his hip, the gold in Baer's trunk and Linc seeing Tathiana's spread legs, the night was clearly charmed — even a skeptic would have to wonder at the day's import.

Almost anything at all could happen.

Sue Cooper!

Linc ran from the basement door to the basement floor taking the steps sideways, dropping eight feet a fraction under freefall speed and setting off a wooden rattle-thunder that shook the house. Mostly frozen in the center, the meat sawed easy, right up the spine. Linc cleaned the blade in the giant basin sink and wiped it down with a rag to prevent rust.

Something about having a stranger and his wife and new baby in the house called for a momentary truce with Frank. The man was his father and to outsiders looking in, they shared a reputation. It was a ceasefire, not a stalemate.

And it certainly was not a foundation for a Hallmark movie ending.

His father was a snake who said one thing and did another.

Frank had proven with his frosty attitude about the stuck F-150 that his words earlier in the barn — about giving Linc his say — were a cheap appeasement drawn from the well of guilt, and not a genuine enlightenment in recognition of Linc's validity as his own person.

Frank thought Linc was a thing, maybe one step above the cows, since he entrusted Linc to milk them. When the strangers left, Linc would find his moment.

Returning upstairs with the split carcass enclosed in untaped freezer paper, Linc found Baer at the door.

"Headed back to the car. Need a couple things."

"Gimme a sec I'll go with."

"Hunh?"

"Wait a minute and I will go with you."

"Uh — if your old man say."

"I'll just go."

"Best honor the man's prerogative."

Without lifting his head from the rug, the dog called Joe lifted his eyelids and looked at Baer.

"Stay with Tat," Baer said.

"Wrrooo woo wrrrgg — gggg."

"Not too long. Enjoy the fire."

"I swear it sounds like he's talking."

Linc held a roaster under the faucet, added the meat, a couple onions and carrots. The rice was done so they could scoop a few cups when the hog was roasted. Linc closed the oven door.

Baer stood on the porch with the glass door closed but the heavy door open.

Linc grabbed his sleeve with his hand to keep it from slipping up his arm and bunching in his coat. The first was easy but the second required him to adjust the shirt on his back to get enough length to grip. His wrists shared the same uncovered torment as his ankles.

Frank entered the hallway with a set of nightclothes rolled under his arm.

"Where you going?"

"Baer needs stuff."

"What stuff?"

"From the car."

"You got that..."

"What?"

Frank looked at Linc's hip. Raised his brows.

"Oh, yeah."

"Mind what I taught you. Awareness, all the time."

That was another thing. Frank was always trying to make him feel creepy about people. Frank waved him off.

Closing the door so it wouldn't slam — there was a baby in the house — Linc watched Frank face the sofa and frown.

THIRTY
"IT'LL COME TO YOU."

"Y'all two hide it but you ain't right with one 'nother."

They were five feet off the porch. Baer stooped and grabbed the toboggan rope.

"I'll get that," Linc said.

"Go on."

Linc took the line and Baer released.

"Why do you say that? I mean, why do you think that?"

Baer walked across the drive circle. Most of his life he'd hidden his preternatural ability to spot a lie or evil intent. That made it hard to tolerate ordinary everyday people, who were so cussed full of wickedness and cruelty toward one another. He'd spent most of his time alone, but for the company of a pit bull. When twenty of his townsmen, including his brother, stole his dog and used him as bait in a fight circle, Baer decided the best way to make right their wrong was to make absolute cruel certain they never repeated their crimes. That meant sending each man forward to whatever was next in his existential journey.

Sometimes Baer wondered: if he'd been straight with folks about his gifts from the very beginning, if he'd called out each deception along the way and forced every person who came near him to deal on a high level of truth, would he have ended up killing so many of them?

How much of his killing had taken the long way around after springing from his cowardice? His fear of being the only voice for truth he ever saw?

"Most folk don't know but they bodies glow. Learn that in school yet?"

"No."

"They won't teach it, neither. It's the rare person get to see it and them that don't, don't know what to make of the rumor. Seein' light ain't like feelin' gravity."

"Then how'd you learn it?"

"Had the curse most my life. Didn't understand none of it 'til a physics professor from Chicago schooled me."

"You see people's light?"

"What they is of it. Mostly I see the dark."

"Okay... Sure."

"You get the higher frequencies from the good stuff. Tat and Moxie, the space 'tween that baby's head an' her skin there, you know: the collarbone and down a bit. That's the color of starlight with a tinge of blue. That boy of mine's feedin' on love more'n milk. Now the lower frequencies is the bad stuff. When people treat each other rotten you get the reds. Comes out the eyes, arms, everywhere. You an' your dad's all the mean colors, mostly."

Linc listened and thought.

There were people near the Amazon River that hadn't ever seen civilization. He'd seen pictures of them taken from airplanes with telephoto lenses. They wore tree bark over their groins and face paint. Nothing else. When white people finally made contact, two of them died from voodoo. Before then everyone thought voodoo only worked on believers. It was in a science article. Weird stuff was everywhere. Linc knew an exchange student from Sweden who was a little plump and carried herself really, really well. Stacked. She said her grandmother as a girl wanted to be a nun and be married to Christ, then one day a ring appeared on her finger. The stigmata was a line of blood pushing through the raised skin, as if the wedding band was underneath. It lasted twenty years and a picture of it ended up on a website the Swedish girl brought up on her cell phone.

But that was other people in other places. Everyone in Oak was regular.

Linc said, "You screwing with me?"

"That's the one thing I don't never do."

"Why are you here?"

"I already said. I go where the Maker send me."

To the Buzzard Farm in Oak, Pennsylvania... Frank always said most travelers passing through were freaks. Linc shivered as his neck hair raised.

"You're in a struggle, son. Your father too."

"The lights tell you that? Or just him being an asshole all the time?"

"Only assholery I seen was when you two was walkin' down the hill with the sled."

Linc attempted to match his stride to the path he'd created dragging the toboggan up the slope before, but with his direction reversed the path his legs took through the snow changed. His progress was awkward and halting.

"Snow ain't too deep. Might be easier to cut a new path."

Linc continued as he was.

"When you watched me at the fire and was hidin' in plain sight on the field — an' by the way, that was smart. Scopin' the scene without committin' to its trouble. Keepin' low with the gun handy... You'd a done better to come up through the woods, but the land's posted and I met the somebody who posted it. What a man in need of the bended knee. Anyhow out there on the field — you wasn't red then. And when you went to the trunk and saw that bucket a gold you wasn't red neither. But comin' back with your dad when I spot you on top the hill it was like you an' him share the same body, just one bigass glow of mean an' hate."

"That's Frank for you."

"Heh heh. No. 'Cause when you and your father ain't talkin', he's got the same white and blue as Tat an' Moxie."

"What's that mean?"

"It'll come to you."

THIRTY ONE
"MOST PEOPLE'S SHIT FOR THINKING..."

At the car Linc stood to the side but visible so Baer could see him while he worked the key into the trunk. If Linc owned that much gold he wouldn't leave it in the trunk of a car and he wouldn't have people at his back while it was out in the open. He wouldn't let a stranger see it at all.

"I bet we have to build a fire again," Linc said. "I bet the water I poured on it froze."

The trunk popped open.

Baer removed his coat and the sweater beneath, then unfastened a wide leather belt that looked like a cummerbund the juniors and seniors wore with their tuxes to the prom. Gold flashed in the moonlight, one piece at a time, as Baer stuffed coins into slots in the belt. Somewhere after ten of them Linc started counting; he got to thirteen.

"Ain't you gonna ask somethin'?"

"You robbed a bank, right?"

"Shit. Banks don't keep money. They keep paper."

"Where'd the gold come from?"

"I run a still for thirty years."

"Everybody running stills end up with a bucket of gold?"

"Them that don't spend but a tenth of what they earn, an' don't trust banks nor government. 'Sides. They wasn't but twenty-five pieces in that bucket."

"Yeah, right. How come you let me see all that gold?"

"You ain't a thief."

"Tell my father."

"Are you?"

Linc observed the snow.

"You ain't a liar. You know the truth of it," Baer said. "I wouldn't tell a stranger neither."

"What's that supposed to mean?"

"A liar's always cagey 'bout the truth. He'll avoid it all he can. Honest man, it's the other way around."

"I don't have anything I need."

"That ain't true, and even if it was, the thief don't have any more when he's finished 'n when he started, anyway. You ever hear the old line, possession's two thirds ownership?"

Linc nodded. "Yes."

"It's bullshit. Folk want the rights to what they don't have and forget the obligations to what they do. To an honest man, possession's nothin' but an obligation. To a thief, it's a noose he can't see, but feels all the time hangin' over his head."

"You always talk in riddles?"

"Can't speak any plainer."

"So why did you say I wasn't a liar?"

"Your eyes was red — you was thinkin' the lie. But you wouldn't say it."

"That's weird."

"I said I see people's light, didn't I?"

Baer removed a blue backpack and placed it on the toboggan behind him. He placed a large cardboard box on the front end of the sled, then a second. "Tat likes her own food. I expect more now we got a son."

"But I do tell lies, sometimes," Linc said. "How can I tell lies and not be a liar?"

Baer pulled a black backpack from the trunk, much larger than the other, and stood with the strap over his shoulder. "Every one of us does things we're not."

· · · · • · • · • · · ·

Linc sniffed.

Diesel?

Linc looked toward Kroh Hill — the wind direction had changed.

The odor was very faint but sometimes it seemed like a blanket of snow changed the effectiveness of his senses. Sounds carried farther. Smells stood out plainer, as if the coldness stilled the air and made it more capable of carrying messages.

Baer waved Linc closer.

"You worn a backpack?"

"My school bag."

Baer lifted Tat's blue pack from the end of the toboggan and held it next to his chest with the straps facing Linc.

"Back into it and feed your arms through the straps."

Linc hefted the pack and staggered. "Man, that's heavy!"

"Lady won't go nowhere without the iron cookware. Turn."

"We have iron cookware. That's all we have."

"Has to be her own."

Baer showed Linc the one-inch straps that tightened the shoulders. "Cinch 'em down and latch the center. That's 'bout it."

"I'm not an idiot."

"Easy. You got no turf to defend."

"That didn't sound the way I meant it."

"Give the pack a bounce an' it'll sit square on your back and ride easy."

"I didn't mean to sound like a dick."

"No harm. Nor need to say it twice."

"I just — I expected you to ride me a minute. My father does."

"Jump a little."

Linc bounced. Metal clanked. Linc adjusted the straps.

"You get the center hooked?"

Linc did so.

"Now go ahead an' I'll get the rest. I need to attend my vehicle a minute."

Linc half smiled.

"That a lie?"

"Some." Baer stepped backward and looked at Linc as if judging him. "Say what you mean without worrying on what you sound like. Life's a balance 'tween showing respect for what other people think and ignoring it at the same time. Do your own thinkin' and be prepared to defend it. If you can't — you may as well not think. Outcome's the same. You get sucked in. Find yourself goin' through motions that don't make sense for you or nobody, as most people's shit for thinking. That's why you don't want them doing it for you."

"You sound like Frank."

"Does he say you're a shooting star, 'less you figure out how to be your own light?"

Linc allowed the words to sink in. Baer punched his arm, easy.

"If you ain't discovered it yet I'll clue you in: your whole life's gonna ask you the same question. Do you follow what makes sense to you? Or do you do what the guy stumbledickin' around with a blindfold on his eyes says, on account he's got the power to hurt you?"

"What do you do?"

"I'm no example. But I never met a man who had integrity and wished he didn't, while I seen plenty who let it slip away and never get it back." Baer winked. "Git on. I'll be after you."

"Want me to drag the toboggan?"

"Take it and we'll swap when I catch you."

Linc set off dragging a week's supply of boxed food on the sled while lumping almost all of Tat's belongings on his back.

Baer Creighton returned to the Eldorado.

He removed a Ruger SR9c — a compact nine-millimeter pistol — from under the front seat. He slid it partly out of its holster, observed the red indicator on top that meant a bullet was in the chamber, checked the white dot on the side — the safe was on — and slipped gun in holster and holster in the small of his back under his gold-bearing belt.

Front door closed, he returned to the trunk and donned his sweater.

He spent a long moment looking at the top of Kroh Hill and when he felt peaceful grabbed the white bucket by its lip and flipped it upside down, and placed a single Maple Leaf on top.

Baer slammed the trunk closed, seated his pack, adjusted the straps and strode after Linc.

THIRTY TWO
INTENT.

Baer drug the sled the last fifty yards from the far edge of the barn, across the driveway area and to the front step. Linc had spent the time wordlessly and Baer understood from his colors he was deep in thought.

Best leave him be.

He had trouble ahead.

Baer had only recently learned to see auras, discovering them one day after falling asleep up near the treetops in late autumn sunshine. He awakened to the brightness warm on his face and a giant ice age boulder (Ma would be proud he finally found one where she said they were, in Yank country) hard against his back.

Moxie was looking like a football in Tat's belly.

Baer had always found Tathiana approximately pretty, but pregnant she became beauty itself. Everything about her incited a kind of unfamiliar lust. He wanted her, of course. But he also craved his future with her. He hungered to feed her and to press his fingers to her shoulders when she complained until she sighed and groaned instead; to bring her water when she thirsted; to add wood to the fire when the flames no longer illuminated her smile.

Lazing on top of the rock after his meditation, looking on Tat from above, Baer wondered if the sun had burned his retinas through his lids. As she moved about tending a small cooking fire below, the barest light followed her like a stubby comet trail, or like dust floating from a drum skin. Easiest to see in the shadow of the rock, the aura disappeared whenever she stepped into direct light.

When she looked up and faced him — the rabbit was roasted — a pale bluish-white glow emanated from her chest to her womb.

The world to Bear Creighton had always been a little different from what others reported theirs to be. He'd first seen the red hues in people's eyes when they lied, often accompanied by a hair-raising sense of electricity on his forearms. Then, only months ago, nearly delusional with mystical torment, he saw beings vibrate out of and back into reality, which he called the porcupine skizzle-fizzle after the first creature to do so. Last, he observed the smoky incarnation of evil itself.

In the months between the expansion of his consciousness and his dreamy meditation on the boulder, Baer realized there was no reality out there, only in here. There were things out there, most likely. Stub a toe and the evidence felt irrefutable. But on inspection, the evidence was always an assurance provided by his other sketchy senses. He believed, and the things they reported were real; until he didn't and they weren't.

His awareness brought him to a new mind.

Seeing colors no one else saw and beings fade in and out like a televised image fighting to survive bad reception, and last, seeing the granddaddy demon swirl about a room while urging him to do murder, Baer was left with a singular impression. Nothing reported by his senses was necessarily honest. All impressions were of something, or nothing, and the mere concurrence of other senses added nothing to their merit.

His senses wanted to be fooled.

In this new recognition, his senses stoked his lack of faith in material things and asserted a new conclusion: existence was a hierarchy, a continuum, a muddy slope. The One who made it all was real; Baer, the mind that somehow dwelt within the created space was mostly real — or was convinced he was real even if he erred. And last, the things he perceived as "out there" were a collaboration between he and the One who made him; a puff of smoke or a dream; an anvil or a mirage, depending on how he chose to see them.

Both were culpable.

The One with the power to create endowed Baer with a lesser version of the same gift.

The entire tapestry around him was no longer a cold reality. He was no longer a wolf hunting in a freezing, unobligated forest.

The universe seemed better explained as an immersive presentation, as if he lived inside a movie and was chummy with the director. He could see within it what he wanted; ignore what he didn't, and create what he desired.

Seeing the bluish white glow between Tat's heart and her womb impressed upon Baer that the colors were always capable of being there, but he had never intended them into his awareness.

He'd always seen the evil. He'd always looked for the lies.

He'd spent his entire life cursing and killing and creating an ugly world, while blaming someone else that it existed.

Intent made things and moved things.

That was what his friend from Chicago had wanted him to see when she said matter doesn't exist without a mind observing it, what Einstein called *spooky science*. Everything is a possibility until a mind selects the truth of the moment and believes it into being.

After a lifetime of pain and bloodshed in pursuit of the good, Baer Creighton grasped his role. The Mind that was greater than his ripped away the veil, revealing the eternal Baer himself wrote the script, directed the movie, tended the projector, and sat in the chair, entranced.

At last, he was free of the liars and their evil, by choosing what was better.

THIRTY THREE
"You saw his teeth."

Linc stood on the first stone step kicking his boots against the second. Baer dragged the toboggan beside the porch and facing high beam headlights coming from far away on the driveway said, "You expecting company tonight?"

"No." Linc turned. "No idea who they are."

"Let's get inside."

The air carried the scent of roasted game. Frank sat on the couch beside a folded blanket. The rifles, pistols and shotguns were gone. Down the hallway, light came from the open door to Frank's bedroom.

Inside, Baer stood behind Linc.

"Pop the center strap and I'll get the pack."

"I can get it off no problem."

Linc swung Tat's backpack from his shoulder, slid his feet to keep his balance and wobbled the pack to the floor. The cast iron cookware inside rattled.

Frank looked.

Baer rotated his shoulders, bounced his pack and slid it down his arms. He returned to the toboggan twice for the boxes and stacked them in the kitchen next to the wall beside the hutch. He shed his coat and left it on his backpack. From the entryway he caught Frank's look then gazed beyond him through the living room window at headlights coming up the driveway. Frank twisted on the sofa and observed.

"Figurin' on company?" Baer said.

"No," Frank said. "What is that? A Blazer?"

"I get a sense sometimes... and this time it's sayin' these people ain't your friends."

Frank turned. "What? You know them? What's going on?"

"I don't know 'em. I just know they ain't right."

"How?"

"Later."

Baer trod to the bedroom carrying Tat's backpack. He spoke to Tat and closed the door. He returned a moment later to the living room. Headlights cut through the kitchen windows over the sink. They remained on and the engine kept running.

Boots sounded on boards, then pounding at the door.

Frank stood from the sofa with his eyes like slits and his head swiveling as if the threat could come from Baer or Linc as easily as the men outside.

Standing at the door, he reached to the small of his back, lifted a 1911 .45 partway from his pants, then tucked it back where it was.

"Yeah, that ain't the right call for the moment," Baer said. "I got your back."

Frank opened the door and Baer stood behind him to the side, unseen by the outsiders but easily within Frank's peripheral vision.

"Help you?"

"Yeah. I want my guns."

His face was long and skinny. His hair oily and long, teeth half rotten. Eyes with too much blood, as if from being strangled or strung out on dope.

Another man stood on the porch behind him, and they shared a familiar look. Their noses, eyes and chins seemed the product of a mold that eroded before the second casting, so the younger had the widest features, the least ruined teeth, the least greasy hair, and the fewest tattoos.

The man at the door was in his forties, maybe. He had glazed eyes and an aggressive stance; he kept shifting side to side like a fighter keeping his opponent wary.

INTEGRITY

"I think you're confused."

"I think you told my father some bullshit and drove off with my inheritance."

"We're not discussing this. Leave my land."

Frank closed the door.

The man pounded on the door and shouted. "That's it? You stole my inheritance and that's it? You think it'll end here?"

"Who are they?" Linc said.

"Run to the potato cellar and bring the shotgun that's leaning on the wall."

"You sure you want that path?" Baer said.

The man outside beat the door and rattled the glass.

"I'm comin' back for you! You won't get away with it!"

Linc stood with his jaw hanging.

"Go now! And yes, I will defend my property. These people aren't even people. They're evil. Linc! Get moving!"

Baer nodded.

Linc strode across the kitchen and descended the steps.

"Talk to 'em, maybe?"

"Come up on my porch making demands? They can go eat bark. I'll send 'em to hell if they come back. Nobody has any respect for anything or anybody. It's always take take take. I want it, I'll take it. They can go die somewhere. Eat mud. These people can go to hell."

"I understand that kinda thinkin', Frank. I get it. But you didn't give 'em nothing. Not even a hello, friend."

"Give them what? Like I owe him something?"

"The man didn't attack. He knocked on the door and said you have his guns."

"I don't."

"He got no claim? And no way to think he got a claim? No way to be confused?"

"He — that's his problem."

"This ain't the moment for easy virtue, Frank. It's the difficult virtue, what sets a man apart."

Frank turned his head to Linc arriving from the steps to the kitchen, sawed off semi-auto 12 gauge in hand. Baer said, "Linc, lean it on the wall next the back door, there."

Baer stepped closer to Frank and his words came easy and slow.

"Frank, hear me on this. Hear me. If you knew where I been the last two year, you'd know I know better 'n any man you ever met the torment you're about to unleash on yourself. Use your head on this. If a man got a claim, if he believe deep down he's right, how's he present himself?"

"You stand your ground. No way in hell I'm even discussing —"

Baer shook his head.

"Hold on. We're not there yet. If a man don't have a claim, and he want to scare another into doin' as he says, how's he come on?"

Frank was blank.

"What'd you just see at the door?"

"The same thing. Strong. He wants to intimidate. Push people around."

"So, here's the money question," Baer said. "You just lookin' to open a bottle of whoopass on this feller? Regardless?"

"Well... no."

"Flip it 'round. If you had the claim and said it, and the feller you said it to started actin' the fool... That the right way to deal with a man like you?"

"I'll hold him to account. People have no personal respon—"

"Uh-uh. Hold on while I conclude a simple point. Then you can tell me how bad the world is. That man could be good or evil, but only his Maker knows his heart. He comes on strong thinkin' he got a claim, and you push back knowin' yours is stronger. All you got is two men hell bent on pushin' harder'n the other. But what if he ain't a thief? What if he ain't determined to push you aroun' and steal your property?"

INTEGRITY

"He should've chosen better words. He said I lied to his father and stole his guns."

"Did you?"

"That took gall."

"So, this whole world's evil an' rotten, but he's wrong for thinkin' you might be? Hell, you boys might be blood brothers, all you know."

"What's that supposed to mean?"

"You go about lookin' for the evil and you see it everywhere you look. So's he. It might be that the only two decent men in the state's ready to kill one another on account they ain't willin' to double check what they think they know."

Frank leaned to the door jamb and allowed his gaze to drift out of focus.

"Point bein', 'til you humble yourself enough to share some words, you don't know what you're dealin' with."

"I know what I'm dealing with. You saw his teeth. All of them. Who the hell has tattoos on his neck? They're druggies. I know exactly who they are and they're not worth talking to."

"Well, maybe. They's plenty that ain't. But every man has a piece of good in him, and that piece is capable of runnin' him. You got to call out his good if you want to see it. Call the bad an' it'll come runnin', every time."

THIRTY FOUR
"IN CASE, IS ALL."

Tat remained in the bedroom.

In the kitchen Baer fixed her a small plate of meat, rice, and carrots. She did not like onions.

Frank sat sideways on the sofa with his back against the arm rest. His eyes roamed from window to window, starting in the kitchen and traversing around each until pausing extra long toward the driveway.

"I know they'll come back. They're drug people. That's what they do. Anything for the next fix."

"Mind if the lady eats in the back, there? She ain't feeling too spry yet."

Frank waved Baer to proceed.

"You said call out the good, but these people don't have any."

Baer paused at the hallway entry. After a moment's hesitation he continued.

Frank rose from the sofa and crossed to the kitchen and looked out the back door. Seeing nothing, he opened it and without turning on the light, stepped onto the closed-in porch. Long ago this was where he and Jenny spent many of their evenings looking out across a lawn he bothered to mow. Then, the porch became a storage shed in the years since Linc's birth. Frank filled it in from the sides with junk he found one place or another, flea markets, yard sales, private dumps, until only a narrow channel remained down the center of the porch. Then he filled the center in as well. So many items he didn't remember them. The only remaining path led to the door.

Items were piled high and low but standing two feet from the kitchen he could see lengthwise to the yard beyond. When the trees had their leaves in the summer he would see only forest.

In the winter Frank saw where he beat Linc into the ground.

No one was coming.

He returned to the kitchen and sat at the end of the table.

• • • • ● • ● • • •

Baer rested the plate on top of the dresser and leaned over Tat. She was reclining in the bed with the pillow rolled at her lower back and Moxie cradled in her arm.

Baer lifted his son.

Tat's nose wrinkled.

"What is for dinner? The smell is awful."

"Whistlepig, my bet."

Tat looked blank.

"Woodchuck. Groundhog."

"I was hungry."

With Moxie nestled close in the crook of his arm Baer delivered the plate. Tat forked a carrot.

"Who came to the door?"

"I ain't sure but I'm keepin' an eye on the situation."

Baer turned partly away from Tat and with his free hand brought his thumb to his son's cheek.

He wished he could see his own light. It had to be burning the hottest, brightest blue-white. He felt it. He'd never burned that color.

Tat mashed the carrots into the rice and cleaned her plate except for the groundhog.

"I haven't slept in a bed for so long... I don't want to throw up in it."

She rested the plate on the bedspread taking care to keep it flat.

Baer smiled at her; smiled at his son. He kissed Moxie's forehead and returned him to his mother.

Then he knelt at Tat's backpack and opened the bottom compartment where she crammed her sleeping bag. He removed a holster and Tat's first baby: a Sig Sauer 9mm pistol. He zipped the compartment, then placed the Sig on the bed beside her.

"In case, is all."

THIRTY FIVE
"NEXT TIME YOU WON'T SEE ME."

Linc sat where he usually did opposite Frank with his back to the front kitchen window. Frank sat with his back to the porch he'd just checked. Baer returned from the bedroom, boots clonking, and said, "I'll appreciate you lettin' me grab a mop."

"This floor needs sanded down and redone anyway. Mopping just makes mud."

"Fair 'nough. That groundhog?"

"Phil himself."

"Every groundhog is Phil," Linc said.

"I was a boy sometimes me an' my brother'd ride in the wagon with the neighbor — farmer name of Brown. He'd pull us along the fields, and we'd take turns missin' 'em."

"All species of rats are wily," Frank said. "Rabbit, squirrel, bear."

Baer pointed his fork but vetoed the words that came to him.

"Mice are pretty stupid," Linc said.

"Help yourself. There's white bread in the refrigerator. Linc —"

Linc slid his chair and got the bread. He brought a butter tray from the counter.

Baer tore a leg from the carcass and scooped rice and the rest to his plate. Buttered two slices and bowed his head.

Frank kept chewing. When Baer lifted his head Frank said, "We used to do that."

"We never prayed," said Linc.

"Before you were born. Until you were born."

"I never did," said Baer. "'Til now this moment."

Frank lowered his fork to the plate. Stared off. "Son of a bitch. They're back." He turned to Baer. "You saw the headlights when you sat down. You have the perfect vantage."

"I did."

Frank squawked his chair and stood. Baer split the groundhog leg at the joint and tore a mouthful from the top.

"Thicker parts is rare."

"Want to put it back in the oven?" Linc said. "I have it at four fifty. Only take a few minutes."

Frank swiped the sawed-off shotgun from the wall where Baer told Linc to rest it. Baer scooped a mouthful of rice and carrots, stood while he chewed and grabbed his coat from where he'd placed it on top of his backpack. He swallowed half of his mouthful of food and spoke through the rest.

"You gonna meet him with that? Or keep it handy?"

"He's gonna know who he's messing with. I'm in no frame of mind — "

Baer shook his head. "Try callin' his good this time. I'll go out the back and watch from the side. Don't shoot me."

"I'm coming with you," Linc said.

"No," Baer said. "Do me a favor and stand at the lady's door. Tell her it's you, and you're there on guard. Do that for me?"

"You just want me to stay inside."

"I want the quickest eye and the coolest head next to what matters most — my girl and my son. Now go."

Baer crossed the kitchen in three steps, let himself to the porch and out the back door. He turned right and stepped through unbroken snow alongside the house, passing the first, then the second kitchen window as headlights illuminated the barn then swerved across the trees and sky beyond, resting again on the front kitchen windows.

The high beams blinded Baer to everything beyond the SUV, but the snow gently falling through the light was pretty.

Two doors slammed and two men — bathed in red, eyes glowing — stepped in front of the headlights.

Baer eased back from the corner and watched Frank through the window as he opened the door. The men arrived at the porch steps and Frank swung the shotgun into the crook of his right arm.

Frank glowed red too.

He stepped onto the porch and closed the door behind. The glass door sprang shut with a screech and rattle.

Baer returned to the corner and stepped into view. He shielded his eyes from the blinding headlamps — there were four — and saw his breath freeze in the air. What kinda vehicle was that? It looked like an old Blazer, but from the smell, a diesel. Did Blazers come in a diesel? All four headlamps were on at the same time, high and low beams both. They must have wired it to do that.

What kind of idiot?

They thought they were being clever, but the bright light would only antagonize Frank Buzzard further. That's what aggressing an aggressive man did.

The first looked at Baer and upon again looking at Frank said, "Called for backup, you thief."

"Who are you? One of Jake's boys?"

One spoke to the other. "See?"

"I knew who you were last time. Your father gave me those guns because he knew what you'd do with them."

"And how's that any of your concern?"

"You ought to be back there with him on his deathbed; instead, you're out here starting trouble. So high you don't even know what you're saying. It concerns me because your father made it concern me and because you're on my land looking for trouble."

'Uh huh. Yeah," the first said. He swayed sideways, back and forth. Hands free, fingers wide.

His coat on but open in the front, Baer stopped his right hand from lifting to the butt of his Smith & Wesson Model 29.

Both strangers glowed, but their hues leaned more toward the rosy red of deception than the burgundy red of violence.

"Your father's an honorable man," Frank said. "What happened to you?"

"You hear this?"

The one elbowed the other and they widened the space between them. They looked at each other without words. Frank advanced a step.

Baer took a deep breath.

"I told you to get off my property. Now go!"

Frank lifted the shotgun into his right shoulder without grabbing the guard with his left hand.

"That how you learn to shoot?"

"Come back and you'll see how I shoot. Now git!"

Frank tightened his right hand on the grip and swung his left to the shotgun's forearm. Forgetting earlier when he'd cycled the weapon a few times, empty, he pointed high and squeezed the trigger.

Click!

"Pfft! Lookit this jackass. You got no claim to those guns. I grew up with them."

Frank yanked the charging handle and released. He jerked the shotgun into a quick aim at the speaking man's head and said to the other, "How hard'll you laugh with your brother's face on yours? Get the hell off my land!"

"Frank! Stop. Put the shotgun down. And you two — this ain't the way to make your grievance! You damn-well know better."

The man in front of the shotgun raised his empty hands.

"This man stole my birthright and I'm supposed to just kiss his ass?"

Baer spoke easy, but through his teeth. "I'm talking to you as a friend. Don't make your last mistake here."

The man turned toward Baer and the porch light showed off his rotten teeth. "Guess I have to kiss the cowboy's ass too."

"Nobody's kissin' nobody's ass. And nobody's usin' his head, neither. If you had a fair claim, you shoulda acted like a fair man and come in the daylight. Respect a man's home. Show some deference. As it is, you made a mess of it. Now it's best you go to the law."

"These people," Frank said.

The man pointed at Frank. "You people."

"Your father's the only decent man I know. In the war he saved my life. What the hell happened to you?"

"I want what's mine."

"This ain't the way to go about it," Baer said. "Now git outta here."

"Next time I see you, I'm shooting," Frank said.

The man cocked his head. He lowered his hands and while he back stepped, said, "Next time you won't see me."

THIRTY SIX
THE HARDEST LESSONS...

Frank leaned the shotgun in the corner by the door.

"Safe on?" Baer said.

Frank lifted the shotgun and flicked the safe. "I get so I can't even think."

"I know."

Linc stepped from the hallway and stood at the far end of the living room watching the taillights get smaller and closer together on the driveway.

Tat stood in the doorway behind him, Moxie in her arms.

Linc said, "They coming back again? Why not call the police?"

"Skip Myers? You kidding me?" Frank said. "I saw him cheat in math class."

Baer stepped past Linc and got close to Tat. He leaned to her and whispered.

Linc said, "At least he has the right to kill people."

"I need to get you out of public schools."

"Better a guy with a badge explaining it than you."

Baer stepped away with his hand still on Tat's shoulder, arm trailing. She closed the door and Baer paused at the noise.

Frank said, "No way. I don't trust Myers as far as I can throw him. Besides, these clowns won't be back. I saw the older one's eyes. He had to put on a show for his brother, but I guarantee once they get to the end of the driveway they'll stop and clean their shorts."

Baer removed his coat and resumed his seat. "I shoulda put that whistlepig back in the oven."

"Let me get it," Linc said. He grabbed the tray they used for baking bread from a lower cupboard and forked Baer's groundhog leg into it. He placed the tray in the oven and turned the dial back to 450.

Frank sat and scooped rice into his mouth. He chewed like it was cud. "I don't understand people like that."

Frank swallowed.

"Anything special, cookin' groundhog?" Baer said.

"Same as any game."

"I knew people'd boil 'em in sugar water, is all."

"Each his own."

Baer spooned some broth onto his rice and scooped. He said, "Bein' a reasonable man..."

Frank placed both of his hands on the table. Nodded while he exhaled.

"How'd it go down? You gettin' all them guns?" Baer ate rice and onion. "Shit. I know what this needs."

He moved to the boxes he'd brought inside. He set the top one aside and opened the next. Closed, restacked, and returned to the table with a block of sharp cheddar in a zipped baggie.

"They ain't nothin' in the world can't be improved by cheddar cheese." Baer removed the block from the baggie and sliced a couple pieces with his deer knife.

Linc dry swallowed. "I'll have some."

"Sure. Eat up. They already made more, I bet."

Baer raised his brows at Frank.

"No thanks."

"You was sayin'."

"You had my back. You have the right to ask."

"I ain't your judge but my son's in your house. If they's more trouble comin', he won't be. Is all."

"The two guys who just came here — their father's the only man I ever knew that saw things the way I do. I always thought it was funny that he had some black in him, or something, you know? With the darker skin."

"How's that funny?" Linc said.

"Because I was brought up to think it was supposed to matter, and it didn't. Hell, I didn't know that — learning otherwise was my first exercise in free thinking. We were kids in a war. Fighting to keep communism from taking over the world. More like fighting to keep the money flowing to the people making the bombs. But here's this guy who didn't look like me at all, and he's the one who took me under wing."

Linc handed the cheese to Baer and Frank waved off Baer's final offer. Baer cut more for himself.

"We were in the same gun section, Jake was gunner. That's the guy who looks in the sights and sets the elevation and deflection."

"What's that?" Linc said.

Frank indicated with his arm.

"Up and down, left and right. I was the new guy, so I had to run out the aiming poles. When a gun takes a position, you have to orient it. There's a process with the sights to make sure each gun in the battery is pointing the same way to start — the azimuth — so when you make a change — the deflection — it's always against the same starting point. Anyhow, the new guy gets the lowest job and works his way up. Time he's the guy on top with the hardest job, he's mastered every task his men have to do."

"Sure."

"Jake was the gunner and I did the poles. Other jobs too, but being the pole man, I had to work with Jake."

Frank looked at Baer and then Linc.

"I'm rambling. I haven't thought about it for so long." He sipped water. "Well, you shoot the bull with people. Make jokes. Laugh at jokes. It doesn't take long to figure a man's character, you know. Where he stands with the world. Gunners were sergeants and the first thing a new sergeant learns is to be a prick to all his friends with less rank — so they respect him. They teach that. Jake was a sergeant, but he wasn't about all that. See, gunners had cake jobs, second in charge, next to the section chief. That meant they didn't dig, didn't put up camo, didn't do anything but lay the gun and aim it, each fire mission. Jake Walsh could've had a power trip, but he was a team guy. He saw I wanted to learn, so he taught me things."

Frank looked off. Shook his head. "You remember things that don't make sense, why they come to mind. One time I was sitting there with rain running down my back thinking how lucky I was to be eating soggy french toast, and out of the blue, Jake said China had more men than the United States had bullets."

"I didn't go," Baer said. "Wrong age. Or right age."

"Service is a thing," Frank said. "On the one hand, the patriot loves his country and wants to serve it. Then he finds out sometime after the fact he didn't serve his neighbors or the other citizens so much as..." Frank looked out the side window. "I don't know who. It wasn't like 1776, you know?"

"I ken ye."

"What about World War Two," Linc said. "What about Pearl Harbor? They weren't real wars?"

Baer sliced more cheddar. Cut a piece for Linc and offered it on the tip of his knife.

"In the field artillery, soon as the projectile hits the other side, if they have the people with the knowhow, they want to figure the angle it came so they can send some back. Or mortar — whatever they have. I was there a month the first time we received return fire, and the first round took out my section. I was lumping powder to the pit — you have to cut the charge. Powder comes in increments, and you only use so many, depending on how far the round has to go. You don't keep the extra powder near the gun — make sense? You don't want to die."

Linc leaned back in his seat and crossed his arms.

Baer nodded. Ate.

"I was running powder and that put me on the other side of the five ton. Jake was the gunner, so he was sitting on the left trail, right up by the breech. Everyone else — we had five men doing the work of seven. Everyone else was either in the bed of the truck or between the trails, and the mortar round fell inside the right trail. Someone yelled Get Down! and I dove. I shoulda jumped instead. The shrapnel that took part of my leg came under the truck. The metal in Jake's chest — there wasn't much of it, but it doesn't take much. It passed the breech and caught his arm and then his lung."

Baer's eyes were soft.

Linc's jaw was hard.

"What about Pearl Harbor? What about the Gulf of Tonkin? What about 911?"

Frank flicked his eyes toward his son.

"I'm speaking real history. What it's like. Not the official line from a high school textbook."

Frank stirred the rice on his plate.

"Jake and me spent a lot of time in the hospital and we talked about the war. About what the hell we were doing there anyway. Where we came from and what we believed, trying to justify why our bodies would be ruined the rest of our lives. Any man'll give up his body for something if it matters enough. But when you give it up and you don't know why... We just did a lot of talking."

"That when he told you about the guns?" Baer said.

"Some. And we talked about the difference between fighting a war your politicians choose verse a war your enemy brought to your door."

"Yeah. Like Pearl Harbor. Like 911," Linc said.

"Not especially. Not at all."

"I don't ken your meanin'," Baer said.

"If I had to do it over the only fight I'd take is the Revolutionary War. That's the only one this country's ever fought that was about freedom. The rest's been by choice, and it hasn't been the little guy making the decision. It's always been the Man. Take kids when they're young and don't know any better. Pump them full of patriotics and fireworks, then turn us into compost so the rich people can grow more money. That's all it is and all it's ever been."

"Whoa! What?"

Baer glanced at Linc.

"Fuck this."

Linc threw his butter knife at the table top. He ground his chair back six inches and stood. His arm flashed; he pointed.

"That hole in your leg's the only thing you ever gave anybody. You gave it to your country and you haven't given anything since."

Linc grabbed his coat, exited out the back and slammed the door behind him.

Frank sat with his eyes wet.

"The hardest lessons don't teach easy," Baer said.

"Anyhow."

"Anyhow," Baer said.

"We were both discharged, and you know how it is. You plan on keeping in touch and you don't. Then a few years back I got a Christmas card, and I don't get Christmas cards. Not after Jenny passed. The address was in a woman's handwriting. Jake's wife. Him and me traded a few letters after that, each time saying how we'd have to find a time to meet up, shoot the bull. Once things settled down. Always once things settled down. They never did 'til I got his letter yesterday, saying if I didn't come right out, it wouldn't ever happen. Plus, he needed a favor. I drove to Pittsburgh this morning. He said to take all his guns and whatever happened, never let his sons get them. One's been in jail for selling drugs. One's served time for beating a guy half to death with a pool stick. The youngest is retarded. In the medical sense, not just stupid. The other, I guess he just fell in line. Jake said all they'd do is sell those guns for drug money." Frank closed his mouth. Resumed. "I use to think the good side always won."

Frank looked out the window.

"You carry a lotta hurt," Baer said.

"Those guns are precious. They're why some people are free and others, not. I'll never give them up."

THIRTY SEVEN
A FLASH OF ORANGE...

Linc crossed the kitchen and closed-in porch, then exited at the back of the house.

There was that diesel smell again...

For all he knew, Frank stole the guns and the two wild men on the porch were justified in looking for them.

Linc headed straight toward the woods. The yellow posted signs looked gray in the moonlight. The Buzzard farm was so far from the road that Kelley James would have to be looking through a half mile of forest with a telescope to see him. These days all the codger did was mow his lawn and scowl at passers by, or stay inside, probably scowling at the television.

How come the world was full of old people who were so pissed off at everything? Wasn't it their world they were pissed about? Would they ever turn around and say, *hey, we're all pissed off. Maybe it's us...*

Where was all that personal responsibility Frank was always talking about?

The stream channel passed between the house and woods. Drifts had accumulated on the near side. Linc jumped into them, crossed the snow-covered ice and scrambled up the other side.

He passed through a short area that long ago held a lot of huge hardwoods that Kelley James sold to a small logging outfit. Their stumps were like rotting headstones. The loggers had left the land a mess and Kelley had refused Frank a decade before when he asked about cutting firewood out of the branches that lay decaying. Now most of the brush had rotted and smaller pines and briars fought for the sunshine. Linc snuck through often enough in the summers that his path was easy to discern through the snow, though the briars snagged his sleeves and pulled nylon threads until the white strands pulled too. In no time he was in thicker woods comprised of the hemlock and white pine the loggers hadn't touched. Much of the season's snowfall remained in the evergreen branches above. The going was easy beneath. With so much snow and so many open places in the woods, the moonlight let Linc see almost as far as he would have in daylight.

Before long Linc was a quarter mile from the Buzzard house, staring into a cave that wasn't really a cave, just a place where two giant rocks were close together, such that their tops pressed each other and a hollow below permitted a boy to creep thirty feet into the darkness.

There were no tracks outside but that didn't mean there were no animals inside.

Linc removed his glove and pulled his .38. Wondered what one of the slugs would do to a sleepy bear.

Wake him up.

Linc stepped backward, looked about fifteen feet to the top of the boulder. That would be a nice place to sit for a while. The other side of the boulder wasn't a rock wall so much as a rock slope that was crawlable in the summer. But sitting in snow wasn't what he had in mind.

The barn would be better.

Linc turned and between the drooping limbs and tree trunks, he saw a flash of orange. He stepped a foot to the side and now the flames were steady. He ran a hundred yards flat out and saw the Buzzard house in flames.

THIRTY EIGHT
"Run!"

"People these days don't have any morals. They think they do. They think they're the most virtuous people — "

"You smell that?" Baer said.

Frank's nose widened. His head rotated left and right.

Baer slid his chair and went to the oven. He grabbed a potholder and withdrew the tray with his groundhog leg. It didn't smell any better.

Tat's feet thudded in the bedroom.

Frank rose from his seat.

Still beside the wood burner, Joe raised his ears, then his head.

Tat opened the bedroom door and stood in the hallway. "Fire!" Tat said. "There is smoke coming from the closet!"

"Downstairs —"

Frank twisted toward the basement door. A tendril of smoke came from around the bottom. "Where's Linc?"

"Tat! Get Moxie outside!" Baer said.

Tat was already in the bedroom. She shoved her Sig into her cargo pocket and swiped Moxie from the bed.

Frank rushed to the basement door and put his hand on it. Not hot. He touched the handle. Not hot. He opened the door, and a wall of smoke was climbing the steps. The lights were off but the fire was bright.

"There's no putting it out!" Frank said. "I smell gasoline."

Baer grabbed his backpack and rushed it out of the house, thirty feet into the drive. He hurried back, stood askance and held the door as Tat rushed out with Moxie in her arms and Joe following.

"Joe, kill anyone threatens her."

Wer wooooop!

Inside, Baer rushed to the bedroom and hooked Tat's backpack on his arm. At the kitchen he knelt at both boxes, lifted with his legs and carried the rest of their belongings outside.

The house was filling with smoke and was getting warm but so far there were no flames upstairs.

Frank joined Baer in the drive circle with an armload of photographs from the wall. Each of Jenny. He looked back and forth wondering where his F-150 was, then remembered Linc had buried it in a drift.

Had Linc disabled the family's transportation deliberately? As part of a bigger plan?

Frank knelt with his armload of photographs. They'd be ruined if he left them in the snow. Standing again, half facing the house, Frank observed Linc scrambling down the bank to the stream. Where had he been? Had he run off after setting the fire?

And now... what? Would he use the .38 to finish his destruction?

Linc raced up the back steps and into the house.

"What did you do?" Frank said.

He hurried to the lower barn entrance and placed his armload of photos inside the cornery on top of the corn in the iron bathtub.

Rushing back Frank saw the kitchen window was orange with flames. Baer had left Tat farther out on the driveway. He stood close to the porch. Frank joined him.

"They's time for maybe another trip inside. Not two. Where we goin'?"

Linc burst out the front door. His face was red. Smoke chased him. He stopped before Baer and Frank. Gagging and coughing, Linc placed his hands on his knees. His nose ran.

Linc wiped his face with his left arm and slapped his right hand into Frank's.

"The money jar," he said.

"What the hell have you done?" Frank said. He looked at his hand and saw the red-rubberbanded wad of bills from the clay jar.

Link stood. "I have to get my stuff!" He ran back into the house.

"Tell me what to get," Baer said. He looked over his shoulder and Tat stood by their packs and boxes. She had Moxie in her left arm and her Sig Sauer 9mm in her right hand.

Joe looked out into the field.

"Stay, Joe! Stay with Tat!"

Frank looked at the front door where his son had vanished. The flames were only on the kitchen side of the house but would engulf the other side any second.

"See if you can get the root cellar open." Frank pointed to the left side of the house. "The guns are stacked on the hinge side. There's a lock but you might be able to stomp through the boards. They're old."

"I could shoot it open."

"Do it."

Baer set off around the side of the house to the root cellar.

Frank rushed into the house after Linc.

The cabinet where he'd kept the money jar was under flames. Frank felt the wad of cash in his pocket. Nothing Linc did made sense. He couldn't have known Jake Walsh's sons were coming — all of this had to be quick thinking on his part. Set a fire and the blame would naturally fall on the Walsh brothers. But they wouldn't have returned to set the house on fire.

They didn't hate Frank the way Linc hated him.

Frank had seen it every day in Linc's eyes, that special mixture of anger and contempt. It was a totally different look than what Frank had seen in the Walsh brothers' eyes, after Frank charged the shotgun and had the barrel dead on the older man's face, a twitch away from a messy porch.

Did Linc really hate Frank that much?

"Linc!"

"Back here!"

Frank stood at Linc's room. Linc was darting here and there, each time returning to his bookbag and shoving small items. A pocketknife, a book, underwear, socks...

"We have to get out now!"

Frank realized he was yelling over the fire's roar. He stepped into the bedroom and the floor gave too much —

"C'mon! Before we fall through!"

Frank bounded to Linc, grabbed the bag from the bed and his son at the neck and dragged him to the hallway.

"Run!"

THIRTY NINE
Sewers...

Baer Creighton shoved the toboggan away from the porch and toward Tat.

He located the root cellar on the left side of the house but the flames shooting out of the nearby basement window were impossible to ignore. The slot had no glass. An orange sheet of flame curled out and climbed the siding to the roof. The snow beside the window was melting but beyond that, a single pair of boot prints circled around behind the house.

Baer dropped on his knees at the sloped root cellar door and swiped with his arms until most of the snow was gone. Again standing, he located the lock on the right side and drove his boot to the board. It was in better shape than Frank mentioned.

Baer pulled his Smith & Wesson and aimed to miss the lock but destroy the end of the board, with his bullets lodging in the dirt.

He fired four times and while he raised his boot, smoke tendrils slithered through the new bullet holes. Baer stomped through the board and threw open the root cellar's outside door, dumping fresh oxygen into the inferno below.

Red embers glowed at the edges of each board comprising the inner door that separated the root cellar from the basement. An intense red glow jittered as cold, outside air sucked through. There were no potatoes or onions inside the root cellar, instead the blued metal of Frank's firearms gleamed in the firelight. Several of the rifles' packing blankets smoked at the bottoms, which folded and ruffled across the floor.

Baer lowered himself into the cellar and gasped. Cool air rushed past him and fed the frenzy of flames in the basement, but the heat cooked through. He wouldn't last a minute and if the draft reversed, he'd be set instantly aflame. He chucked pistols by their barrels to the snow. Frank arrived as Baer switched to the rifles. Frank caught one and placed it in the snow. Linc grabbed the next. Frank. Linc. Frank. Linc. On and on. Now the rifles were wrapped in blankets.

Baer noticed a blanket was on fire and the bottom of his pant leg as well. He jumped for the corner of the root cellar, got his hips over the edge, and wriggled forward. Frank grabbed both his hands and dragged him out, then rushed to Baer's feet and buried them in handfuls of snow.

Sitting up, Baer saw Linc prone with his face and shoulders over the edge of the root cellar, lifting a rifle barrel with each hand. Frank hurried there and took them from Linc and placed them side by side in the snow as Linc shoved two more into the air.

The flames rushing up from the basement window now consumed the entire wall. The house had no two by fours, no insulation between them. It was constructed of three layers of one-inch boards.

It would burn hot and long.

With the root cellar empty of firearms, Linc rolled away and kept his face in the snow a long moment.

Frank dropped to Linc and rolled him. Linc sucked a deep gasping breath and Frank dragged him away from the house toward Baer, presently on his knees before the majesty of destruction that was present in the abandonment of form and purpose of the house where generations of Buzzards struggled through each and every day they sheltered there.

Linc popped to all fours. His face was red like sun burn. The place where he stood a moment before now boiled with orange flames.

Baer shielded his face with his hands and strode several more feet away.

Frank knelt and leaned the rifles nearest the fire against his outstretched arm. He turned to Linc.

"Finish loading me up."

Linc stacked more rifles into his arms.

"To the barn!" Frank said.

"Ain't time! Just get 'em out the driveway with the other stuff," Baer said.

Frank rushed away.

Linc knelt for an armload of rifles.

Baer took his turn and in a rotation of effort the men saved all of Frank Buzzard's firearms: the four rifles, two shotguns and three pistols he'd started with, which he'd combined with the twenty-one rifles, five shotguns and eight pistols Jake Walsh bequeathed to him with the eternal charge of preserving them, so that one day men and women of courage might defend the rights of humankind against the tyrants who never failed to arise, and who fought with the depravity of sewer rats, even after generations of wealth lifted them from their sewers.

FORTY
"Linc did it."

They stood in the turning circle watching the house burn.

"Hog's done," Linc said.

Frank stared.

Baer stood with his side to the burning house, his gaze off toward the driveway. He rotated and allowed himself to take in the full scene, the driveway to the horizon, a gentle knoll a few hundred yards away, bending to the right, following a posted tree line.

Turning to his left he took in wave after wave of the silver-gray field that crested at the top of Kroh Hill. He looked the length of the ridge, down the wooded slope on the far-left side, guessing the whole thing was at least a hundred acres. Sizes were harder to figure back east; now that he'd been west. Continuing to his left he took in the roll of field that hid the slope and the tractor road to the Eldorado.

Baer studied the barn and discovered Frank watching him.

"See anything?"

Baer shook his head. "My bet, they's long gone."

"Yeah," Frank said.

Baer studied the thin, tan-flecked-with-magenta glow about Frank's face, heavier on the side next to Linc. He observed the yellow emanating from Linc, and Tat's white-blue love peppered with tiny purple star bursts of frustration. He was still learning the colors and half of his cues came from facial expressions.

Joe alone was unfazed.

I know people. Nothing surprises me.

"We better get you folks situated in the barn," Frank said. "We'll take a couple dozen bales from the loft to the bottom level. We've only got ten cows down there, so we'll build a wall with the bales — it's cleaner on the milking side. We can make a bed of them. It'll stay above freezing and your camping gear can do the rest."

Baer looked away as he noodled the situation. "You milk twice a day?"

"Uh-huh," Frank said.

"Them cows'll only be in the stalls twice a day. Heat'll go as fast as they do. An' how'll they get through the wall, back an' forth? How 'bout we build Tat a little cubby, instead?"

"Sure. Roof it in with a couple old horse blankets. Linc'll show you where. Keep more heat in."

"I like it," Baer said. "An' what if the tattoo people come back? Defense-wise?"

"They won't. No way. I saw straight through that man. I scared him." Frank met Tat's look. "Anyway, if they do come back, that's what these are for." Frank waved his foot toward the pile of guns on the packed snow and ice. "Linc and I'll take positions in the loft. Spell each other. Baer, you do as you see fit. Roam around. Tat and Moxie'll be in the lowest level — the walls are eighteen-inch rock and cement."

"Tat?" Baer said.

"Okay," she said.

"You need anything right off? We don't have much to work with but keeping you and the little one in good shape comes first."

"I want to get off my feet."

"Linc," Frank said. "First job: take Tat and Baer with you to the lower deck. Tat can sit there while you and Baer go get the bales. Baer can do the arranging how he likes. If he needs more, get them. Then grab the shovel and chains and get after that truck. I want it up here tonight."

"I'll give you a hand after Tat's situated," Baer said. "Joe'll keep an eye on her."

Frank said, "The truck needs to be up here tonight. Just so everyone knows, all the ammo Jake gave me is behind the seats. The shotgun I used before is the only gun loaded. I'll get them inside the barn and then put the distributor on the tractor. Linc, if you don't have the truck out when I'm done, I'll bring it down. Tomorrow morning we'll have all our resources, and we'll figure out what to do." Frank faced Baer. "Can you see to getting your lady situated? Whatever you need to do."

Baer nodded. "Will do."

"What if they come back?" Linc said. "They just burned the house. They're not going to stop after something like that. Shouldn't one of us be on lookout or something?"

Frank bit his lower lip. He opened his mouth and snapped it shut. Opened it again. "Take Tat to the lower deck and get the bales. Tat, Baer, you'll find the entry to the lower deck on the right of the slope there. See the door?"

"I see it."

"C'mon. I'll show you inside," Linc said.

Frank shivered. He zipped his coat tighter to his neck. "I don't know if it's getting colder or if the whole thing's just settling in."

"Colder," Baer said. "Every which way."

Linc said, "Since we're all headed for the barn, maybe we can each take a load of rifles."

"Good thinkin'," said Baer.

Frank stood shaking his head.

Linc and Baer loaded up and walked together. Frank loaded up too. The bay door remained open from earlier and inside, Linc turned to Frank. "Want them at the ladder?"

"Yeah."

They filed that direction while Tat and Joe stayed just inside the barn. His arms still loaded with rifles, Frank ensured Tat had a place to sit by kicking a tarp off a rocking chair he'd made out of a reclining driver's seat from a Lincoln Contintental. Tat switched Moxie to her other arm and drew his blanket closer around his face while backing uncertainly into the seat. Situated, she raised her brows in delight.

"I will sleep here," she said, but Frank had joined the others on the far side of the bay.

Upstairs on the main deck, Linc climbed to the loft and unwound a rope from a flagpole cleat mounted on a sloped roof timber. The line fed a pulley suspended above the edge of the loft, where hinges attached a sliding board the elementary school had disposed of several years before, when they built the new playground and left the old at the dump.

Linc shot bales down the sliding board to the second level.

Frank passed Baer on his way to the boxes and backpacks.

"I'm sorry for all the trouble while you're my guest," Frank said.

A burning rafter settled and the crunch caused Frank to turn. Baer looked at the swarm of sparks floating into the sky.

"Earlier back there," Baer said. "The window to the basement. Wasn't any glass there."

Frank shook his head. "No, it was plywood. Few years ago, Linc broke the glass with a baseball and I used plywood to fill it. Had some laying around."

"What was under the window, in the basement?"

"Work bench. A few hand tools. Screwdrivers. What are you thinking?"

"Dunno."

"You sure? Maybe you don't want to say it."

"I tend to speak my mind," Baer said.

"Linc did it."

"Nah."

"Like the Walsh brothers knew where to kick in a window without the sound of breaking glass."

"Luck."

"Well, like I said. I'm sorry for your trouble, while you're staying with us."

Frank continued to the barn and Baer drug the toboggan to his boxes in the snow. He placed Tat's backpack partly under the round nose and used the boxes behind it to jam it tight.

Strange, that a man would apologize for his lack of hospitality after losing his house to a fire he believed his son responsible for.

Dragging the sled to the barn, Baer wondered what he didn't know.

FORTY ONE
GRACE...

Baer dragged the toboggan to the lower barn entry and unloaded boxes and backpacks right inside the door. He went back up for bales and brought them from the pile Linc had tossed down a silver playground slide. On his return he brought the toboggan. Leaving it at the door, he looked deeper inside the barn and discovered Tat on the Lincoln chair, smiling.

Since he'd reached his lowest low, the single turn he'd spent most of his life descending toward, he'd found Tat had supported his goodness when it mattered and stood beside him as he rebuilt his outlook based on the peace he felt when he connected his mind to the eternal, instead of the fury he felt seeing all of human crookedness.

Tathiana was so good to him, so common and natural with him that he didn't often think of her origins. Her life hadn't been easy. When she was barely a teen her parents were murdered. She set off with her younger sister knowing almost nothing about the world except it contained men so wicked their existence insulted the security of the species such that they ought to be put down whenever encountered. She'd outrun them for a while, but she and her sister were eventually kidnapped and trafficked.

Baer rescued Tat and she rescued her sister. After that, Tat became a stone-cold killer. Baer didn't know how many pedophiles she'd sent forward.

Looking back at him Tat said, "Moxie is warmer now, out of the wind."

Baer crossed the floor and stooping, dropped the bales and put his arms around Tat and Moxie.

"I'll have you situated with your feet out in no time. Maybe give 'em a rub."

She smiled, mostly.

"What you thinkin'?"

Her eyes flicked to the loft. "Was it the boy?"

"His father seem to think so. You?"

She lifted her shoulders.

Baer said, "He's a good kid. Just ain't enlightened to it."

Baer lifted his bales and said, "I'll be back for more, an' we'll get you set up."

Turned back toward the loft, Baer spotted Linc standing at the edge, a bale ready to pitch to the sliding board.

"We usually drop 'em through the chute for feeding but I don't want to bust the bales. We'll have to carry them down." Linc motioned toward the pile. "That look like enough?"

"I'll let you know."

Baer carried two bales to the toboggan, then two more. He slid them around to the lower deck and brought them in one by one.

Each milking stall was partitioned by head-high, round metal bars that protruded from the wall to the cow's shoulder area and then bent back to meet the wall at knee height. Baer chose a stall two slots beyond the damp circle that represented the most recent cow mud cleaned earlier that evening, after the day's last milking.

He placed the first bale longways against the stone wall. Looking at it a moment, it seemed very large, filling the width of the stall, but also tall, so two bales made a headboard. He used the next two for a bed.

Baer brought his backpack to the adjacent stall and removed his sleeping bag. He whipped it over the bales and unzipped it all the way. He placed Tat's sleeping bag inside his, with her camp pillow at the top.

He returned above and escorted her down the snowy slope to the lower deck's door. Inside, Baer held out his arm and Tat gave him his son.

She crawled onto her sleeping bag and sat with her boots over the side. She looked at Baer.

"Can I take them off?"

"Any trouble comes, we'll see it. Frank's a decent man. His boy's a decent man."

"They fight."

"They don't know how good they are."

"But if the boy burned the house... How long would it take to light all this straw? These boards are dry."

"The boy didn't burn the house."

Tat pried the heel of her left boot with the toe of the right. Baer knelt. With Moxie in his left arm, he untied Tat's boots and pulled the laces sloppy with his right.

"I learned these last months that the bigger man ain't the judge of another. The bigger is what he is, knows what he knows, owns whatever ground he stands on just 'cause he's standin' there. He credits the lesser man's character as if he achieved his best, instead of calling him to account for whatever measure he fell short. And because the bigger man is also a fair man, he credits himself the same way. It ain't justice, I know. But it's the mercy we seek. An honest man appreciates the mercy more'n the justice."

"What does that mean? Gibberish."

"It means it don't matter, even if he did burn the house. He's a boy that can use some grace."

Tat removed her Sig 9mm and placed it beside her. She folded her legs and slid them inside her sleeping bag.

"Want to lean? Or lay flat?"

"Lean, while you are away."

Still one-handed, Baer placed her backpack against the headboard bale at an angle. Tat skooched back to it. He placed Moxie in her arms and shifted her Sig closer to her hips.

"I'll be back."

Baer ferried bale after bale until the cubby walls were built, then lay several long-handled tools across the top with old horse blankets for a roof. He closed the end with a foot-wide gap and placed two bales there for him to stretch on; if the hour came when he could sleep.

FORTY TWO
WHISPERS...

Linc imagined the build of the bed and walls Baer had described and dropped twenty-four bales down the playground slide. Baer moved four of them on the toboggan but after his first trip to the lower deck, he hadn't yet returned.

Linc waited.

Sue Cooper!

What would her face look like when she learned about the Buzzard house fire?

Would her eyes go wide with terror at the thought of how close her secret love came to perishing in the flames? Would she kiss his singed eyebrows? Would she imagine him as wonderful as he really was? Would she imagine him with his aura, the way Baer might have? Then, seeing him rescuing the rifles with flames about his head and arms, would she shriek? Clutch her breast, both of them? Would she squeeze them hard? Would she sigh?

What would her sigh sound like, right next to his ear?

What if she moaned before putting her tongue in his ear? Just a flicker — before she stabbed it all in?

What if... what if she just grabbed him? Reached out with her hand opened wide, took his whole throbbing blood engorged purple helmeted warrior —

But Sue Cooper would really say, "Who? Linc the turkey Buzzard or whatever? He lived in a house?"

Sue Cooper.

The way Frank had glared, he thought Linc set the fire.

Someday Linc would be gone. Someday he'd gather what little he had and leave. All he needed was bus fare to someplace warm. He'd survive with his wits, same as now. Take a deer rifle, a pistol, an axe and a knife, and set off into the woods. Early timers could do it. Why not him?

Linc looked over to Frank on the other side of the loft. He'd spread the rifles and pistols across the hay bales and leaned several against the barn wall, as if he was in a western movie prepping for a siege. He stacked bales in front of the window, blocking most of it, and created a platform to sit on like he did on the other side of the barn when he was hunting deer that would come out from the woods onto the side of Kroh Hill. This time, he built his blind on the house side of the barn.

The burned house side of the barn.

Baer still hadn't returned for more bales. He must have decided to do something else.

Linc slid down the slide and upon landing, caught his boot heel on an awkwardly positioned bale and twisted his ankle.

He growled, then stifled his noise. Frank could go to hell, probably crept close enough to the loft edge so he could watch Linc suffer. Linc hopped on his right leg until he found his balance, then eased his weight on his sprained left. Pain rushed through him, other-worldly and sharp. He kept most of his weight on his right foot and bent at the waist until his hands arrived at the last bale, then shifted his weight to his left sprained ankle.

As a boy running through fields or woods for one stupid reason or another, he'd twisted one stupid ankle or another many times. This one wasn't the worst, but it was bad. But even the worst he'd had was bearable. He'd been playing tackle football in a friend's back yard and didn't' even hit a groundhog hole or uneven patch. He'd been carrying the football and running like mad when he'd made a cut, landed bad on his right foot, sitting inside a sloppy fitted, high-top sneaker, and almost broke it off. He was ahead of his pursuers and the touchdown was his — until his ankle snapped so loud, he could hear it. He rolled and drew up his knee. The others stopped and gathered in a momentary truce, jaws fallen and looking at each other.

"I heard it," one said. "That has to be broken."

Linc scrambled across the goal line untouched. Then he removed his shoe — which he'd taken to wearing loose, like Frank — and saw his ankle was already the size of a small melon.

He'd worked it back and forth and didn't feel any bones gritting against each other. The pain was from the side, below the anklebone. Figuring it was a pulled muscle or tendon accompanied by popping joints, he'd laced his high-top sneakers tight and continued the game, but now as a partly mobile, nearly useless lineman.

Seated on a bale Linc removed his work boot. Even with a badly messed up ankle, he could get around. This one wasn't that bad.

A full-sized boot laced snug would have likely prevented the injury but having only one pair of shoes (aside from the sneakers he needed for gym) and needing to wear them to school and for farm work, and for hunting, Linc preferred the ones that didn't go so high on his leg they cut off circulation and were too hot in the summer.

Linc worked his foot back and forth, testing to see what gave him pain and what didn't.

Digging out the truck would suck, bigtime. But the sprain wouldn't prevent him from carrying on. If it was just him and Frank, he might push to wait a minute and see how bad the injury was. But with Baer and Tat and the baby, it seemed like a bigger family was depending on him and stepping up with a little bit of self sacrifice was the right thing to do.

Linc stopped rubbing his ankle.

Stopped breathing.

Cocked his ear and heard words so faint, he wasn't sure if he imagined them:

What you thinkin'?

Was it the boy?

His father seem to think so.

It was Baer and Tat, talking about him in the milking area, below.

Linc remembered a lesson he'd learned two years prior when he sat terrified in his room on his bed with his back oozing blood and lymph. He'd been getting up, readying himself for a painful trip to the toilet when Frank's boots thudded down the hallway and then glass shattered in the bathroom.

The lesson he'd learned: *most pain didn't matter.*

Linc shoved his foot back into his boot, laced it tight, and gathered the tire chains and shovel.

FORTY THREE
THE RUBBER...

Linc limped out of the barn and Frank watched from the loft. He'd heard Linc land hard from the bale slide, then groan while rubbing his ankle.

Frank had said he wouldn't say anything more about Linc stealing and lying to him, but that didn't mean he had to blind himself to what his son was. The barn and cattle, machinery and land was all Frank had left.

Should he allow guilt over something that happened — admittedly, he beat his son. It happened. He could never escape! It happened! — Should he allow his guilt to harry him into trusting a person he didn't trust? Risking what he couldn't afford to risk?

Linc limped to the far wall and removed the tire chains, placing them over his shoulders, and pulled the flat shovel from its nail. At the bay door he looked up at Frank.

Frank said, "I'll be down with the tractor when it's running."

"I don't need the tractor. You said that."

Linc left.

Of course, the 8N would help. Most of the reason for having Linc dig out the truck was to teach him to think before he acted.

Frank shook his head. Maybe Linc did think. Maybe he thought if he got stuck while trying to save the young mother and her baby, it wouldn't be a big deal because the tractor would be fixed the next day...

Frank strode across the planks to his gun nest, unlatched and pushed open the door. He limited his gaze to the driveway, the field, the stretch of woods.

At last, he was out of options and looked at what remained of his home.

From the distance, if he let his eyes go out of focus, assisted by their watery film, his house resembled a campfire. Some logs jutting this way, some that. Flames having a royal time, dancing about. Coals glowing. Smoke lifting. Embers floating like evil snow.

Almost everything that made his house his home was gone. All he'd taken was his photos of Jenny and his guns. The clothes on his back. His wallet. The money roll Linc had saved from the fire.

The breeze shifted as he stood and after a moment of feeling the new cold against his face, the smoke arrived.

The wind shifted again, and it was gone.

Frank was thirteen and his father drove a Chevy truck. That's why Frank drove a Ford. One day they were in the turning circle. His father never washed the truck — why bother when it rained every few weeks? He never cleaned it inside, either. Work trucks required jumper cables in the footwell and fast-food wrappers behind the seat. His father changed the oil by unscrewing the plug and letting fluid drain from the oil pan into the dirt. By age thirteen Frank had seen his father change the oil enough to know the procedure. This time his father assigned him the task to perform alone. He told Frank to move the truck to the side, over close to the fuel tank, so they wouldn't be tracking a mess into the house. Then he left Frank to do the job. Frank waited for the oil to settle back to the pan after running the engine. He'd seen the pile of cheeseburger wrappers, along with paper fountain soda cups, Dr. Pepper bottles, leaves, cakes of mud, a couple empty caulk tubes, shotgun casings, a map of New York — the truck had never been to New York — and a box containing a portable citizen's band radio, for emergencies. While the oil drained, Frank went inside the house and took a trash bag from the box under the sink. His mother opened the oven and set out bread to cool. Frank stood with his nose over the warm loaf, inhaling the magical scent. "Not yet Frankie. Let it cool." Frank took the trash bag to the truck. He knelt and looked under the frame. Oil still dripped. Frank started on the driver side and when the trash was removed from under the seat as far as his skinny arm could reach, he tilted the seat forward and cleaned the area behind. He toted the bag to the other side and when he stooped over, the first thing he saw down by the seat bolts was a shiny piece of transparent plastic or latex or something with a ring around one end. He lifted the ring end between his thumb and index finger. The mysterious object stuck to the carpet, and stretched, until Frank knew what he held. There was still fluid inside. The bottom released from the carpet and snapped into Frank's hand. The condom dangled. Frank's face flushed. He'd heard about rubbers but had never seen one. He couldn't fathom being lucky enough to ever need one — but there were these two Cooper sisters from school, golden haired twins, each as pretty as an angel from heaven — and he was holding someone else's used rubber between his fingers — which was exactly as gross as holding someone else's dick.

"What you got there?" said his mother.

His back toward her, Frank dropped the condom. He turned and while the plate with two slices of buttered bread caught his eye, he couldn't erase the confusion from his face. Why was a used rubber on the passenger side of the truck?

What was the slime on his hand?

"What?" his mother said.

"Uh, bread. That smells good. Is that for me?"

"What's wrong, Frankie?"

His mother wasn't the sort to wait for someone else's conclusion when the evidence was there to appraise for herself.

She shifted Frank out of the way while placing the plate in his hand.

That evening after a wordless supper, he opened the door a crack while he was supposed to be doing his homework. He sat on the floor with his ear to the gap.

It turned out his father screwed a McDonald's manager he met because he cussed the girl at the register for giving him a five and a one back, instead of two ones. He demanded to see her manager and ended up going for a country drive with her.

"I was tryin' to do the right thing... the mind is willin' and the flesh weak."

But before his father confessed to his mother, he said three times the rubber was Frank's.

FORTY FOUR
Spare Her a Terrible Decision.

Linc lowered the tailgate and stood leaning backward; he dropped the tire chains from each shoulder. The truck had planed the snow flat between the wheel tracks with a depression in the middle where the differential was lower. Linc closed the tailgate and scooped a shovelful of snow from behind the left rear tire.

He stopped.

The truck was saddled. Removing snow from the tracks meant the truck would want to sit lower, and more weight would rest on the snow underneath the body. He was working against himself because he didn't have a plan.

Linc stepped back from the truck and thought.

Shovel in hand, he started beside the bed on the passenger side.

He found his rhythm quickly; Linc shoveled in steps, lower and lower, chucking heavy loads just far enough to leave the snow near him unmolested. The pack was heavy, but the weight afforded an advantage: the walls of his path stayed true, and didn't crumble the way dryer, more-powdery snow would have. He heaved, advanced.

Almost every time he changed position, his twisted ankle slipped, jolting him. The pain served as punctuation, each stab marking his advance forward, the job one increment closer to being completed.

With the path to the front tire finished, he switched to the other side of the truck and worked the opposite muscles.

He cut a little wider at the driver side door so it could open most of the way, then climbed inside and started the engine. In a few minutes the heat blasted. Linc removed his gloves and hat. He switched the air flow toward the snow clumping his socks above his boots, unzipped his coat and leaned back his head.

Eyes closed, he recalled the snarling face of the wild men, the drug addicts on the porch.

Next time you won't see me, the one had said.

And Frank thought Linc set the house on fire.

After the beating, Linc's wounds took months to heal. The lashes kept getting infected. Linc hid the fact from Frank in case the news prompted another round of violence. Frank was like an animal in a cage, the world around him poking sharp sticks through the wire, and Linc was hidden within, frozen in the back corner hoping to remain unremembered. The next year in school he had to be careful when changing clothes after gym and showering, as some of the wounds remained red long after healing. Mostly his back was scarred and bruised. Kids saw him anyway and said nothing because part of being a kid was hiding. It was the smart thing to do.

But part of being a man was not hiding. It was the opposite. Learning to stand up was what becoming a man was all about. A boy could reach eighty years of age and never stand up.

Linc would, he was certain. But Frank would soon accuse him, and at that point Linc would have no choice but defend himself against the lie, and that would mean Frank would go totally apeshit berserk on him —

He wasn't ready to stand up. He would, because he had to, but he wasn't ready.

The best thing Linc could do would be to get the truck unstuck and then drive until it had no gas — which wouldn't be very far. The needle showed close to empty.

So what?

INTEGRITY

Linc knew how to siphon gas; he'd just toss a piece of hose behind the seat before he left. And he could grab the red gas cans Frank had left at the pump.

Every winter the helpful weather people on the nightly news said a candle could keep a vehicle warm inside — or at least keep it above freezing. No, screw that wimp shit. He'd drive the F-150 to Sue Cooper's place, stand by the truck door with his chest wide and his shoulders broad, and spare her a terrible decision. He was leaving without her. He loved her with all his soul, but he had to chart his own course....

Oh! She'd weep and cling to him in her pointed nightgown as snow fell through the yellow porch light and caught in her hair. Her back quivering under his hands, Sue clamped her fingers to the base of his skull and pulled until their lips —

Rapping on the tailgate.

Linc jumped and searched the mirror. It was Baer.

Linc opened the door.

"I was getting warm."

"Back to help in a couple minute," Baer said. "Need to see 'bout the Eldorado."

Baer angled into the field and joined the established tracks.

Linc turned off the engine. He grabbed his shovel.

Fifteen feet away, Baer turned. "Keep your eyes open. Them boys is still out there, I bet."

"Yeah," Linc said. "I will."

He dug around the front driver side wheel, back far enough to get a jack under the frame.

Baer watched him a moment and left.

FORTY FIVE
SPITBALLS...

Minutes before seeing Linc at the truck, Baer stood at the lower barn door looking at the sky. To his right the house smoldered, though it no longer held the form of a house. While he'd spent most of his life living in a cave or under a tarp stretched tree to ground, he'd owned the house he grew up in. He remembered it after it burned, and how it put him in the mind of a shipwreck collapsed into a basement. He remembered wandering about in a daze, punched in the gut, fearful that the flames had consumed his memories and not just the location where they happened.

It hadn't, though.

He could still close his eyes and see Ruth — the woman who held his heart captive for forty years — holding baby Mae, with his brother Larry glowering behind her.

He still saw his mother on her bedroom floor, shotgun in pieces, dead because she'd been unable to defend herself with a weapon Baer had carelessly left unloaded — after she urged him not to.

Living even a few hours amid the Buzzards sufficed to remind Baer that no man was entirely or even mostly virtuous; no man ought call himself good. And knowing that, some men just kept after it because they knew civilization rested on their shoulders, even though nobody talked like that anymore.

Up above in the barn, Frank leaned his prized photos of his dead wife on the bales where she could keep an eye on him.

The fire wouldn't get rid of the memories but telling Frank would be no mercy.

Would the arsonist brothers return?

Baer stepped sideways, back, and forth, not quite possessed of the will to advance from the barn.

On any other day, Tat could take care of herself. She moved like the wind and regardless of the instrument she chose, knife or Sig Sauer, her aim was true.

But with a newborn in her arms?

Likely so. She'd have even less tolerance for stupidity than normal. If the rough-looking brothers showed their faces in the lower deck, they'd lose 'em.

Tat could handle herself, but leaving her for even a moment felt like desertion, now that Baer had a son.

Having the truck nearby with a heater available made sense, and getting the Eldorado unstuck made sense, and that meant fixing the tractor made sense. Leaving Tat vulnerable wasn't prudent but keeping her vulnerable was less so.

The men had work to do, and every bit of it existed so the woman, Tat, could do hers. Hers was more important — one woman with a child commanded the instant defense of three men.

She would be safe.

Baer climbed around and up the dirt ramp to the middle deck and Frank descended the ladder from the loft.

"Gonna check on things. Lend Linc a hand at the truck. You be here?"

"I'll be here."

"Keepin' an eye out?"

"They're not coming back. They didn't set the fire. They're gone."

"Just same I got Tat an' Moxie below."

"I understand," Frank said. "I'll be at the tractor there, the bay door open. Tat's just down those steps, over there. I'll keep watch."

"Appreciate you."

Baer set off toward the Eldorado and soon stood fifteen feet behind the F-150.

The engine ran. Exhaust fumes gathered in a low cloud.

The boy had made good progress — worthy of a word of praise.

The job of digging out the truck was big enough a man would need to steel his patience before beginning. Get himself accustomed to the idea the next hour or two were going to be a mix of labor, discomfort and frustration. For a teenager the task probably looked close to insurmountable, but all Linc had left to accomplish was put the chains on the tires and dig out some of the snow below the body.

Baer stood at the tailgate. Linc sat in the cab with his head against the rest. A tinge of white glowed around him. Best leave him be... Far be it from Baer to interrupt a man dwelling on purity and love.

But it wouldn't do to go waltzing by and have Linc mistake him for one of the Walsh brothers.

Baer rapped on the tailgate.

Linc opened the door.

"I was getting warm."

"I need to see something at the car, and I'll be back to help you finish. You done good work here. Fast."

"I was taking a break. Warming my feet."

"Sure. Accourse."

Baer cut through the drift, reversed after two steps and resumed toward the Eldorado on the established trail. Soon as he rounded the bend and began descending the knoll, he knew what he would find at the car.

His gold Eldorado was a gray shape in the moonlit dark. The hood was wide and long, the roof, low. The back of the car had no fins like the older models, but looking at it now, the car did seem to have fins.

The trunk lid was open.

When Linc left the house before the fire, where did he go?

Keeping the same measured pace Baer arrived at the Eldorado to find the metal below the trunk lock was twisted at the edge and the paint chipped off. The pry bar that performed the feat was lodged in his rear window. The bucket that he'd placed upside down had been hurled thirty feet into the woods.

The gold piece he'd placed on top of the bucket was gone.

His tent remained. The crossbow he used for silently hunting game remained.

Baer observed the latch and guessed he could bend it back to the right shape with his vice grips. Leaving the trunk open he moved to the passenger side. The ambient light was insufficient to see inside, but the handle hadn't been pried open. He pulled and found it locked.

Baer spent a minute bending the latch straight again so the trunk would close, then considered the evidence as he walked up the grade to join Linc.

The pry bar remained in the back window. The person who used it could have broken into the car, but did not — yet had seen the bucket of gold — otherwise why break into the trunk?

Linc had seen the bucket, but the glowing headlights on top of Kroh Hill — whoever was in that vehicle likely saw the bucket of gold too.

Good thing he'd pulled a fast one.

Earlier that night, after Linc brought Frank down to the car, they returned to the farm to get the toboggan and to bring the F-150 as far as the upper bend on the tractor road. While they were gone, Baer packed an iron roaster in the middle of Tat's backpack and with his back to Kroh Hill, filled it with gold specie. From the weight he'd guess Linc had carried about three hundred thousand dollars' worth of Double Eagles, Maple Leafs and Krugerrands back to the house. Baer had put a roughly equal amount in his own pack, leaving twenty-five pieces in the bucket for him to flash about while loading into his gold belt, and one to place on top of the bucket, a friendly spitball to the face.

Someone didn't like spitballs.

FORTY SIX
SIGNIFICANT STORES OF JOCULAR FIBER

Frank sat on the front tire of the Ford 8N tractor. He held the distributor box in his hands.

Linc had said the only thing Frank ever gave anybody was his hollowed-out leg. Sometimes words hurt because they were intended to hurt, not because they packed a cruel insight.

Sometimes it was both.

Sitting on the tire, shocked into a higher awareness by the realization his home had burned, and his family disintegrated, Frank entered a moment of rare lucidity. He saw himself from a distance sufficient to reveal a pattern.

He was angry *all the time*, but not because he preferred being provoked and mean. No; the world around him was unrelenting with its pointed stick.

Jesus flipped the money changers' tables. Should Frank just sit there?

Evil was on the march and doing nothing was tantamount to joining the other side, becoming one of the tricksters who would say or do anything to get ahead. Raging against the world's wickedness, even accomplishing nothing, was better than being crushed under its relentless advance.

Except, the old adage was true: fighting fire with fire made more fire.

Sitting on the tractor tire with the grand view, Frank mused about himself as if from a distance, as if seeing himself from the perspective of an older and wiser version of himself — by happenstance, one possessing significant stores of jocular fiber.

His anger and violence surprised him.

If Frank didn't already know his motivations were pure, judging his highlights from a distance, he might believe himself one of the bad guys.

He blinked as if bringing his eyes out of a dream but found himself in the same barn.

Frank pulled the new distributor from its box and flipped the cardboard aside.

He could get lost sometimes, immersing himself in the problem-solving tasks involved in mechanical work. It used to be a haven, but when the tractor quit running, whatever future Frank had ahead of him was already spoiled. Whatever days he had ahead were empty of promise and felt more like a sentence to surrender to and someday emerge from, than a regular life with regular goals and dreams.

Except, emerge from what... to what?

Every place Frank had found meaning in life he had also found himself unworthy. His son had been stealing from him. His wife was still dead. The farm was dying — or was now dead, since the house burned — and the work ahead was enough he could labor around the clock and not complete half of the tasks required to maintain a modest farm. His finances were depleting so rapidly, his only move was to sell it.

Emerge from what... to what?

Emerge from a period of suffering... but it didn't matter where he emerged. Anyplace he went he brought the same poison because he was the problem. Frank was the poison.

He knew it.

When the tractor quit running this last go-round, Frank had studied his check book register. He'd earlier set aside the dollars needed to pay the big annual insurance bill, but a new distributor would put him under, and then he'd be short on whatever expense came next. Cow feed, fertilizer, electricity, fuel... he'd miss the dollars one place or another.

When the tractor quit running and Frank was sure of his diagnosis, he took the only item of value in the house, a brooch that remained in Jenny's jewelry box, and polished the gold until it shone like the day he and Jenny married. Something old, the saying goes. The brooch, made of gold with pearls and tiny pieces of emerald, had one hundred and eighty years behind it.

When the tractor quit running Frank knew what would be required to fix it. He'd been working around Ford 8Ns and 9Ns all his life. They had short distributor shafts; he'd always speculated they wobbled, and that contributed to how they wore out their bushings so quickly, in tractor years. Bad bushings led to the point gap being too wide at operational speed.

The first time it happened, shortly after Frank and Jenny bought the farm, the tractor ran like normal in the morning but was nearly dead by afternoon. Frank suspected the loss of power had to do with a lack of fuel. The tractor idled fine but coughed and sputtered attempting higher engine speeds. He cleaned the carburetor in the field — all it took was a 9/16" wrench and his pocketknife — but that didn't solve the problem. Next, he thought it might be a clogged strainer in the fuel shut off that screwed into the bottom of the gas tank, or a leaky fuel pump not putting out enough pressure.

Nothing restored the tractor. Eventually Frank realized it wasn't the fuel system, and without any reason but his curiosity, he removed the distributor. He discovered the worn shaft bushing and created a makeshift repair by splitting a piece of copper pipe, which worked until it spun in the body, causing him to have to order a new one. That was years and years ago, but Frank liked mechanical work and remembered details easily.

This last go around when the same lack-of-power symptoms presented, Frank guessed it was the distributor and quickly confirmed his diagnosis. He took Jenny's gold, pearl, and emerald brooch to the pawn shop, ordered the distributor, and put the money in the clay jar.

The pawn shop in town gave him thirty days to return with a hundred dollars for the brooch, but Frank knew when he left, he wouldn't be back for it.

FORTY SEVEN
"Pretty sure two could."

Linc paused to catch his breath. He'd jacked up each front wheel, put the chains on both front tires, and dug most of the snow from beneath the frame. With the engine weight on the front of the vehicle, that might suffice to get the truck backed out.

But any time Linc had ever heard Frank say *put the chains on*, he'd never meant *put the chains on the front wheels, and not the back, because that might suffice*.

If Linc successfully backed the truck out and Frank saw the rear wheels were chainless, he wouldn't take it as a triumph of his son's intelligence or pragmatism.

Linc stepped to the truck bed and saw Baer. Linc said, "Gold still there?"

"All I left was stole."

Stunned, Linc drifted backward into the snowbank. "All of it? How?"

"Pry bar. Trunk was open."

"No way. There was so much. No one could carry that much."

"Pretty sure two could."

"People are rotten. Frank's right about that."

"Some."

"Seems like almost everybody to me."

Baer shifted back and forth, appraising Linc's progress. "You done fast work. I'da figured you'd be here a good couple hour, an' lookit this. Fucky fucky. How much diggin's left?"

"Just the back wheels, and under."

"Need a hand?"

"I'll finish. 'Sides, with all that's happened you haven't had much time to look after Tat and the baby. And it's getting colder."

Baer drifted a few steps. He stopped.

"Your father's tryin' to figure who burn the house."

"Yeah."

"Shame, you left when you did. Didn't help his thinkin'."

"I'm sick of him. I don't care what he thinks."

"Make you so mad you can't get your head right sometimes… somethin' like that?"

"Something."

"You stuck him pretty hard there at the end. What you said 'bout his leg."

"It's true. You don't know him."

"Yeeaah — I know a little. I know he bleeds. Man give up a lot for his country. For his ideals and for you."

"You're taking his side."

"No side. Two men live under the same roof and don't know one another. He don't have a clear view of you, neither — what you give up on account of him. But if you hadn't left, you mighta understood him better. And if you was in the house the whole time, well, they'd be no way to suspect you did what you an' I know you didn't."

"I didn't burn the house."

"I know. You didn't steal my gold neither."

"Well great. That's settled. Tell my wonderful father."

Linc returned to the front wheel and grabbed the jack and handle. He placed it on the tailgate while he shoveled snow from the area in front of the passenger rear wheel.

"Can't be good, two men workin' side by side an' neither trustin' the other."

"It is what it is," Linc said.

Baer smiled, big. "Things is rarely what they ain't."

"Yeah. Rarely."

"Not often."

INTEGRITY

"It's unusual."

"Singular."

"You win. Frank's a hypocrite. Always talking about his morals and trying to show off. I got frostbite on my ankles."

Linc stabbed snow under the side of the F-150 with his shovel.

"I confess I don't see all you do," Baer said. "I been elsewhere and don't know the history. But if you keep one thing in mind, it'll help you navigate the world and maybe save you from some regrets later on."

Linc returned to the end of the truck for the jack and handle. Then, kneeling on the ground ready to place the jack under the frame, he looked at Baer.

"What?"

"No one measures up to anybody else's ideals, and no one measures up to his own — and that's discouraging. The bad quit trying, but the good keep on. If you got to judge a feller, long as he ain't give up on himself, you'll do better and have more friends if you judge him by what he wishes he was, instead of what he's proved himself to be."

Linc withdrew his shovel from under the truck and chucked the snow aside.

"Good stuff."

FORTY EIGHT
MERCY, NOT SACRIFICE.

Baer lowered his head, turned, and continued toward the barn.

Sometimes the words did their part, but the listener couldn't add them into a meaning.

That had to be the reason grace existed: each instance provided one more opportunity to grasp what was so obvious, all that was required to see it was to confess one's blindness.

All of humanity could be rescued from evil in an instant if every person looked inward for the darkness that was wrong with the world, instead of outward. A mustard seed versus the mountain kind of feat, for folks convinced the mote they spotted in their neighbor's eye made them unique and gave them worth.

To some folks, those like Linc who, for the moment, unfortunately, didn't *get it*, the whole string of thoughts probably sounded like gibberish.

Before Baer's enlightenment a few months prior, all the time he spent marching toward the lowest low of his life, he believed his ability to see evil in other people, combined with his hatred of it, meant he was good.

And then one day after going toe to toe with satan himself, Baer discovered Evil was real. The way gravity was real, or electricity. It was a force, not a perspective. It didn't have a personality. You couldn't kiss its ass. Evil wreaked havoc. It wasn't a side of a spectrum, the less-desirable outcome between two survivable possibilities, the other being Good. As in, good, evil, whatever. It's all relative. Relax. (As Baer overheard at a gas station, one lad to another: *Take a chill pill, bruh —*)

Hell no.

Evil was a force recognizable by its fruit: destruction. That meant whatever brought about destruction was its vessel. The greed that animated some, the power lust that animated others, the inferiority that animated most...

But a vessel filled with evil wasn't evil. The man is separate from the force he serves; he gets to choose, and he always chooses what he believes is best. His only confusion is in believing he gets a pass because his evil is the special kind, that is secretly good, because the shit that happened to him that made him who he is wasn't his fault.

I'm only an asshole because —

He demands grace because he knows he didn't deform himself. He arrived broken, and if God is going to call himself fair, then he better recognize the bad people deserving the fire and brimstone are the ones who caused him the hurt, who made him what he is.

That serves justice, to him.

Never-mind that punishing him serves justice to everyone else.

If a man has the conversation with himself, he inevitably reaches the point he no longer accepts his own bullshit. A vessel filled with evil wasn't evil... it remained a vessel — and capable of carrying other contents, as soon as it had the conversation.

Hating a man because he struggled with evil was as misguided as hating another because a tornado threw his house four miles into your lawn. Why punish the first and extend grace to the latter?

Linc couldn't see it yet.

Nor Frank.

Baer didn't neither, most of his life.

Baer entered the barn through the lower entrance and found Tat asleep with Moxie next to her in her sleeping bag. He remained at a distance. Hours had passed since dark. What did that make it? Nine PM? He was glad she slept.

Joe lifted his head and Baer discovered him on the bales with Tat. She'd pulled the bottom of her sleeping bag out of Baer's, and Joe snuggled at her feet in downy warmth. That was fine.

Baer didn't plan to spend the night snoring.

From above grumbled the engine of the Ford 8N tractor Frank had been working on. After a moment the sound smoothed to a steady purr. Frank had to enjoy making something broken whole again. His life didn't seem to have given him many opportunities there, but Baer didn't know. Men were what they believed they were. What they chose in the littlest choices.

Sometimes a man remained susceptible to evil because he believed he was. Sometimes he missed opportunities to build a better life because forgiving felt like giving up anger he believed was righteous, while accepting grace felt like accepting charity, or taking ownership of a treasure he didn't merit.

Yet forgiveness and grace were inextricably bound, differing expressions of the same higher plane.

Seeing the math that solved the problem was the very definition of enlightenment.

Mumbling dreamily, Tat shifted farther onto her side around Moxie and Baer could no longer see her face. Joe rested his head below the roll in the sleeping bag.

Baer stepped back outside and began up around to see Frank. The hour was late, for country-minded folk whose only after-daylight illumination came from a lantern. Baer and Tat tended to bed down shortly after dark. If they couldn't sleep, they could play. Being outside in the cold again, he realized how much warmer he'd been in the barn. That was good.

Baer stood at the bay door and since Frank was occupied with some minor adjustment or another, hovering close to the engine, ear cocked, screwdriver eager for another quarter turn, Baer stepped to the side and arced a mighty braid of wheat-gold whiz over the steep side slope. If the tractor wasn't running, he'd be able to hear his stream cut through the snow.

He stretched his shoulders forward and back, then steepened the arch in his spine until the muscles felt short of cramping, and relaxed. His body felt good.

Meanwhile Frank Buzzard's house was a black rubble sitting atop a wreck of embers. Much of the house had collapsed. Orange flames were still plentiful, but an equal amount of color came from the red glowing coals at the bottom, up the jutting rafters, up the bottom sides of a wall that had been the last to fold inward. Much had collapsed but much still resisted.

Baer stood at the side of the barn bay door and the elevation combined with light from the fire was good enough to illuminate something silver in the snow, on the far side of the house, beyond where Baer and the Buzzards retrieved the weapons from the root cellar.

The tractor engine died.

Baer turned.

Frank sat on the seat with a half grin. The moment wasn't right for a full display of self appreciation, but Frank smiled as if the amount he gave, he needed.

"Sound like new," said Baer.

"Just a little fix. The distributor shaft is short on these things. I think they're prone to wobble — and you don't enjoy mechanic work as much as I do."

"Not quite I bet. But c'mere and look at this."

"What? I thought you were with Linc. Is the truck out already?"

Frank turned to look back the other way.

"He all but got it out. I checked my car and time I come back up the hill he'd dug it out an' had two chains on. Wanted to finish on his own. So c'mere." Baer nodded. "What's that, shiny over there? Twenty paces past the corner of the house in the snow. See that?"

"Round, maybe what, a foot or so in diameter?"

"What you call a deer with no eyes?"

"Hunh?"

"No-eye deer."

Frank huffed. "Good stuff. Let's go see what that is."

"Hold on. See these tracks cut fresh? — the ones I just whizzed on, there — they yours?"

"No. I keep to the slope here. There's loose rocks and other stuff, boards with nails, all kinda junk under the snow on that side. I don't go near it."

"Is Linc aware?"

"Of course he is."

"Uh huh. I wonder why run across those nails, is all."

They tramped down the slope from the barn's mid level and Baer saw the chicken coops off to the side, tucked away almost, by a small depression at the lower corner of the barn. He hadn't even known they were there before. They passed a fuel pump standing tall in the snow, what looked like an eight-inch pipe reduced to a four inch, with a waist-high spigot and a curved hand pump drooping down like a long-dead tree limb. Below the pump in the snow sat two red plastic fuel cans.

"Interesting," Baer said.

"How's that?"

"Don't know yet."

They passed the fuel pump and at the back corner of the house stopped.

"Those prints off the back steps here, headed to the woods. Anything back there?" Baer said.

"Neighbor has the woods posted. I don't go there."

"Any reason Linc would?"

"When I was a kid, I used to mess around on some boulders back there. Big ones. They sit like to make a cave, almost. Good stuff for a kid looking to break bones."

"Place to hide out, maybe. Do some thinkin'."

"Could be. Sure. I did sometimes. But it doesn't take a minute to run out and back, then say I was in the woods the whole time."

"These other tracks I show you, from the top there, they come 'round like the path we took but not so close the fuel pump."

"I don't know what you're meaning."

"I don't either. Just noticin'. But they join us here and circle behind the house, and I bet they stop at the basement window over there, had the flames comin' out."

"Uh-huh. They do."

"I guess he got the truck out," Baer said.

Frank shifted and looked. Linc backed the truck up to the upper bay, with the door still open, and went inside.

"Twisted his ankle. He rode the hay slide."

"Uh-huh." Baer said, "So, when you and Linc join me getting the rifles out, you come from the front."

"Right."

"Okay, we got the lay. So, what's that fuel can doin' over there?"

Frank turned. From the new angle and closer location, the silver orb reflecting firelight resolved into a five-gallon metal gas can laying on its side.

"That's my can."

"Anything special 'bout it? Fuel mix? Something?"

"It's two cycle, we keep it mixed fifty to one for the chainsaw. Last good can I have. Now all they sell is cheap plastic garbage with spouts that won't let any gas out 'til you break them off. Climate nazis."

"But the yellow can out there, the metal one. That got a regular spout?"

"Yeah, you know. The old-fashioned kind. Flexible." Frank booted snow. "I don't know what you're driving at."

"I don't either. Why'd somebody go to the barn for a gas can when they's two bright red ones over by the pump?"

Frank nodded toward the barn as Linc drove down the ramp and across the turning circle. He continued fifty yards down the driveway and stopped. He left the engine running and the driver's door open — the cab light was on — while he stooped in front of the vehicle, out of Frank's line of sight.

"What's he doing now?" Frank said.

"No-eye deer."

"Anyway, I don't think he would have used the red ones. Linc doesn't like them any more than I do. He knew where the other was — we use it getting firewood. He must've wanted the good spout."

"Didn't you say the basement window was plywood?" Baer said.

"Uh huh."

"Then he didn't need a good spout. Kick the plywood in and take the spout off and dump the whole five gallon in one minute."

"That's true for anybody. Not just Linc."

"An' that's my point," said Baer.

"But the rest doesn't look good for him."

Frank removed his knit cap and ran his fingers through his hair. "Another thing that's bothered me. Why would they burn the house if they wanted the guns that were in the house?"

"Intoxication don't produce the best logic, sometimes."

"Were they high? I couldn't tell."

"I wouldn't say they was especially high. But I wouldn't bet they had much in the way of mental perspicuity sober, neither."

"Perspicuity, huh. There's no reason for two brothers who don't know anything about the farm to go poking around looking for a fuel can in the barn when there's two full out in the open."

"It do seem unlikely."

"So, it was Linc. My son set my house on fire."

Baer allowed the words to float away unchallenged.

"I should have known sooner. I did know sooner. He was a firebug. I caught him one time a couple years ago, out there in the woods farther down. Where it's not posted. He had two-foot flames burning pine cones. Lucky I didn't come back to see the whole farm gone."

Baer turned toward the house and held his hands to the warmth.

"I caught him stealing, too. I kept a money jar in the kitchen. We don't have much but I've always been open about that. Not trying to hide it and pretend we have money we don't. He's been swiping singles out of the jar."

"Sounds like you just about got it judged."

"I don't see how the evidence adds up any different."

"Connect three dots an' you paint the Mona Lisa."

"Not the Mona Lisa, but without a good reason for a hoodlum to go poking around a barn — "

"If he didn't see the fuel cans — "

"If. You don't build a case on if."

"Hold on, play fair. The case agin Linc is *if* he wanted a fuel can without a gizmo on top to save the planet, he knew to get one in the barn."

Frank titled his head back and forth as if weighing his ears. "Yeah. That's fair."

"Ain't my business, how you raise your boy."

Frank turned to Baer and held his look.

"But?"

"Sayin' he did it. Sayin' he set the fire... Is he broke beyond repair?"

"I don't..."

"Is he the sinner can't be saved?"

"Well, c'mon. Damn."

"Irredeemable?"

"Lord, I hope not. I hope none of us are."

"Maybe keep that top of mind when you talk to him."

Frank held out his hands to the heat.

"Irredeemable. I didn't take you for the evangelist type," Frank said.

"I ain't. Never was. Man's soul is his own business."

"Glad to hear it."

"But I want to share one thing I learned long ago, and it didn't make sense 'til recent. The words *mercy, not sacrifice*. I went through a hell of a struggle, tell the truth. Lookin' down on myself, can't do nothin' right, felt like my every move shamed humanity and humbled the Almighty, since he made me. You know that feelin'. As a boy I learned Jesus said *I desire mercy not sacrifice,* and it didn't make sense 'til I run out of sacrifice and was just as broke inside as the day I started."

"I know the words."

"And you know what sacrifice is? That I'm talkin' Old Book faith here, the Law of Moses — how they slaughtered animals to make good on sin."

"Okay. Keep going."

"Like I said, none of my business how you raise your boy."

"But?"

"Mercy, not sacrifice. Love him, is all. The rules, all the justice, all the struggle to make the world this way or that... and all the heartache when it don't happen. They's one potion cures it all."

"Mercy," Frank said.

Baer slapped Frank on the shoulder and left him at the giant campfire.

FORTY NINE
YesYesYes!

Linc parked the truck at the fuel pump and limped to the fuel cans sitting below it.

His twisted ankle had swollen so much his foot wouldn't bend, but at least the sharp stabbing pain no longer occurred with every step. In a few days the sprain would likely feel almost normal.

Linc toted both red fuel containers to the F-150's fuel cap and stopped.

He looked in the bed of the truck and verified a block of ice he'd placed there still rested in the contour between the sand bags Frank used for weight.

Frank stood at the far corner of the burned house. Baer had been talking to him when Linc stopped at the barn for a wood saw. He remained while Linc gathered the chunk of ice evidence from the driveway. Now Baer walked toward him.

"Good job," Baer said.

"Just some digging."

"It was a big job. You done good."

"Thanks."

"Outta gas?"

"I shoulda filled it before getting stuck."

"Was it you, pumped the gas in the cans?"

"Frank did after he got home. I saw 'em after milking."

"Ah. Well. I got to see 'bout the lady."

"Sure."

Baer continued toward the barn and Linc removed the truck's fuel cap. He slipped the nozzle inside.

Sue Cooper!

She pressed her breathy mouth to his ear... *Yes Yes Yes! Take me now! We'll run away — Tell me you're mine forever!*

Linc pressed the green button, forced the entire can downward on the nozzle and the internal valve opened. Fuel gushed into the tank.

"Soon," Linc said.

The gas gizmos worked fine. They were just one more thing Frank was always in a storm about.

Speak of the devil.

Frank had approached while Linc meditated about copulation to the sounds of a whooshing, gurgling gas can.

Standing back, Frank looked at the chains on the front and then the rear wheels. Linc placed the empty can on the ground and dropped his hands into his coat pockets, then pressed his right against his hip.

The .38 was still holstered there, beneath.

"Any trouble getting her unstuck?"

Frank's voice was slow, as if his real thoughts were more violent and remained unspoken.

"Just some shovel work. It came right out."

"Good. I'll have a minute with you, when you're done."

"Sure."

Frank returned to the fire and stood facing away while Linc drained the second can.

Afterward, walking awkwardly to reduce the weight on his twisted ankle, Linc joined Frank, and both faced the embers and ashes of their home.

"Seems like more than a house burned down today," Frank said.

"That fire's been burning a long time, right?" Linc said.

"I know it."

Linc stubbed his toe into a nub of grass. The blades had dried and burned off, but the base was still wet from melting snow.

"When I was just a couple years older than you, I used to run with John Senior. John's the fella that owns the Tractor Supply. We were on the varsity football team. I knew I wasn't college material but then everybody had a plan, because of Vietnam. Some joined right up after high school. Some figured to go to college, and maybe the war would be over by the time they got out. I know a couple that went to school thinking they'd become officers. I didn't have a plan. Mostly I just wanted to drive fast and mess around with your mother."

"Why not just go?"

"Anyway, John and me took the test at the same time. The aptitude test."

"The SAT."

"I don't remember what was on the test or whether it was the kind that a calculator'd be useful for. But John slipped one in. They didn't use to be so thin you could put one in your wallet. They were these big, boxy jobs. I saw him get it out while we were in the math section. He's over there trying to jab down between his legs. Think of trying to keep one of those things flat between your thighs on a school seat, and you leanin' forward, so you can see past your junk..."

Frank huffed.

"Well anyhow he dropped the thing. Sounded like a bomb going off, the room was so quiet. And while all these heads are turning, he kicked it all the way under my chair and out the other side. I jumped so it wouldn't hit my feet, and that made the test person — the whachamacallit — "

"Proctor."

"So, he thought it was my calculator."

"But your fingerprints — "

"You think they're going to dust for prints?"

"What happened?"

"Long story short, I got drug out of the SAT. I went to the war and caught some shrapnel. I didn't give my leg to anybody. I didn't fight for freedom. I went because I had to and came home as soon as they figured I was no use to them."

"What about John Senior? He got away with it?"

"No, he didn't."

"Well, how'd it turn out? Don't you know how to tell a story?"

"Coach Peterson got wind of what happened and made a stink. He said he'd been coaching both John and me for three years and knew there was no way in God's creation I'd think to cheat on a test. And if it had to be one of us, it had to be the other, John. He told the principal — with John and me there in the room — that a man's integrity is all he has, and when you see someone hold himself to a high standard, he ain't a liar, ain't a cheat, ain't a bully, and treats the girls with respect — when you see him do that every day of his life, you know he's a class act. You know he did it the same way the day you didn't see him, too. Or something like that. It's been a lot of years."

Frank looked at Linc.

"That make sense? What I'm trying to say is, your integrity is yours. You live a certain way, choose what's right, you get to own that integrity. I didn't like being called a cheat, but if you always do what's right, the truth is your strength. You can stand firm on your reputation and know you never need to back down. If people don't like the truth, they can go to hell."

Linc looked ahead.

"So, about this fire. Anything you want to say to me on that?"

"Yeah," Linc said. "I have something to show you. Let's get Baer."

"If you did it, I forgive you," Frank said. "If you burned the house, I say so what? We'll move forward."

Linc cocked his head. "You know, what sucks balls is that you don't know me at all. But whatever. I want Baer to ride along. I trust him."

Frank dropped his gaze.

"Sure. I do too."

FIFTY
"I CAN BEAT THEM!"

The three assembled at the truck.

"I'll drive," Linc said.

Frank opened the driver side door and skooched to the middle. Baer took the passenger side and sat with his legs angled tight to the door. Frank lifted his left leg but couldn't get it over the shifter.

"Go easy," he said as Linc lurched into the seat to his left, his legs still astraddle the shifter. "Careful my nuts."

"We're only going fifty yards out, at first."

"I would have walked."

"Someone fart already?"

Linc engaged first gear and crept along until he spotted where he'd sawed a twelve-inch square block from the driveway ice. The hole appeared black on the driveway and was easy to locate.

Frank leaned toward the windshield. "What is that?"

"Evidence."

Linc turned the wheel and cut a new path through the snow. He stopped.

"Baer, can you hop out and give me the signal when that black square is right behind the tailgate?"

Baer exited. Frank jostled into the open space. Linc eased the truck forward and watched the side mirror. The moonlight was strong and with the surrounding snow, illuminated Baer like early dusk. He clasped his hands.

Linc stopped, put the truck in neutral and pulled the parking brake.

Baer stood to the side.

Frank glanced at the block of ice in the truck bed and standing at the tailgate, observed the dimensions matched.

"What'd you cut it out with?" Frank said.

"Crosscut saw."

"What are we seeing?"

Linc removed the block of ice from the bed and placed it beside the matching hole in the driveway ice. Frank nodded; Linc moved the block a few feet to the side, on top of the new track he'd just made in the snow.

"That's a different tread pattern," Linc said. "The only other vehicle that's been up the drive since the snow began was the guys in the Blazer. The ice shows their track."

"Okay." Frank got on his knees. "Totally different zig zag going on. Baer — when you drove the car back, was it snowing yet?"

"No."

Frank stood.

Linc placed the ice block back in the truck bed on top of the sandbags.

"Let's load up again."

"Where to?"

"I'll explain in the truck."

Baer shrugged.

"You're not legal on the road."

"I know."

Frank opened the passenger door and slid to the middle, keeping his legs to the right of the shifter. Baer climbed in with a grin and Frank flashed one back.

Linc sat behind the wheel and drove. He said, "Baer, I don't know how much driving around you did before picking your campsite, but there are two ways to the top of Kroh Hill." Linc pointed with his right hand over his left shoulder. "That's Kroh Hill — it was behind me when I came up on your car through the field. You can turn left out the driveway or right, and as long as your next two turns are the same as what you started with you wind up on top of Kroh Hill. Left, left, left, you're there; follow me?"

"Uh-huh."

At the end of the driveway Linc turned right.

"We're taking the longer way — what is it, Frank? Six miles?"

"Five and a half."

"The short way's only four miles, but it's steep in a couple places, with really tight turns."

"Sure," Baer said.

"Why are we going to the top of the hill?" Frank said.

"You know how the wind changes direction in the evening."

"I taught you."

"When I spotted Baer's lantern, I set out through the field so I could approach from the lower ground and not have him spot me, and even though there was only a little breeze, it was still going from the bottom to the hill. I'm just saying it because I was mindful at the time."

"Did it work?"

"No."

"Why?"

Linc slowed and took the first right turn.

"Baer has eyes in the side of his head."

Frank looked at Baer.

"I see people's light," Baer said.

"Oh. Sure," Frank said. "Yeah? I always thought that was, you know. Crap."

Baer nodded. "Lotta folk do."

"What color am I?"

"Blue-white."

"That good?"

"It's where you want to be."

"Anyway," Linc said, "when I was watching Baer, I could smell the car's exhaust. The breeze wasn't much, but what there was of it came from the bottom. After we got Tat and Baer up to the house, Baer and I went back to the car for their backpacks and food, and that's when I smelled diesel."

"The wind changed," Frank said.

"Right. It was cooler on the hill and warmer at the bottom."

Linc slowed, then stopped at the next right turn. Ahead was a steep bank. To his right, a road that gradually ascended three miles and crossed the top of Kroh Hill before zigzagging down the other side.

Most roads, Linc had noticed, tended to go around hills. He never knew why this one went to the top and stayed there. The land on the other side of Kroh Hill had a lot of soggy marsh land, a mile-wide flat with a silty river that seemed to overflow every couple of years. Big trees couldn't grow there because their roots rotted, Frank said. So, it was just scrub.

"What are we looking for?"

Linc pulled right onto the lookout and parked as soon as the F-150 was off the road.

"I haven't been up here, but in science you're supposed to come up with a theory, make predictions, and see if the predictions come true."

"Sounds like I remember."

"What's the theory?" said Baer.

"When I watched you from the field, the wind was coming toward me, and I smelled the Cadillac's exhaust. When we went back for the other stuff, the breeze was coming from up here, blowing down. That's when I smelled diesel. I also smelled it when I left the house, after supper."

"Right before everything burned," Frank said.

"So, my theory is, what happened is... Your friend Jake Walsh: before his sons came to the door at supper time, they watched up here. What time did you get back to the house with the guns, from Jake's place?"

"Shortly before you got home after school."

INTEGRITY

"They probably showed up right after that. There had to be some time between you getting the guns and them finding out. If they came as soon as they figured it out — "

"How'd they know to come here?" Baer said.

"I wondered that too," Frank said. "Jake told them, most likely. He'd just written me a letter, so the address was handy. His sons could have gotten it from him or found it on a letter."

"So, let's say they were up here watching by the time we got back from the tractor supply. Why didn't they go to the house for the guns then? We were both gone."

Frank shook his head sideways.

"No eye deer," Baer said.

"They had a different goal. They knew about the gold."

"The gold, what? Like a ruse, on a western?"

"No, not like that. Listen. Baer, did you have the trunk open anytime in the hour before I was there?"

"Several time."

Linc looked at Frank. "Then they saw me go across the field and watch Baer, and they saw him fill up his gold belt and leave the rest in the trunk."

"What gold belt?"

"He wears twenty some pieces of gold around his waist, all the time."

"Are you serious? Baer?"

"I do."

"Oh."

"He also left a bucket full of it in the trunk — and they saw that too. Baer — grab the binoculars out of the glove box, would you?"

"A *bucket*?" Frank said.

Baer withdrew the binoculars and adjusted them to his eyes. "Be better if I wasn't lookin' through trees, but the field glasses bring the car in close."

He handed the binoculars to Frank.

"Eldorado. You could land a Huey on that hood."

253

"Could you see a bucket of gold in the trunk, if it was open, and daylight?"

"I can make out some of the detail on his wheel rims, so I'd say yes." Frank said.

"My theory is that they weren't after the guns, unless you gave them up easy, when they asked. They were after the gold in Baer's car. It was worth like a zillion times more than the guns, and for all they knew, it was in the car, unprotected. That would be way easier than stealing from a house with a bunch of people with guns in it. They switched plans."

"A bucket of gold," Frank said.

"Next point: these are city folk. They don't know how the wind'll make each roll in the field bald on top, and how the folds are where it gets thick. I walked in low where it drifted, and they saw how hard I was working through the snow. When they made their plan, they thought the whole field was covered deep. Instead of walking across all that way, they parked with their headlights at the house. You said there were four brothers, but only two came to the house. The other two went down to the Eldorado for the gold while all four headlights were in your eyes."

"Any sign of robbery when you went down to the Eldorado, after the fire?"

"Trunk pried open, and the bar lodged in the rear window."

"The gold?"

"What I left of it was gone."

"How much you lose?" Frank twisted in the seat and studied Baer. "I know who they are. You can press charges."

"Not necessary. I only left one piece in the car, on top of the bucket so they'd know I punked 'em."

Linc leaned close to the steering wheel and swung his backside around to square him with Baer. "What? You had a whole bucket."

"Remember how heavy Tat's backpack was? You carried half the gold to the house. I carried the other. They didn't know that."

"But you did," Linc said. "You tricked me."

"I let you shine. They was no way to give you the answers and have you pass the test on your own."

Still watching Baer, Linc noticed a far-off vehicle at the bottom of the hill, miles away.

"Who are you to test me?"

"All life's a test, every minute, every day. Has to be. Who was you to watch me deliver a baby? *Who you had to be.* They's no shame in bein' cautious, 'til you get a sense of people. No shame in doin' your own thinkin'. It's your right, and how you keep from being stampeded with the herd."

Linc was quiet.

Frank said, "So Linc, if your theory's right, we ought to find matching tire prints up here. And we might find some footprints on the driveway."

"Probably not on the driveway. I think they set the house on fire as a second diversion. They were supposed to come back to the Blazer the second time they had the lights in your eyes, but you drove them off really fast. What if the others didn't find the gold and spent more time looking? By the time they came back, Tat would have been in the driveway, and we would have been hauling the guns and everything else there. If they set the fire for a diversion, the others would have had to walk through the field to get around us, as a last resort."

"If we find their prints, that's a good indication," Baer said.

"Looks like you've thought this through," Frank said. "Let's get out and see if we can find a matching print."

Baer unlatched the door and eased out. Frank followed.

"Oh! Look!" Linc pointed. He slipped getting out of the truck and caught himself on the door. "That's them!"

Frank spun.

Baer turned.

The vehicle Linc had spotted earlier had turned on the road that led past the Buzzard driveway and was less than a mile away.

"Look at the headlights! Remember how they had all four lit at the same time?"

"All it takes is to ground the yellow wire coming out the low beams," Frank said. "We did it all the time. Low beams are low, high beams show both."

"Don't see it much anymore," Baer said.

"It's them!" Linc said, bouncing on his feet. "I can beat them!"

Linc raced across the frozen lookout and crashed into the narrow stretch of woods.

Frank turned to Baer.

"Tat's down there," Frank said.

"If the bad guys surprise her, they'll rue it."

"Let's go," Frank said.

FIFTY ONE
WHAT REMAINED WAS SPIDER WEBBED.

When Frank beat Linc two years before, Linc hurt for months. In the beginning the pain was sharp and forced Linc to spend most of his time trying to be still enough to sleep because the aspirin didn't help. Frank prepared food in the morning and evening and spent the full day outside the house working on one task or another. That lasted two days and a breakfast.

The first day, sleep came easy. The second, not so much. He was sick of laying on his stomach or side around the clock. The third day as he lay awake on his stomach, facing the wall, he heard boot steps in the middle of the day.

Why was Frank coming inside the house?

Boots clodded on the porch. The screen door screeched open and thwapped closed. The front door slammed...

Frank was coming back to finish the job.

Frank was coming to kill him.

Without thought, Linc's volition moved him.

He locked his stomach, kept one leg straight and rigid while folding the other at the knee. He shifted to his side then he squirmed to the edge of the bed. Clonk, clonk, across the living room.

The bandages Frank had applied with tape rolled beneath Linc and tore against his wounds. Linc closed his eyes and tears pressed from beneath. His throat was silent but his mind shrieked. Sitting on the edge of the bed, his loose bandages touched his skin. They were cool and wet.

Clonk, clonk... past Linc's door, to the bathroom. Frank slammed that door too.

In two and a half days on the bed, Linc hadn't used the bathroom one time. He'd eaten little and drank little, but the shock to his body stilled his normal evacuation processes. But as soon as he sat up on the side of his bed his bowels rumbled and pressed. Erecting his spine pulled more bandages and triggered more pain, but Linc blinked away the water.

He sniffled. He was sitting despite the pain. He'd moved, despite the pain. He would do what he had to do to live.

Most pain didn't matter.

Glass shattered.

Linc imagined Frank hurling a coffee mug against the stone fireplace or throwing the bathroom sink through the window.

Linc braced himself. His pocketknife was in his pants pocket and his pants were on the floor. He shifted forward and lowered himself to his knees. He grasped his pantleg and pulled until he sank a hand in his pocket and discovered the knife wasn't there.

The other pocket was also empty.

Linc's bedroom door opened, and Frank stood there. His face had the look of pure hatred. His eyes were red and watery. His skin was flushed beneath his sun burn, and blood trickled from his forehead to the bridge of his nose and along his left nostril.

Frank's mouth twitched — he was ready to speak but didn't.

After a moment that felt like ten, Frank closed his eyes, backed a step from the door, and left the house.

Assisted by adrenaline, Linc went to all fours and then — maintaining the same curve of his back so not to aggravate his wounds by changing posture — Linc stood. His bowels cramping, he quick-stepped to the bathroom and after sitting on the toilet lifted his head and looked to the sink, and above.

The mirror was shattered. Glass from the center had fallen to the sink, and what remained was spider webbed.

FIFTY TWO
Don't quit lookin'...

Linc pushed off on his good right ankle and adrenaline shot through him, a bolt of can-do alertness born of both courage and fear. He landed on his bad ankle in a small depression cut by a tire and frozen hard. A healthy ankle would have absorbed the minor twist and driven his stride forward. His injured ankle flashed pain and if he hadn't simultaneously remembered most pain didn't matter, he would have quit.

The snowplow had cleared the lookout but snow drifted back into the cut. Linc angled toward a section where the snow was lower and like a hurdler leading with his bad ankle and launching from his good, bounded into it. His ankle was still mostly immobile in his boot and the snow cushioned the impact. If he didn't twist it again, he would be fine. He felt pain but it didn't matter.

Tat was in the barn.

Moxie was in the barn.

The dog — bad guys always killed the dog.

The headlights were at the driveway; the vehicle slowed and turned.

Knees churning high, legs wide apart, Linc pushed himself forward. The snow thickened as he entered a short width of briars; he stopped for a moment and gulped air, heaved, ripped his jacket in a dozen brambles and crashed to the field. The snow on top was thin — the cornstalks showed four inches.

Running downhill, Linc lengthened his stride. Every other footfall sent a shock of pain until after a few dozen steps his ankle loosened, the pain reduced, he caught his wind and began pumping his arms for speed.

The snow thickened and Linc swerved for the dome of the first false summit. The route would be a fraction longer, but the thin snow cover would allow him to maintain speed.

His lungs burned from the cold air. Linc backed off his stride and coughed. Again, his energy surged. The four-lighted Blazer was halfway to the barn.

Linc reached to his holster and the .38 was gone.

He slid to a stop.

Turned.

He turned again. Frank had stationed all of the rifles and pistols in the upper loft. What would be faster? Retracing his steps looking for a gray .38 in the snow? Or climbing to the loft?

Linc burst toward the barn and maintained his sprint all the way. He ran through the headlights of the approaching Blazer. His lungs on fire, his ankle screaming, his shoulders aching from throwing his arms back and forth, he darted up the slope to the barn's second level bay.

"ARM YOURSELF, TAT! They're here!"

Linc pounded across the floorboards, leaped the first three ladder rungs, and scrambled to the loft.

A door slammed. Headlights lit inside the barn. Linc scrambled and slipped on loose hay as he arrived at Frank's sawed off semi automatic shotgun leaning on the wall next to the window.

What did he want?

There were so many rifles, pistols, everything! But which had ammunition? The only one he knew for certain was loaded was the shotgun. The rest of the ammo was in the truck and there was no time to get it.

Linc grabbed the semi automatic shotgun and pulled the charging handle back an inch. He observed a shotgun shell in the breech. He drove the handle forward and flipped the gun to its side. The safe switch was on. He flicked it off, then on again.

Voices carried from outside the barn.

Linc stood at the edge of the loft. The opening at the bay door was fifteen feet wide and twelve high. From his perch the opening was clear. Linc aimed to the upper left corner, dropped the barrel and shifted rightward because he'd never fired a sawed-off scattergun and didn't know how wide the pattern would be.

He pressed his finger to the trigger and froze.

What if Tat came running out of the lower door?

What to do?

They were coming — possibly spreading out to attack!

Linc aimed at the open back loft window. The field was plain snow. He pulled the trigger and the shotgun blasted out the part of the barn wall.

He raced to the edge of the loft. The Blazer's headlights went off.

"Next one takes your head off!"

The bale slide was still down. Linc jumped.

He lifted his knees, leaned on his back and dropped twelve feet in two seconds. At the bottom of the slide, he kicked out his feet and landed on them while swinging the shotgun toward the open bay door.

Four men stood gawking at one another in front of the Blazer outside. One had a pistol.

"Drop it!"

Linc marched toward the brothers. He'd been aiming from the hip but as he stepped forward, he lifted the shotgun stock to his shoulder.

"My warning shot took out six feet of barn wall. That's why I'm aiming in the middle of you skuzturds. Drop the gun!"

The man stared at Linc.

Beyond the Blazer, the lights of the F-150 appeared on the driveway.

From Linc's left arrived the sound of barn wood groaning. Tat appeared with her pistol trained on the four brothers.

"Don't be stupid," she said.

The pit bull Joe growled in a voice that sent a chill down Linc's back.

"You burned my house. Drop the gun."

The man on the left of the one with the pistol whispered something. The one on the end took a half step from his brothers.

"Tat — cover that asshole."

The oldest brother dropped his pistol. The barrel landed partly on his boot.

"Put your hands up," Linc said.

One by one they complied — except the one who'd held the pistol.

Frank parked the F-150 behind the Blazer and got out with Baer; their pistols drawn but pointed at the ground.

From his peripheral vision Linc noticed Tat disappear in the lower-level door.

"Four guns on you. Put your hands in the air."

"You're outgunned, son," Baer said, coming up on the left side of the Blazer, but wide of the shotgun's line. "Don't make your last mistake here."

Joe growled a concurring admonition.

Linc heard Tat's boots lightly strike the barn floor behind him. She appeared at his side and drew on the grinning Walsh brother with his hands down.

Linc caught Frank's look.

"Zip ties by the tractor," Frank said.

Linc switched on the safety and walked to the Ford 8N. A jar with twenty zip ties was beside the tools Frank hadn't yet put away. He brought eight.

While the other three kept their pistols on the Walsh brothers, Linc stepped to the youngest on the end and pulled his arms behind him. He zip tied his wrists, marched him six feet and turned him facing the Blazer.

"Stay."

He zip tied the next two and positioned them the same way.

As he approached the last, the man who grinned and kept shifting side to side, Baer said, "Let me handle this one."

Baer stepped forward and getting partly to the man's side, drove the butt of this Model 29 to his skull, crumpling him.

"These other three is worth something. This one sold his soul," Baer said. "Gimme one of those ties."

Baer knelt and pulled the man's wrists behind him. He secured them with a plastic tie and said, "One of you has a gold coin. I'm gonna knee each your nuts 'til I get it back."

"Me. In my coat pocket," said the one in the middle.

Baer trod to him.

"Left side. Don't kill us. We didn't mean any harm."

Frank huffed.

Linc clamped his mouth.

Baer extracted the coin from the man's pocket and said, "They's a decent man in you somewhere. All of you — I promise. Don't quit lookin' 'til you find him."

FIFTY THREE
THE ONLY THING THAT FEELS PEACEFUL

With the four Walsh brothers zip tied and sitting on hay bales, Frank found a corded telephone in a junk bin in the barn and plugged it to the line in the barn that hadn't been used since he ripped the last phone off the wall after the umpteenth call from a telemarketer six months before. Jenny had wanted a phone in the barn in case an accident happened, and even though it struck Frank as foolish, he'd always believed that giving her what she wanted, especially when it didn't matter, was how to keep the marriage running smooth.

Glad to hear a dial tone, he called 911 and explained what happened. A half hour later Skip Myers and another deputy arrived and took the four Walsh Brothers into custody.

"Need to bend your ear," Baer said. He tilted his head away from the four being marched to a Blazer and walked with Frank to the steps leading to the first level.

"That scattergun... Might not be the kind of weapon a fella wants in a law abidin' house. If you want rid of it I'll give you a — let's see — "

Baer opened his coat and lifted his shirt. He pulled a coin from his belt.

"Give you a Krugerrand for it."

"That an ounce?"

"Yuhp."

"What's gold going for these days? A grand?"

"Round there."

"Sounds like charity."

"You give me shelter in the storm, brother."

"I don't know. Doesn't seem like a fair trade. Tell you what: Jake gave me a Winchester .308 and I already have the same gun. Has a nice scope. Take that and the shotgun. Fair?"

Baer hesitated.

"What? You already have a Winchester .308 too?"

"You're a generous man, Frank Buzzard. I'll take the deal."

The deputies took statements from Frank, Linc, and "Alden Boone." For some reason, that was the name on Baer's license. Frank wondered if he used the name Baer because he'd done something bad under the name of Alden Boone...

He grinned at a wild speculation: what if Alden was a wanted man or something, and Baer was a fake name?

Or... what if he was an Angel? It was uncanny how he arrived at the exact moment he did, a voice of calm and reason through both the greatest crisis and most extraordinary revelation of Frank's life. That whole thing about seeing people's auras was flat out weird. Angels probably saw auras.

But it would be a strange angel that relied on profanity so much as Baer.

Most likely he was just a stranger passing through. The pendulum had swung against Frank for so long, maybe it was finally on the return path, swinging for him.

The deputies drove away the Walsh clan and by midnight Frank realized he'd just lived the longest day of his life. Only sixteen hours before he'd set out in the F-150 to visit with his oldest, best friend on his deathbed. The day ended with him having all four of his friend's sons arrested for arson.

Myers had said they'd tack on a bunch of other charges and Frank shook his head.

"You do what you want, but the only charge I'll press is arson."

"What about you, Mister Boone? You said they stole a gold piece and damaged your car."

Baer shook his head. "I'm inclined to show mercy. They won't use it for good 'til someone give it to 'em first."

• • • ● • ● • • •

Frank stood at the edge of his burned house looking at the rubble. Embers glowed and rippled in the basement; sparks lifted here and there, smoke rolled along into Kelley James' posted land. Maybe it was time to visit and see if his neighbor needed anything. The fellow was getting up there in years and didn't have family around. It'd be the decent thing to do.

There were a lot of decent things to do, now that his thinking was different.

The ground he stood on was grass burned to the roots, hard and dry as the driveway in the middle of August. Behind him where the snow had melted but the grass hadn't yet burned, the grass was green and reminded Frank of the renewal of the spring.

The truck door closed behind him and Frank turned. Linc had been toting the many boxes of ammunition Jake Walsh had given him from behind the seat in the Ford to the barn's upper deck with all the weapons.

Linc faced the house. Frank waved him closer.

He resumed his thinking while Linc walked, favoring his left, sprained ankle.

How would he find the words to say what he needed to say to Linc?

Frank had considered releasing the four brothers before the police arrived. They'd made a mistake… but everyone makes mistakes. There was no call to be vindictive about it. They were like anyone else, in a way, capable of bad decisions, capable of harming those they hated and protecting those they loved. Focus on the bad and they had plenty to hold attention.

Focus on the good and there wasn't much to see. They stood beside one another; that was something.

Maybe the real takeaway was they needed more love in their lives, like everyone else. More forgiveness, starting with themselves.

Frank's mind was blown. Paradigm change. Mystical wonderment. Witnessing Linc burst out of the boxes Frank had put him in — liar, thief, hateful, selfish — revealing himself to be a young man capable puzzling out a mystery, then instantly dashing off, putting his life at risk to protect those who needed protecting — including Frank, and the farm — if Frank could be so wrong about his own flesh and blood, living in his house, how much more easily could he misunderstand others, whom he knew almost nothing about?

Earlier that night he'd listened when Baer said to one of the brothers, so they all heard: *They's a decent man in you somewhere. All of you. Don't quit lookin' 'til you find him.*

What was a father's duty, if not helping his son find in himself a decent man, that he might nurture it?

What was a neighbor's duty, or a citizen's duty, if not helping others find in themselves decent people?

Thinking about cutting the Walsh Brothers loose, though, didn't seem like it would be doing them a favor. The longer they sat in the barn with their wrists behind their backs, the more they mumbled and the angrier they sounded. By the time Myers arrived under his swirling red and blue lights, the oldest of the Walsh boys was a fountain of belligerence, going on and on about Frank stealing his birthright. He pressed his head to his shoulder and had drool coming out of his mouth. Once, earlier, he barked three times at Joe.

The greatest challenge on earth seemed to be knowing when to show mercy.

Without any of them indicating contrition, affording them grace would only assure they returned to their ways sooner. If he turned them loose, he may as well expect them to burn the barn too.

There was no good in that for anyone, even them.

Instead, Frank was sad for them.

The feeling resulted from the greatest revelation of Frank's life, which Baer had brought to him:

Virtue doesn't increase hatred; virtue doesn't clamor for violence; virtue doesn't apply a label to a person and use the label to remove the person's humanity, his agency as a thinking being, the way Frank had labeled Linc a thief and a liar.

If Jake Walsh's sons went to prison, Frank decided, he'd visit. Their father would be gone. Maybe Frank could help them to a different path, somehow. He wouldn't know until he tried.

"Hey Dad," Linc said.

Hands in his pockets, Linc stepped to the very edge of the foundation and looked downward.

"How's that ankle?" Frank said.

"Swollen. I feel things grind when I walk."

"Maybe it's time to stop walking. We can put the truck in the barn, and you could sleep on the seat if you want. Or up in the loft. That's where I'll be."

"I'll take the truck. You snore."

"You saved us," Frank said.

He approached and stood beside Linc at the foundation.

"You saved Tat, Moxie. Baer's gold. Most of all you saved the farm — and that means you saved me. I all but accused you of lighting this fire, right here, and after that you saved me, most of all."

"I guess so. I didn't really think about it. Just seemed right."

"A lot's changed today."

"I lost the .38 you gave me in the field somewhere."

"Shouldn't be too hard to spot. We'll find it tomorrow."

"You said you dropped the insurance on the house today."

"I did."

"What are we going to do?"

"Move forward. Get through it. So much has changed in my heart, I'm not saying it very well. But whatever happens we'll get through it. I've been seeing you all wrong. I think with you owning half of this place it's going to do fine."

"Were you serious about letting me help figure out the money and bills and all that? The business part?"

"I'm saying more than that. Yes, I meant it, but I'm saying a lot more than that." Frank reached to Linc's shoulder and turned him so they faced one another. "In my code, when a man's wrong he needs to come clean. I was wrong about you. What you did today... I don't know how else to say it. I look up to you. You're a hero. You showed me mercy. I'm grateful to you."

Linc matched Frank's gaze.

"I don't understand why you did it," Frank said.

"When I twisted my ankle, I remembered something I told myself after — you know. Two years ago. I told myself most pain doesn't matter. My ankle hurt. When I remembered that, I also remembered you breaking the mirror with your forehead."

"I don't understand."

"Two years ago —"

"I remember. I just don't understand why you did it."

"I get that angry with myself sometimes too," Linc said. "Sometimes I do dumb stuff and don't know why."

"The human condition."

Linc stubbed his toe into a rock by the foundation. He looked to the space in the basement that contained the ashes of his bedroom, and then to the space above it, now empty, where his room had been. Life moved like that.

Linc imagined standing in his father's boots, trying to make sense of all the sudden changes, and he took pity.

He lied.

"I guess I figured if you were that mad at yourself, I didn't need to be that mad at you too."

INTEGRITY

Frank dipped his head and pushed out with his fists inside his coat pockets. He clamped his jaw and spoke through it. "I'm sorry for what I did. To my core I'm sorry for what I did."

Linc saw him.

A father looms, sometimes like a giant. Sometimes like other things — but he looms.

At age sixty, Frank had spent most of his years working himself ragged as a vessel of one form of misery or another. Whatever shape his light took when he was born, it now conformed to the pressures of the world he hated. Fighting it in every direction had spent him in every dimension, and he stood now with elbows jutting, hip out, mangled leg inward, head tilted, a scarred veteran learning the second war he fought was also a war of choice, with him the one who made the decision to fight, serving as the general, the enemy, and the cannon fodder, but nowhere the victor.

Frank looked small next to the charred remains of his house, slightly confused by the results of his life.

He looked even smaller against the scale of the farm, more akin the dirt than the snow that covered it.

Whatever philosophy a man held, Linc imagined, it ought to produce a better result than standing next to the rubble of your life, begging forgiveness.

Frank was his father, but he was no longer the giant who said what the world was. He was a man, confused but doing his best by the code he thought most honorable.

Linc paid attention to Frank.

As Frank relaxed his jaw, he pulled his balled hands from his pockets and looked toward the sky.

"I have to let it go, Linc. What I did. I can't keep hurting myself out of guilt because I hurt you. I won't be any good in the future if all I am is the worst of my past. I'm not trying to get over. Not trying to pretend."

"I get it."

"I can't be different until I see myself different," Frank said. "The only thing that feels peaceful is letting go."

Linc inhaled cold air. He straightened his back.

"It's time to move on, Dad. I forgive. It's time to live again."

CODA: ~~BAER~~ TAT, AND ~~JOE~~
WHO SEES EVERYTHING, AT ONCE?

Baer Creighton spent the night asleep next to Tat with his Model 29 Smith & Wesson on the barn floor and his arm across Tat's side, with Moxie warm between them.

If he could have seen his own light, he would have been dazzled by the intensity of the whites and blues spinning and pulsing between the three of them, nurturing Moxie and restoring him and Tat.

A year before, the professor from Chicago had told Baer that the universe consisted of a kind of trinity. Everyone knew about two of the three, matter and energy, because everyone experienced them. Most had heard of the equation that proved they were essentially different aspects of the same thing: $E=MC^2$. Energy was a particle or a wave; matter, or an energy field with the possibility of becoming matter somewhere within the waveform.

She said, "Energy equals mass multiplied by the speed of light, squared. Which is a fancy way of saying energy equals mass that's moving around very, very fast. And that means, if you somehow remove the speed, freeze the energy in one place, then you have matter."

"Uh-huh. Yuhp."

"What do you suppose is required to freeze the energy in one place?"

Baer grinned.

"A hammer."

"No. Mind. Awareness. Consciousness."

Einstein was mute about the cause, or volition, implied by the equals sign in his equation. But at roughly the same time in history, quantum physicists proved Mind was essential to the mix. The possibility of matter contained in the waveform does not collapse into actual matter with a concrete form and location — until Consciousness observed it.

It turns out, the third, most necessary element in $E=MC^2$ was the part that was ignored or summarized in the equals sign. Like energy and matter, it was also something human beings had a direct experience with: Mind.

Albert Einstein called it spooky science.

Materialists — those who preferred to believe the world was nothing but what their senses reported — chose to never address the ramifications of the axiom that nothing exists without Mind observing it. They preferred to believe consciousness was an illusion projected by a mush of chemicals in their skulls, instead of their eternal, singular identity, or Mind, which they tacitly agreed was master of their bodies every single time they said the word 'I.'

Some folks kept themselves blind. They denied themselves so they could deny the eternal. For some reason they preferred believing their lives were empty of significance, their actions useless and their fates beyond their control.

"Imagine that." Chicago Mags said to Baer. "Imagine how empty they must feel."

"Buncha bullshit," said Baer.

"Yes. The first truth of quantum physics is that energy does not become matter without consciousness observing it. So, think about all the matter you can observe right now, plus all you can't. That's everything. Who sees everything, at once? It can't be us. The universe would disappear if we all took a nap."

"The Almighty," Baer said.

Chicago Mags shrugged. "Not for me to say. It's for you to discover."

"But they's something out there," Baer said. "You can say it as a science person."

"Of course."

Baer's life took a different turn after meeting Chicago Mags, a direction that couldn't have happened without her. Almost as if she arrived when she was supposed to arrive.

Like Baer, Tat and Joe arrived in Frank and Linc Buzzard's life, when it was time for them to change course.

Like they all arrived in the Walsh brother's lives too.

Baer and Tat slept well that night, and Moxie spent the rest of his first night on planet earth bathed in their love.

• • • • ● • ● • • •

Baer was in the main bay of the barn when Linc climbed down the steps the next morning. His ankle had swollen again over night. He walked gingerly to the hay bales where Joe groaned in Baer's sleeping bag, and Baer rubbed slow circles behind his ears.

"If the Buzzard farm was a country you'd get a medal, what you did yesterday."

Linc leaned backward and stretched. He yawned and it turned into a giant smile.

"You figured out what those Walsh brothers was up to, restored your name. Run on a messed-up ankle right into the middle of the arena and, took on four squealin' hyenas. I tell you boy, you chose some high virtues and lived up to each 'em. Rare stuff, and worth a medal, anywhere."

"I guess so. We don't have much money for medals."

Baer pulled a gold coin from his pocket and pitched it to Linc.

"Ever see a Double Eagle?"

"No?"

"It's reward money. I never made a wanted poster or nothin', but I sorely wanted to find the fella, what left a pry bar in my back window. Keep the coin."

"You serious?"

"That'll trade for 'most a thousand dollars of government fiat money. You know what fiat means? Lemme school you on economics real quick. It'll be the second most important lesson of your life..."

CODA: FRANK
THIS TOWN KNOWS YOU.

Frank came down from the loft at first light and fired up the Ford 8N without coffee or breakfast. He spent the morning using the tractor to dig a path to the Eldorado and before lunch returned to get Baer. They towed the car out by noon. The front wheel drive Cadillac pulled better on snow than Frank would have guessed.

With the Eldorado parked at the drive circle Frank and Baer stood at the trunk looking at the hole in the back window. Tat was in the upper bay of the barn preparing lunch on a propane camp stove. Linc was there to help, so she could mind Moxie at the same time.

Paws twitching as he chased the eternal dream rabbit, Joe snoozed surrounded by Baer's sleeping bag, which he'd placed on top of the four bales the Walsh brothers had sat on.

"I know a guy in town that can handle that glass for you. Does good work."

"I'll go see him."

"Maybe get Tat and Moxie to a hospital," Frank said. "Let a doctor look them over."

"Maybe," Baer said. "Lady has her own mind. Slow to trust, you understand."

Frank leaned against the Eldorado's trunk and Baer watched. Something dark flickered behind his eyes but it passed, and Baer smiled wide.

"I appreciate you," Baer said. "Pulling us out, not gettin' too bent about the trespassin'."

"I never have figured out why you were there. We're far enough from the highway, you had to do a bit of looking around. And if it wasn't for the mailbox, most folks wouldn't know the driveway leads to a farm."

"I go where I'm told, is all."

"Where you're told."

Baer dipped his head.

"Have to do with the colors?"

"Roundabout way."

"Well, I'm glad..." Frank stood from the trunk and turned. "Wonder who that is?"

Baer looked down the driveway.

"You have better ears'n me."

Frank slipped his right hand toward the sidearm on his hip. His shoulders tightened.

"Feller in the car's happy. Got a good surprise for you."

"What — you know from his light?"

"I do."

"So, I won't need to draw on him?"

"You won't."

Frank tucked each thumb into his jean pockets and waited.

"That's my insurance man."

The white Toyota Camry crunched over the ice. Walter Truby parked beside the Eldorado and popped out of his car. Before he'd taken two steps he said, "Frank Buzzard, you're the luckiest man I know."

Truby stopped. He turned and looked at the ruins of the Buzzard house. "That's not what I meant to say. I got excited to tell you — your insurance didn't cancel yet. The home office hasn't even opened since you told me to cancel, and — did you see me flagging you down at the door? When you left? I needed your signature to cancel the policy. Otherwise the policy would remain in force as long as unearned premiums remain from your last payment. So, the good news is you're covered, and hot dog, under the best policy I've ever read. I added up some numbers

INTEGRITY

and... the replacement cost of your home — your policy has a limit but it's high. Really high. And with the cost of building materials — "

"You didn't cancel the policy?"

"That's what I just said. Right. Without your signature, even if I was able to enter the change into the computer, which I wasn't, the coverage wouldn't end until the premium you've already paid for this year's coverage expires, and that's not for another thirty days. Not only are you covered, but you're covered under the best policy we have. I already stopped and talked to Skip Myers at the police station. I used the police report to file your claim this morning, and I have a check to cover a week's lodging or whatever expenses you have right off, until you can get a builder under contract. Then we'll go from there.

Frank fell back to the Eldorado's trunk.

Baer clamped his jaw. Smiled.

"I don't know what to say," Frank said.

"Don't say anything. I'll stay in touch and keep on top of the claim. If you have any questions, call me, day or night. Oh look," Walter said. "Who's that coming up the driveway?"

Frank again turned.

"Popular," Baer said.

"I'll get out of here once they pull in."

Walter Truby climbed back in his car and circled around while the next vehicle — a Ford Excursion — parked beside the Eldorado.

Frank clamped his teeth as John Senior opened the door.

"How you doing John," Frank said.

"I'm okay." John looked at the burned house and shook his head. "I had breakfast at the County Seat and Chief Myers was there. Everyone heard. I wanted to come out and holler at you real quick, let you know what we decided."

"Uhhh."

"But I got something else to say first. Been needing to say it a long damn time, is the truth. But it's hard, you know? Being wrong, and carrying it around..."

"Lord, I know," Frank said.

"You know what happened with us at the test. Well, I carried that around a while and if you wasn't off serving the country, we'd a tangled. But after a bit, I quit my grudge. I realized I didn't get to go to the college I wanted, and I didn't get the life I thought I wanted that came after it. But I got the *right* life. My daddy was so pissed about that test, and what I did to his name, when my number didn't come up for the draft he made me work at the Tractor Supply. It was almost like he knew something, you know, because he made me learn how to run the business when I was nineteen. And it was a good thing because he died of a heart attack when I was twenty, and I had to do everything, or else my mother and younger sisters, they'da had nothing."

"I didn't realize that. I'm sorry he passed so young."

"I guess what I'm trying to say is your integrity served us both. I never would have married my high school sweetheart — I was planning on ditching her after high school. Get some of that college tail. Well, she got pregnant right after I didn't go to college, and I had a good job learning the ropes at the Tractor Supply, so I married her. My whole life, everything I love most; none of that would have happened if anyone believed you was capable of cheating on a test. I've had the best blessings of my life because of that."

Frank drifted backward until stopped by the Eldorado.

He sat.

Baer grinned, hard.

"But here's the thing," John Senior said. "I never in all that time stopped to think where you might be on everything. You're the one I wronged, and I never said it. I was just grateful. Well, it's time to fix that. I'm here to apologize. I did something rotten to you. I regret it. And I regret being so ashamed I never came and apologized sooner."

Frank blinked. Swallowed. Blinked again but the water was forming.

"If you'll accept my apology, I'd like to offer you the maintenance job at the Tractor Supply. I know you have work to do here getting your life put back together, but I also know you're in a tight spot. So, the job's yours if you want it. I'll pay the same hourly rate as I paid Lou Fortunato when he ran it, and give you the same cut of the revenue you bring in. The work'll be steady once word gets out. I know what kind of man you are. You run it your way."

Frank swallowed. Nodded. Grappled.

"Sue's hoping you'll take the job too. She told me to tell you that. And that she's sorry too. Didn't know all the history with us, and she didn't mean any disrespect."

"I don't know what to say," Frank said.

"Hold on, there's more. You just saw Truby, and I don't know any particulars, but he was happy at breakfast — he was at the County Seat too. So, I expect he had decent insurance news for you. Anyhow, you know the Lingenfelters? We went to school with Pete. Him and his wife run the motel, other end of town..."

"I know them."

"They have a room for you and a room for Linc. It's the slow season, they said. No trouble at all for them to help out."

"They musta been at the County Seat," Baer said.

"I... I don't know what to say."

"I know at least three general contractors that'll work with you on the budget, that can build your house and do it right. I don't know what else you'll need to get back on your feet, but whatever it is, Frank, this town knows you. We're here to see you through."

Finally, Frank allowed tears to spill from his eyes to his cheeks.

"Thank you, John."

John Senior stepped to Frank and offered his right hand. Frank grasped it and shook.

CODA: LINC
IT'S CALLED JOCULAR FIBER...

Looking good in new boxer briefs with superior elasticity and roominess, jeans, and a heavy plaid shirt, Linc noticed Sue Cooper at her wall locker. The day's last bell had rung; most kids were gone from the hallways. Those who rode busses home had to wait five to fifteen minutes before their rides arrived. Most loitered outside where the busses staged around a loop, filled with kids, and departed.

Linc veered and in a moment stood a couple feet from Sue. He leaned on a locker. Stood with his leg folded like James Dean.

"Linc," Sue said.

"Hey."

"The essay you read in class was so good! That end — you held them off at gunpoint! — you'll be in a movie before too long. What an amazing story."

"I thought you'd think it was... you know. A dick move."

"What? No way. I didn't mind."

"I told everyone I had a crush on you, before telling you."

Sue grabbed two books and shoved them into her backpack. "Uh, that's not exactly true."

"What do you mean?"

"You've been broadcasting two things all year."

"Yeah?"

"You're really shy, and you really like me."

Sue stopped cramming books into her bag. She held Linc's stare.

Linc said, "I guess one's still true."

"Which?"

"Guess."

"You don't seem quite so shy."

"Yeah."

Linc remembered a particular moment reading his essay in English class. He'd slowed down and looked up from the page to see Sue's face when he said the lines about drizzling melted chocolate on her bare skin.

"So, you're not mad I put you in my essay?"

"No. It's sweet. I just..."

"Yeah?"

"This is so hard. I just don't know if I feel... the same way."

"When you didn't run up the aisle and leap into my arms at the podium — "

"Yeah — "

"I got it."

Linc offered his hand.

Sue took it.

He shook.

She said, "You don't seem... I dunno... phased."

"It's called jocular fiber. I'll see you around."

Linc released her hand.

Sue held his.

"Wait! Walk me to the busses."

What's Next?

I have a vision of writing a collection of novels focusing on virtues, written for both younger and older audiences.

Long ago I read a short story called *Trust*, by Jack London. (You can read *Trust* free, online here: http://www.online-literature.com/london/104/)

Trust is about a man who understands that being entrusted with something creates tension between him and his highest virtue. He is obligated to uphold his values, but at risk of death, will he? In the end, the man learns that maintaining his values in the face of a life-or-death challenge is heroic — even if his life is absurd and has no meaning.

Of course, London didn't say that. I read that out of the story. (Readers create far more of the world the author takes them to than the author does...) Looking back, I probably read London's story in seventh grade. I've been a fanatic about trust, ever since. I don't give my word unless I'm prepared to do whatever necessary to keep it.

I formed my lifelong definition of the word *Trust* by experiencing the feats of a Jack London protagonist who would do anything at all required to keep his word, once he gave it. I think that's better than reading a dictionary definition and then trying to use the word in a sentence.

The bottom line, of course, is that I'm contending a novel is a better medium to convey a profound, life-course altering meaning than a twenty-word dictionary entry. Since I write novels and believe our virtues ought to be understood so well they serve as guiding lights for our lives, I anticipate writing a series with titles like these:

INTEGRITY
COURAGE
FAITH
LIBERTY
AUTHORITY
COMPASSION
PATIENCE
RESTRAINT
JUSTIFIED COUNTRY ASS WHOOPINS

If you enjoyed this book and would like to see more along this line, please be sure to mention the book to your reader friends, and if you think it might benefit them, especially to those people closest to you whom you thought about while you were reading the book. One of my beta readers suggested the book could be read by fathers and sons at the same time, so they could get together and discuss at different milestones in the book. I think that's a great idea. If this book got you thinking and left you smiling, please consider paying that forward by recommending this book to everyone you know who enjoys thinking and smiling. :)

If you have a moment to review INTEGRITY, please do so. Nothing helps folks weigh a prospective read as much as genuine reviews written in the voice of the people who read the books.

To post a review on Amazon, go here:
https://www.amazon.com/review/create-review/&asin=B09RQ86FQY

• • • ● • ● • • •

The second book in my Virtue Series is called COURAGE, and the eBook is available for preorder on Amazon here: https://www.amazon.com/dp/B09VCM82KC

Aloysius Horatio Smith is used to getting picked on. Thirteen years old and called an old soul by his grandmother, he's also nearly six feet tall, uncannily smart, and known for screeching when pranksters startle him at school.

Einstein, his best friend and confidant is a wiry pit bull pup that his mother rescued from a kill shelter. One day in November after the first dusting of snow, eleven-month-old Einstein catches a scent and disappears into the woods.

He doesn't come back.

Instead of waiting for the school bus, Aloysius hides under the porch until his mother leaves for work.

He gathers a few survival items and six peanut butter and jelly sammiches, then leaves a note vowing not to return until Einstein returns with him.

Nine days later...

From Clayton

Hello! I appreciate you reading my books—more than you can know. If you've read this far, you and I are fellow travelers. I suspect you sense something is not quite right with the world. It's not as good as it's supposed to be. We human beings aren't as good as our ideals. Yet, we prize and want to fight for them.

I do my absolute best to write stories that portray the human situation with brutal transparency, but also I strive to tell stories that are not as bleak as the human condition sometimes seems. There's no limit to the darkness. Light is rare. But it exists, and I hope when you complete one of my novels, you find your values validated.

I'm grateful you're out there. Thank you.

Remember, light wins in the end.

Printed in Great Britain
by Amazon